The Legacy of Ma Jun

The Legacy of Ma Jun

BOOK I OF THE DRAGON SCRIPTS

By Stuart Cotterill

ISBN: 0692355715
ISBN 13: 9780692355718

Acknowledgments

Special thanks to my many friends and colleagues in Beijing and Inner Mongolia who inspired me to write this story, but above all to the China I love and whose culture warms my heart. Thanks also to my editor, Susan Snowden, whose guidance on this project proved invaluable; and, of course, to my family, who are always supportive and understand what writing means to me.

Prologue

_⤳_

Beijing, January 12, 2014

THE CALL CAME IN AT 10 p.m., later than scheduled. Mathers was irritated with the caller before she spoke. He muttered to his wife how insensitive his fellow countrymen were to the time differences between them. He let it ring for several minutes before picking up the phone, knowing he would answer it but half hoping the caller would ring off.

"Yes?"

"Is that George Mathers?"

"Professor Mathers, yes. You're calling later than planned. Who is this by the way?"

"It's Susan Henning of _National Geographic_ in the U.S. I'm sorry to call so late. My editor, David Shaw, was called away urgently. He asked me to call you instead; I couldn't get through for some reason. Is it too late now?"

"Yes it is; I guess you might as well tell me though why _National Geographic_ is calling _me_ in particular. Can you make it brief?"

"David Shaw didn't send you anything?"

"No, just an e-mail and a time to talk to me."

"It's about your find, Professor."

Mathers shifted uncomfortably in his chair, pausing momentarily before responding. "And what find might that be Ms., or is it Mrs., Susan Henning?"

"It's Ms., and I have no idea what your find is. The information came from someone in our Beijing office. Rumor has it you've found something spectacular in antiquity. Our editor thought we could collaborate on it; apparently, you have something of a reputation in that area."

"I have no idea, Ms. Susan, what you're talking about; there's nothing to collaborate on."

"David told me you might say that; he also wanted me to be sure and tell you we have this information on the very highest authority."

"Well, tell your David to contact your highest authority and not to bother me again. I don't know what he's talking about."

Mathers brought the conversation to an end and rang off; his wife, Xiao Ping, had been listening with a puzzled look on her face. "What on earth do they want, George?"

"Someone has talked. I need to call Diao tomorrow and tell him. I don't think the authorities want any publicity right now."

"I'm sure you're right; anyway, Diao will know what to do."

Susan Henning was surprised when her phone rang so soon after her call to Beijing; she checked the caller ID before taking it.

"Susan, David here. How did your call go?"

"You're calling very late . . . what's the big deal on this? If it's so important why didn't you call him yourself?" Susan was irritated by what seemed to be a waste of her time.

"Just tell me how the call went; that's all I need right now," David huffed.

"It went nowhere at all. He claims there's no find to talk about and referred us to the Chinese authorities. He certainly wasn't happy to hear from me so late. What's really going on here, David? Are we *National Geographic* or the *National Enquirer?*"

"Relax. All I can say now is that I promised management I wouldn't personally follow this any further, so I used you instead. Sorry about that, but part of what I told you was true. Our Beijing office did get word of a great find from someone highly placed. When they followed up through official channels we were told there was nothing to the story and basically to back off. Apparently when we pushed further there were some veiled threats, carefully worded of course, about our business in China. At any rate I was told in no uncertain terms by you-know-who to back off, to make no further calls on this."

"So you used me to double check this? Just to protect yourself? Who is this guy anyway?"

" George Mathers? I have his bio in front of me actually. Professor Mathers lived in China since the country opened up to the West. Let's see . . . originally invited in 1980 to assist with the interpretation of ancient scripts found in the DunWan Buddhist caves of Gansu province in western China. Says here, 'These were unlike any writings previously seen.' Chinese scholars apparently knew his experience in languages and pictographic scripting from his earlier books and lectures in the U.S. He was given an official government invitation via the State Department to go there—partly funded too, it seems. According to his own comment here in a *China Daily* news article in 2011, it led to what he called a lifelong adventure in China."

"Anything else about what he's actually doing there now?" she asked, wondering why she never thought to ask more about him before the call, not that she expected it would have changed Mather's reaction to her.

"Not too much; he's got a small team working closely with the university there, but they remain independent. They have funding from both Chinese and U.S. government entities that deal with cultural cooperation apparently."

"Doing what?"

"Studying old myths . . . in association with the antiquities department of Beijing University. According to the same article they've proved that some of the great legends passed down over the centuries were as told, though modified by storytellers. And they've *disproved* some of the fanciful stories with their Chinese counterparts, especially a Professor Cai Levee and his team at Tsinghua University in Beijing."

"How old is Mathers, David?"

"Doesn't say, but looking at his photo in the file I'd say late fifties. Bit of a throwback though, judging by his clothes. He looks like a walking ad for Goodwill compared to this younger Levee character in the same photo."

"Married?"

"Oh yes; she's right here too, one Zhang Ping or 'Xiao Ping,' as she's called by everyone apparently. A beauty by her looks in the photo; well educated too. Similar field. Christ, she must be half his age though, lucky beggar!"

"Okay, enough of that. Typical you! What do we do now?"

"Nothing, Susan; nothing at all. We have to back off. I was hoping we could work with them on whatever they've found. But if he won't talk and the authorities are controlling this, it's not worth the hassle. We have the other work on the digs in Xian with the government; no one here wants to jeopardize that."

"So that's it. Use me, pique my interest, then tell me to forget it?"

"Exactly. Sorry, thanks for trying the call anyway. I'll see you in the office in the morning. I have a different project for you to get started on. Go to sleep and forget the whole thing."

CHAPTER 1

Beijing, February 2013

MATHERS AND HIS WIFE SCHEDULED their latest trip to one of the lesser-known areas of China to listen to local stories—part of their efforts to ensure that legends and verbal histories would not be lost. Their project involved recording and storing them until they could eventually be registered and published. There were many concerns that traditional tales from ancient periods would disappear under the pressure of modern times.

Traveling to a small village near the larger city of Zhangjiajie in the province of Hunan, Mathers first heard rumors surrounding a particular family, which would lead them down an ancient path. The team, in association with the antiquities department of Beijing, arranged to meet the village leaders to explain their work. They were hosted at a lavish banquet and treated by the locals to seemingly endless dishes of food, and toasted with locally made baijiu, a fiery liquor best described as Chinese moonshine.

After describing to the locals several classic tales that turned out to be true, Mr. Huang, the senior political party member of the small community, related some of their local legends. Most of them were variations on stories the team had heard before. One intriguing tale, however, was his outline of this old character, Ma Jun.

There were a number of village rumors about the family itself and their history. Now, close to the end of its line, the Ma family supposedly had come from great wealth and importance. They apparently were burdened with some secret, partially revealed in the village when Ma tried drinking himself to death after his wife passed away. That was also the last time anyone ever recalled Ma taking a drink.

"Do you think we can meet with this Ma fellow tomorrow, Mr. Huang?" Mathers asked. "He sounds quite interesting." Mathers thought it better to request it before more toasting muddled his brain. He never handled drink well, unlike his wife, who for her size had remarkable capacity for any kind of alcohol.

"Professor Mathers, I can try, but I must warn you Ma keeps to himself; he's a most honored member of our community but few really know him well. He may refuse to see you."

Mathers struggled to understand Huang's heavy Hunan accent until Xiao Ping whispered in his ear exactly what was said. The three finally joked about the Hunan accent, which then called for yet another toast to celebrate their ability to communicate with each other.

"Don't worry, darling, I'll find a way to get to Ma Jun." She smiled as she gulped down her full glass of baijiu in one fell swoop. "Gambei!" she shouted to the people at her table, forcing them to similarly drink up, some having to fill their glasses again with the white liquid to match her. Only her husband was allowed to down the smaller amount sitting in his cup.

The couple woke the next morning a little sore-headed from the endless toasts. After meeting again with Huang they tried to see old Mr. Ma Jun. They were told Ma would not see them. Xiao Ping determined to approach Ma alone. She prided herself on her ability to charm men, especially older ones. They always seemed to harbor a strong desire to protect her. She used her looks to advantage, accepting her good fortune in that regard as a gift from her parents, yet she'd found it troubling when unwelcome advances were made.

Walking down the narrow unpaved lane to the home of Ma she was struck by the quietness of the surroundings. The old buildings were in poor condition, although villagers had done their best to keep things tidy compared to other villages she visited. There was no trash to be seen anywhere, and a thin whitewash covered the outer mud walls of the homes, now brightened by the morning sun. When she finally arrived at Ma's front door, she was struck by its ornate nature compared to all the others she had passed; nevertheless, the home's shabby outer appearance indicated years of neglect.

It took a while before someone answered her knocks. She sensed at first that the person inside was waiting for her to leave, but she continued to rap on the heavy wooden door.

Finally a small opening appeared in the door and a weak voice told the caller to go away. Hearing the frailty in the voice of what surely must be Mr. Ma, she spoke gently. She asked him to at least meet with her if only for a few moments, to at least listen to what she wanted to talk to him about. She could make out tired eyes moving back and forth taking her appearance in, just as she hoped they would. His eyes betrayed something she could not quite register at the time. It was not that they knew her, but they seemed to see something strangely familiar.

After halfway closing the opening the old man paused momentarily, finally uttering the words she hoped for. "All right, you've come a long way . . . but only for a short while. Then perhaps you'll leave me be."

"I assure you, Mr. Ma, it won't take long, but if you want me to leave I'll go right away."

"You'll have to take me as I am; my cleaner comes only one day a week now."

"Don't worry about me, Mr. Ma, you should see our apartment in Beijing. I'm sure your home will be just fine."

The opening slid shut and Xiao Ping smiled inwardly; she had not lost her touch.

She waited at the door while Ma opened it, the clang of more than one lock sounding. This fact spoke directly of Ma's desire for privacy even in this isolated village.

When the door was finally opened she stepped inside and was surprised by the sight before her. "Why, this is quite lovely, Mr. Ma. I can see you've collected some very interesting things, and they are so beautifully arranged."

Ma blew his nose on an old rag, still looking Xiao Ping up and down with a strange expression. Surprisingly she did not find it uncomfortable. Finally he motioned her into the main room. He wore a long gray gown and shuffled along in his tattered silk slippers.

Xiao Ping felt she'd taken a step back in time. The rooms could have been used for any Chinese TV melodrama set in the 1920s, especially those set in Shanghai.

"This is exactly as my wife left it," Ma said in a low voice. "We had so much more than you see here. She loved beautiful things. But that was a very long time ago. Please come in. You are?"

"Huang probably told you, my name is Xiao Ping; well that's what everyone calls me instead of Zhang Ping. My husband is Professor George Mathers, an American, but he loves China very much. I hope you can meet him later while he's here. He'll be fascinated by all these things."

"That won't be possible, my dear. Now, what is it you really want? I am not well and you should be leaving soon." With that Ma graciously led her to an ornate sitting area, just under an open window looking out on a small courtyard.

Their meeting lasted longer than Xiao Ping had expected. No matter how she approached the family's past he avoided any discussion of it. He seemed more ready to talk to her about his wife, always looking directly at Xiao Ping as if searching for something or someone. Although his initial reception was a little cool, she was surprised when he agreed to see her again, if only to talk more of his wife and her tragic passing away. It seemed to have little to do with their project, yet she was touched by how he responded when talking about it with her.

During each subsequent visit she tried to get him to agree to see her husband, though George had said to forget about trying to coax anything out of Ma. Yet something continued to draw her to continue talking to him. She was surprised when Ma finally agreed to meet her husband, almost as she'd given up. She tried to hide her pleasure when he finally said he would meet George.

George was as surprised to hear Ma had changed his mind as he had been with his wife's obsession with talking to the old man. And he'd been a bit annoyed with her, given that they had other work to do.

When George finally met Ma and saw the ornate furnishings in his simple villa he sensed, like his wife, that something was very special about the man. From the moment he walked in and introduced himself he saw quickly how Ma's eyes brightened anytime Xiao Ping was near or said anything. It eventually became clear why. While Ma and Xiao Ping talked George was left browsing through some worn photo albums of the Ma family's arrival in the village. The photos Ma had lovingly caressed of his young wife, long since passed away, caught his attention. She looked very much like Xiao Ping.

Over the next four days Ma warmed to Xiao Ping more than ever and began to open up. He quite often hinted of a particular family legend, which he claimed only his family and their ancestors in the whole of China had been entrusted with. When prodded about the story he would immediately change the subject and say no more.

In those few days Xiao Ping clearly became attached to old Ma Jun and would disappear from the team for hours on end just to sit and talk to him. He seemed to Mathers to be in failing health, his life already drifting away, even before their eyes.

On the fifth day of their stay, it was time to move on and the team needed to get ready to leave. They duly thanked Mr. Huang and the villagers for all the time spent with them, and their great hospitality, despite the relatively hard living conditions the villagers endured. As they were preparing to leave, a man rushed up to Xiao Ping begging her to come alone to see Ma Jun. Ma, he said, was deteriorating at an alarming rate. He said Ma Jun was asking for her only, alternately using her name and his wife's.

When Xiao Ping looked at her husband with pleading eyes, he immediately urged her to go; the team would wait as long as she needed. The village elders thanked the professor profusely as Xiao Ping hurried away.

She strode alone as quickly as she could, once more to the small house at the end of the narrowest lane in the village. Considering the imminent death of this frail and very sick old man now overshadowed the brightness of the white-walled homes she passed.

When Mathers himself arrived later at the house he saw Xiao Ping on a long couch holding Ma in her arms, cradling his head to her bosom. Ma was looking directly into Xiao Ping's eyes, mumbling his way through many words, moving in and out of consciousness. He was addressing Xiao Ping as Wan Yan, his wife of twenty years before she died. Xiao Ping would listen carefully, then gently respond to him as if she was indeed Wan Yan. She was mopping his brow with a cool damp cloth and trying to keep him comfortable.

Mathers could see how ill Ma looked; he was not long for this world, but with Xiao Ping holding him his passing might at least be peaceful. Mathers bent over Xiao Ping's left ear and quietly whispered, "There's nothing I can do here, my darling, spend as much time as you need."

"But don't we have to leave right away?" she said, tears glistening against her delicate skin.

"Don't worry about that," George said, dabbing at her tears with his handkerchief. "We'll unload the truck and stay at least over the weekend. I know this is important to you. Hopefully, he's at peace with you here, or his Wan Yan as he sees you. He must have loved her dearly, as I do you."

"Thank you, George, you are so very special."

"I'll remind you of that in the future!" George said over his shoulder as he finally left the house to talk to the others. He knew Xiao Ping was heartbroken but happy to take care of Ma and ease him into the next world; perhaps he would finally meet Wan Yan there once again.

CHAPTER 2

MA WAS CONFUSED; HE KNEW something was desperately wrong. All the traditional medicines he had tried failed to halt his illness. It was engulfing him, a darkness that closed around him and frightened him more by the hour. His strength was slipping away, but the joy of Wan Yan's return comforted him in what he knew were his final days. He determined he could no longer keep from her things he should have passed to an elder son they never raised. Only she could find the way to continue. Would he have the strength or time to tell all she needed to know? Would she be able to carry out his wishes? He had no choice but to try.

He heard her through his fog; he felt the cool moist cloth and softness of her hand on his brow. He ignored her whispers to rest and be quiet. To be at peace with her was everything he had dreamed of, yet this was not the time. She must listen to his final words.

"Wan Yan, I have failed our honored ancestors. Only you can help me now. The son we do not have now burdens our ancestors and me. Never in all these centuries has a son not graced our family. You must help me now. You must find a way."

Again through the mists, when darkness cleared and her face appeared before him, he heard her begging him to rest. He told her he could not, there were things he had to speak of. Eventually she relented and her sweet voice told him to take his time, to drink the soothing nectar she raised to his lips. The darkness lifted as the light of her words shone through and his mind cleared enough to begin to tell her everything his thoughts had drawn together. His body was frail but his memory sound. How could he forget such a story handed down over the centuries? And yet he was the first to have failed to nourish the seed of a son to succeed him.

"Wan Yan, there is much to tell you. Promise me you will try to find a way to honor our ancestors. I need you to promise me that you will believe all I tell you."

The face floating before him told him she would carry out his wishes, that he could take his time and tell her everything. He was pleased when she told him she had gathered paper and pen. She would write down all he said, but he must not rush; they could take as long as he needed.

"I should have told you this story a long time ago, Wan Yan. It goes back far in time."

"Take it slowly, from the beginning, I am here; I am with you, and what has to be done will be done."

"To begin, I go to a time when all had gone well with our ancestors over the centuries; that is, until the time of the Taiping Rebellion. Our Ma family then still maintained ancestral landholdings in the Tioayaun area. That year the Taiping rebels suffered great losses at the hands of the Qing armies. With money running out they took to looting and confiscating property to keep their soldiers and armies financed and fed in those final days. Advance warnings arrived of the Taiping approaching our own landholding. Like hordes of locusts they were stripping everything bare. My great, great grandfather and his son, Ma Cai, anticipated this and removed treasure that they were guardians of from its hiding place. These are the things I must tell you of, treasures our family has watched over for generations.

"What kind of treasure do you speak of, husband?"

"Wait a little; you will understand soon enough; my time is short and there is much to tell you."

"I will not interrupt you again. I am listening. I am recording your words and will do whatever needs to be done."

"They were careful to move the contents from a special hidden casket into two plain, ready-made coffins for children. Knowing the villagers always spread rumors of a hidden treasure the old man figured he would still need something for the Taiping commander and his thieving troops. He understood they would not believe there was nothing left. It was known that many people were tortured to confess where valuables were hidden. So wisely, the family treasures were divided into two parts, one small part placed back in that very splendid casket but the main part squeezed into the two children's caskets. The ornate casket was returned to its original hiding place. The two children's coffins, that same dark night, were buried temporarily in the family graveyard to be moved to safety some time later."

Ma continued the story as told him by his father. It was clear in his mind, and the gentle voice he had missed for so many years gave him the strength to go on.

"As our old ancestor expected, within the next two days the Taiping commander and his soldiers arrived at the main villa. His servant was dragged behind them, a rope around his neck, into their large reception hall. As he was flung before Old Ma the blood flowed freely from the poor man's head. My father told me the servant cried out how sorry he was to the old man. In terrible ways they had forced him to divulge that there was indeed treasure hidden in the Ma family home. He had confessed to his captors that it must have been there for years, but he did not know where it was hidden.

"Denying existence of any such treasures, our family head played the commander as long as he could, until his son, my great grandfather Ma Cai, was dragged before him. With a knife against his throat, Old Ma was given a count of ten to reveal the hiding place or his son would not live to comfort him in his old age. The commander guaranteed they would leave the landholdings unharmed if their treasure was turned over to the Taiping commander.

"Not knowing if his plan would work—and sure they would be killed anyway—the old man led the way to a special cupboard. The cupboard looked bare when opened, as if it had been emptied already. The soldiers were puzzled until Ma pressed on a small piece of wood. Resembling no more than a raised knot, a hidden door opened to reveal the splendid-looking casket. Ornately covered it both startled and pleased the commander.

"Two soldiers hauled the casket to the middle of the hall, but neither could figure out how to open it. Again, Old Ma was dragged over and given one final threat on his life. According to the story told me by my father, Ma drew the commander close and asked in a low voice if everyone needed to know how this casket could be opened. The commander of course wanted the casket for him alone to open. Old Ma bargained; he asked that the commander show good faith by releasing the son; only then would he complete his part of the agreement. Fortunately the commander agreed.

"Sadly, neither father nor son was allowed even the smallest gesture in parting. In their hearts I'm sure they knew escape was unlikely and suspected what was to happen next. With the son, Ma Cai, led away, the room was cleared while his father led the commander to the casket. He pointed to three gemstones on different sides of the casket. Pressing these released a locking device and the casket opened.

"Knowing which three to press was important, Wan Yan, but more critical was that they be pressed in the correct order. Ma demonstrated several times before the commander fully understood how it was done. Inside the casket lay monies and valuables Ma had left in it. While they were indeed valuable, they did not match the so-called 'treasures' the servant had spoken of. Ma was accused of lying to his captor.

"Despite pleading that times had been hard in those years, that their family wealth had been used to keep their estate running, the commander would hear no more excuses. He ended any hope of Ma seeing his son again; he flung the old man to the ground in a rage and killed him with one blow to the head."

"And what of the son, Ma Cai? What of him? Did he survive?"

His wife's question lingered in his mind as he paused to gather his strength. He again felt the moist cloth and touch of her fingers on his brow.

"My love, this is but a small part of the story. You will hear soon enough."

"You are weak, my husband, rest and we can talk again later; I am here with you."

Ma Jun rested for what seemed only a short time in her arms before he stirred and opened his eyes. He was relieved to sense the enveloping darkness clearing again.

"My dear, there is little time. I must go on. I must finish. Where was I?"

Once more he felt Wan Yan's touch and heard her echoing the part about Ma Cai being taken from old Ma, and of Ma being killed by the commander.

"Yes, oh yes! But somehow Ma Cai evaded the soldiers who had taken him from the villa. How he escaped? My own father never heard, nor his before him. They did learn that he hid for several days in a nearby village. Former employees of their estate hid him at great risk to their own families. These were men who could be trusted; they had worked for his family for years. They had watched Ma Cai grow into someone who helped them whenever they needed it. They respected him as a fair and compassionate landowner's son.

"Within hours of his escape word arrived of his father's murder at the hands of the commander. He then understood that his father's plan had one aim, to protect his life and the secrets entrusted to them by their ancestors so very long ago. Such is the fidelity of a fine son, Wan Yan. The kind of son I could never raise for my dear wife.

"Ma Cai heard of other villagers less friendly to the family telling wild tales of great treasures on the estate. Soldiers were forcing villagers to begin digging in and around the main villa in search of this wealth. The story tells that they even broke through floors in the rooms of the main house, which was magnificent in its own right. The floors had cost earlier generations of our family a great deal of silver to install, a fortune in itself.

"Our great grandfather, Ma Cai, knew he must act quickly if he was to prevent the two small children's coffins from being discovered. As new coffins in freshly dug graves with no small children in the area having died recently, they would be suspicious the moment they were found.

"That very night he stole back to the family cemetery; it was far from the main house and surrounded by thick woods. Thanks to the lack of moonlight it was engulfed in darkness, and the villagers generally avoided the place and the spirits that dwelt there. He brought with him a small two-wheeled wooden wagon to help move the two coffins. Even in the dark Ma Cai knew where to find the two coffins, and since they were freshly dug graves it took little effort to uncover them again. But moving them into the wagon was more challenging than he had imagined. Despite the noise caused by the wagon's donkey, all went surprisingly well. Surely our ancestors' spirits were looking over him. Ma Cai was able to leave the cemetery in relative silence under the darkness of the night.

"In an effort to get far away from his ancestral home before the dawning of another day, he left the village area and continued to journey through the night. The friends who harbored him and sold the cart and donkey to him were well compensated for their risk. A few gold coins hidden in his shoe took care of them. He was still not sure, however, that their secrecy would prevail were they to be questioned by those searching for him. The less they knew of his plans and where he was headed the better. He told them he was moving far away to a town called Hengyang to start a new life. His real destination was somewhere different. He already had plans in mind for the two children's coffins. He hoped the new location would protect them and allow him to honor the obligations of his father for generations to come.

"To know why he went where he did is important, Wan Yan. The story tells us that Buddhist monks had visited his father's family several times; they were from Mount Tianmen, the sacred mountain near Zhangjiajie. They came to advise Ma Cai's father of the building of a small temple of rest and recovery on a pathway halfway to the top of Mount Tianmen. Pilgrims and travelers could rest and pray there as they climbed the mountain to the original main temple.

"They said that building had begun and the smaller temple would favor donations from devotees, that they would provide honorable recognition for the families of those involved as major contributors. Ma Cai's father had been such a contributor.

"The plan itself had evolved rapidly in the son's mind. He determined to undertake the journey there and see if his idea might work. Traveling alone, he and his donkey cart drew little attention. The two small coffins visible on the rear kept people away, fearful that the spirits of the dead would bring them bad luck, or that the deceased had suffered death by some terrible disease.

"It took several days to reach the village at the foot of the mountain. Ma Cai asked local peasants if there was a way to access the temple of rest and recovery being built along the route to the top of the mountain. They assured him there was a trail up to the site that a donkey and cart could manage. He thus began a slow journey up the twisted pathway to the top of the mountain. The journey grew more difficult as they climbed higher, but the small donkey was sure-footed and Ma Cai had securely tied down the coffins.

"They did not complete the journey on the first day; they rested for the night in a staging area before completing the climb the next day. When they finally arrived, the monks who visited his father earlier that month welcomed him. The monks were distressed to hear what was happening in the area and especially to Ma Cai's father, who provided much monetary support for the temple buildings. Ma Cai described for them one last wish of his father. This was for two of the family's children who died to be entombed for all time in the new temple. A request which, if granted, would of course be covered by more monetary support for its construction.

"The monks were delighted to accommodate their benefactor and gave him a tour of the building work and its progress to date. The building was not large, limited by funding as much as the difficulty for such a small group of monks and workers to carry the needed materials up the mountain. The temple was simple in design, a large main hall with covered walks to the monks' quarters on three sides and a large entryway looking to the hall. To protect the entrance an elaborate wall had been constructed, not only to shield the temple from the mountain winds, but also to keep out unwanted spirits that might wander across the mountaintops.

"The story tells of the temple floor being laid in a pattern, drawing the eyes to a central area where the head monk would be seated during prayer sessions. Behind this a large base was already in place for a statue of the Buddha Siddhartha. Over by the corner of the floor an area as yet unfilled caught our ancestor's eye. He asked if it were possible the coffins might be interred there and fulfill the commitment to his father to prepare the children's final resting place.

"Ma Cai asked that he be allowed to carry out the interment alone, as an act of fidelity to his father. None of the laborers were to be present. The monks thought the request strange but they needed the funds. The artisans could finish the flooring once his work was complete. The monks offered to help, but he assured them he was skilled enough to handle it alone. He agreed the monks could hold prayers and read sutras for the safe passage of the children once the temple was completed.

"Ma Cai asked that there be chiseled into each slab over the coffins the figure of a horse, rather than the family name of Ma, the name also meaning horse. He wanted future generations of his family to know the area of the temple where the coffins lay. Since the gift his father provided for the temple was relatively large they were more than ready to agree to any requests from the younger Ma, especially when he assured them of the new fund.

"Nothing changes in this world, Wan Yan; money through the ages still speaks. Money and blood, so much of both spilled in our history."

CHAPTER 3

MA JUN STILL FELT WEAK, but she was there. Without her he could not continue; he would simply let go and slip into the darkness drawing him in. How would his ancestors treat him beyond this world? Would they forgive him? He thought not. He knew he must go on with the story; somehow Wan Yan would find the way.

"Forgive me, my dear, perhaps I slept too long. Do not leave me again to sleep, please. I need to finish. Where was I? Oh yes, I remember. The next evening, when workers were absent from the site, Ma Cai set about preparing the burial of the coffins. He spent some time planning how this would be carried out, determining it should be accessible to future generations of the Ma family. With materials on site he made a resting place that would protect the coffins underneath and on all sides from any intrusion. He allowed for a separate lid to cover the entire area. On top of this lid he placed layers of stone followed by a gravel mixture, using materials left behind to level the area before the final flooring was to be laid.

"He spent some time working on this until there was no way the workers themselves, other than the monks, would ever know there was anything underneath the area. The drainage around the temple was good. Ma Cai could see that even in periods of rain or snow on the mountaintops, he would not have to worry about the coffins or their contents deteriorating. Prior to interring the coffins, Ma pried open the heavier of the two and withdrew a few of the large stones inside, making sure both coffins were fully sealed and tight before finishing his work."

"Just stones, my husband? Only placed there to hide the contents? That's what was inside?"

Those few words from Wan Yan brought a smile to his sunken cheeks. "Oh no, my dear wife, not mere stones. They were stones of precious jade, but not the typical jade you find. These were rare gem-quality jadeite, finest in this world, from the region of Kachin, close to our border. These precious stones were needed to enable him to carry out the next phase of his plans for the future.

"Ma Cai determined that once the coffins were safe, he would stay and live in the general area. He would establish a new life, perhaps not as grand, but one of comfort. He was confident that with hard work he would be able to succeed anew. The large stones in his possession would enable him to get started again, assuming he could find a small holding to purchase and develop around the foot of the mountain."

Ma Jun struggled to continue—the darkness had come again—but he began speaking of the terrible period during the Cultural Revolution and remembering all that happened. His wife tried to soothe him, aware that he seemed to be slipping away.

"Do not sound so worried, my dear. I am with you," he said. "I may not have much time but I must tell you everything. You know it was only as the Cultural Revolution began that my own father, Ma Yu, grandson of Ma Cai, finally sat with me for a good many hours to relay the story of Ma Cai and the great treasure hidden in the temple on the mount. This was a story he planned to tell much later but could not delay, a story I could never tell anyone, even to you, my most precious wife. With news of the attacks of the Red guards, he took me into his private room and told me of plans that had been developing in his mind for the past months. He would need my assistance to help him, but there were still risks ahead; he said our lives were likely to be in turmoil for some years to come.

"The next day we set off up the mountain to reach the temple as quickly as we could, promising to be back before we were to leave for our cousin's protection in the next county. You must remember when that happened. The climb of the mountain was tough for me; it was late winter, the paths were slippery, and the temperature fell as we climbed higher and higher. I had to help my father as the going grew ever more difficult. When we finally reached the temple my father was shocked to find so much damage there; the monks must have already fled some time before.

"Much of the temple's treasures were stolen by Red Guards or moved away by the monks. Many walls of the temple had been defaced. It was heartbreaking for him. There were slanderous slogans against the temple and its faithful, covering areas of the temple building that carried sacred scripts and paintings from times before. My father determined to complete the task he came to carry out as soon as possible. In some ways the tragic events helped us, as the building and surroundings were deserted. We were able to work without interruption.

"We swept the debris around one corner of the temple. I was truly surprised to see the figure of the horse representing our name of Ma set into two old flagstones, exactly as my father and his father before had told. I had listened patiently to my father's story but in my mind I figured it was simply that. A mere story handed down that became a legend to pass along with our family history, no more than a fable. I was excited to call father over to the place with the horse symbols. We set to work trying to lift the two slabs that, according to the story, would allow us to dig up the two children's coffins. All the time I wondered if our ancestors had really buried anything there at all.

"Levering up the first slab was not easy; the passing years and daily traffic of monks had set the floor solidly in place. It took almost an hour before I was able to break a portion of the slab out. I don't think my father could have done it alone. Once free, the first slab could be raised enough for us to drag it away from the area. After my father rested it was much easier to move aside the other slab with the small horse engraved upon its corner.

"Under the removed slabs we found stonework, aged and well set over the years. My first strike on the compacted surface produced nothing, just the flat resonance of a solid underlay. To me it seemed the very rock of the mountain below. After several failed attempts to dislodge more of this bedding, my father wavered in his faith and belief in the stories told to him. I remember him now sitting on a stone step nearby, head in his hands. He told me how foolish he had been all these years to believe his father Ma Ping's stories. Now here we were, senselessly hammering away at a floor because two slabs had our family symbol chiseled in them! Maybe our ancestors simply worked on the temple and left their mark for future generations, spinning a fanciful tale to pass to us children on long cold nights by the fireside.

"I do not know why but my father's grief and cursing of Ma Cai and all before him made me strike the ground even harder. You have never heard such a scream from me when suddenly a large wedge of material broke free. It revealed the edge of a different material and color, as if indeed there might be something else interred there.
"With renewed vigor we worked our way across the area. To our joy we discovered a burial area about the size that a child's coffin could be buried in, but only one. We worked deeper and after about a third of a meter came across a small, very plain coffin. It looked in remarkable condition for its age. Father put that down to the conditions in the temple floor and how well it had been buried and sealed. It took very little time to remove the coffin and set it aside on the temple floor."

Again he heard the voice of Wan Yan calling to him. "So, my husband, at least half the tale was true? There was a coffin there. Did it contain treasure or the body of a child? Was this entire story simply made up around the loss of a family member?"

Ma Jun remembered his own thoughts at that time; to him, the weight did not seem right, especially after a body's decomposition. My father and I held our doubts until we were able to see what was really inside. I wondered, would we answer the mystery passed down through the centuries from Ma to Ma, father to son?

"I was surprised when the lid of the casket was finally off to see some kind of ancient covering, which still seemed in good condition. We carefully peeled the layers back to get our first look inside. The breath seemed to pass from my father with the deepest of sighs as we beheld the contents. Brown shells; that's all they were! Shell upon shell! Every available space in the casket filled with shells. Father fell to the ground burying his head in his hands, crying over our useless findings. But I did not give up, Wan Yan. I carefully looked at what the shells really were and saw these were no ordinary shells at all.

"On the pale underside of each shell there was a form of writing. Some looked like pictorial renditions, writings unlike anything I had seen. No, not even in old temple writings or on ancient workings. Thanks to a good education paid for by Father, I recognized that these in some way could be a treasure. How, I did not know at the time, but it did tell me that the story our fathers had passed down was somewhat true. I again wondered if there were indeed two coffins as in the legend. Did they really lie side by side? Was this coffin placed to fool future thieves into giving up after finding the first one?

"As my father continued to bemoan our findings I went back to dig even farther down. It was not long before a distinct thud rang out, announcing that something might be deeper below. The recovery of this object, however, took more time; removing it was difficult but finally the ground gave up the second coffin to us. This coffin was clearly heavier.

"As we hurried to open it our excitement grew. Once again we removed the tightly fitted lid to find similar wrapping; gently peeled back it revealed more shells. That sight threw my father into a bigger rage of disappointment; he stormed around the temple room shouting abuses to his ancestors back to the very beginning of time.

"But as Father raged on, I began to lift out piece after piece—more hard shells, each one on the underside beautifully covered with scripts I could not comprehend until I noticed a board set lower in the coffin. With some excitement I was able to pry back this false floor, which wouldn't have done much to hold back a suspicious thief. With the box's weight and size, anyone would have recognized something else was there.

"I could not help but smile when calling Father over to show him there was more to this story. Maybe indeed the casket contained treasure. Momentarily my father's ranting eased and together we looked at what lay before us. I am ashamed to tell you, Wan Yan, when I saw what at first appeared to be useless stones, I too let my disappointment fill the room, storming from wall to wall like my father, cursing this useless Ma legend that so many fathers committed themselves to.

"In the midst of my wailing I was halted by screams and laughter coming directly from my father, now dancing around the room, yelling and shouting his thanks to his ancestors. I thought he had gone mad. When he finally settled down my father told me the news; these were not common stones, they were raw jade, not the kind of jade people like us could ever own. They were real jadeite, the very stones of the emperor. These so-called "Stones of Heaven" had traveled great distances from the mountains of Burma. They were worth a fortune, more than gold or diamonds!

"But, Wan Yan, that was not all. Oh no! There too in the box and under the stones was a container; inside there was a large number of objects and handwritten notes we could read. The objects consisted of many pieces of precious jewelry, finished jade pieces, and a large gold ring, too big for any human finger, perhaps the size of a wrist but definitely not a bracelet.

"The notes were handwritten by the Ma ancestor who originally buried the caskets; the notes laid out part of the early story I have now told you. It said that by reading this, we had either come to preserve the contents in accordance with our ancestral charge, or there was trouble again in the land requiring the treasure to be moved again, or whoever or whatever was the origin of these writings had returned.

"The letter cautioned finders of an overriding curse if these contents were destroyed. If the reader indeed was a Ma descendant he was still obligated to safeguard the contents. It said we might take only what we needed to ensure the survival and well-being of our lineage and to protect the remainder of the contents. I could never tell you this in those times, my dear, yet in truth that is how we survived many dark days." Ma Jun then told Wan Yan how his father, Ma Yu, had taken some of the jadeite stones before sealing the coffins back up.

"In the morning while the temple was still deserted, my father stood watch over the coffins while I made a tour of the area. We knew we could not safely drag the coffins down the mountain. We would have to find another well-hidden and secure resting place. Scouring the mountainside took me precious hours; most of the places where we could install them would also be easy for others to find. Finally I found an old pathway off the main trail used by monks that had gone into disrepair. It was passable, but not a route anyone would choose to take unless desperate for some reason.

"At around two hundred paces from the main path, at the end of this broken and unused off-route, there was a narrow slit of an opening in the mountainside. It appeared to have been a place that some traveling monk had used as prayer refuge, away from the rest of humanity. I figured we could push both caskets into the opening, line it with rocks, fill the cracks with stone, lay on some dirt, and finally plant some roots of the material growing nearby to create a safe hiding place.

"My father agreed with my idea and we used old tools lying around the site to drag both caskets to this new resting place and inter them safely for future generations. We took one piece of fractured temple slab and placed it at the entrance leading to the buried caskets in such a way it could be seen, but only if you were looking for it. As we made our final way back after completing our task we were careful to make the track we had used less noticeable. We even damaged it more in some areas, pulling loose rocks down and laying old dead branches as big as we could manage across the trail to deter others from using it.

"We returned to the temple and did the best job we could to put back the slabs, less the one part we used as the marker. We filled everything in, in such a way that with the damage to the temple no one would see any difference. We counted our steps back down from the temple to the side path again. It was exactly five hundred paces to the side trail. My father chisel our Ma family symbol into the rock, a marker for where to turn off in the future. He made it difficult to see unless someone knew it was there or looking hard to find it. This would become part of the story for future generations, of course, when I passed the story to my son, or if for some reason the family needed financial help."

"It seems Ma Cai must have done well in the end, dear. Was it not so?" his wife asked.

He thought for a while before responding to her question. "Oh indeed he did! Within five years Ma Cai became a successful farmer and businessman; he married a local girl who bore him a son, my grandfather Ma Ping. Two more children were added to the family, but both were daughters. Despite the preference in those rural areas for sons to carry on the work and family duties, Ma Cai and his wife loved both girls and raised all three children with much love and pride. Our families prospered, but strangely have been limited to one son in every generation—something of a mystery to all. Most families in this area, you know, were large with many sons to work the landholdings.

"Great grandfather Cai died in 1909; his passing was much honored by our family and neighbors. Each elder son learned the story of what was hidden safely in the grotto near the temple. Just up the mountain above we could sense its presence every day, but none of us sons fell to temptation; what my own father took from the coffin when we moved it was of little significance in some ways but provided security for us too. Now it is to you to find the marker. It may not be easy, Wan Yan. Your steps may be small, but it is there, believe me, it is there!"

CHAPTER 4

MA JUN HUNG ON FOR another eighteen hours before passing away. A little later Xiao Ping returned, exhausted, to the room the villagers had provided for them. Before she could tell George of the experience, she almost fell asleep at the foot of the bed. He helped her undress and climb wearily into bed, tucking the sheets and quilt around her. He kissed her good night and told her to get as much sleep as she needed; they would talk in the morning.

Xiao Ping arose late to find the others preparing to leave, already overdue for the next scheduled stop in Changsha. They were heading to the city of Zhangjiajie where they would overnight en route; Zhangjiajie was a modest city by China's standards with fewer than two million people. Its history dated back to the earliest of times. The city used to be called Dayong, with roots going back to the Stone Age, the ancient Lishui River still running through the city boundaries.

Charles and Arthur, two Americans on their team, reloaded all the bags onto the lead truck. They also managed to arouse Zhao Feng, the other member of their team, from another of his lazy mornings, urging him to get ready to move on.

Even though Xiao Ping was eager to talk to George about Ma and his dying moments, he ushered her along to leave as soon as they could. The village was reluctant to let them depart so quickly without staying for Ma's funeral, especially with the kindness shown to the old man by Xiao Ping. But Mathers assured Huang they would return in the weeks ahead; he explained that the team was already late for their next assignment and could delay no further. A large number of the local inhabitants gathered to see them off, insisting they come back so the village could show its appreciation.

George and Xiao Ping were in their four-wheel drive Land Cruiser in pursuit of the other three members, already some fifteen minutes ahead of them. George could see right away his wife could contain herself no longer.

"George, I have to talk about this. You need to hear what Ma revealed to me. I feel so guilty about never trying to tell him I was not his wife. I just couldn't do it, you know. I couldn't bring myself to spoil the warmth and pleasure in his eyes. I even called him 'my husband' when I talked to him."

"Look, Xiao Ping, don't worry about it; you did the right thing. He would have been confused at the end if you tried to tell him otherwise. Anyway, I doubt you'd have a story to tell me otherwise, whatever it is."

George tried to concentrate on his driving while she recalled how Ma talked often of their childhood together, always referring to her as Wan Yan. He retold how their parents and the village match-maker brought them together, but expressed sadness over never being able to raise children. He told her repeatedly there was a story he must tell her before it was too late. His pain in somehow breaking an oath his family guarded from earliest times in China seemed to run deep within him. She told George she could see the anguish on his face, despite his illness.

It was a story handed down from father to elder son, an obligation passed between the generations of Mas for who knew how long. As Xiao Ping told more of the story George began to feel the hair on the back of his neck rise. This was clearly something special. He knew if only half-true it would make a terrific story, even if played simply as a dying man's family tale and no more. He listened to everything she told him, despite looking away from the road a few times, which drew caustic remarks from Xiao Ping to watch out. They decided at that point to meet with the others in the evening; they could hear the whole story too and decide as a team what actions they would take—if any. For the rest of the drive, as the gap narrowed between the two vehicles, George's mind raced with the details of the story Ma Jun had revealed.

They finally stopped for the evening on the outskirts of Zhangjiajie after traveling for several hours. Given the fading light and dangers from heavy truck traffic, it was a good place to rest for the night. The hotel they found was small but clean, the restaurant a popular gathering place for the locals. They usually avoided town centers and the typical modern hotels thrown together with such speed during the recent years of economic expansion. Staying in smaller, budget friendly hotels, they often met more interesting guests, and were closer to the local culture of the area.

They were able to reserve a separate banquet room allowing privacy in what seemed a boisterous restaurant crowd. It would give time for the others to hear the story told to Xiao Ping. Feng ordered food for the evening, as always seeming to select enough dishes to feed a dozen people. The variety of food available and how the dishes varied between towns and provinces never ceased to amaze Mathers. It amused him greatly when friends traveled to China and dined with them. "Oh we know Chinese food" was always followed by exclamations of how incredible the food was, "never tasted anything so good in our lives."

The food their team member Feng ordered was in fact not the best, but the hospitality of the restaurant was special. The owners were clearly pleased to see foreigners eating there, especially because they were able to speak reasonable Chinese. The owner insisted on depositing a bottle of local baijiu on the table as his gift to welcome them. He led the first of three ceremonial toasts, after which his visitors were clearly established as "lao pong yo" (old friends) who would be welcomed back for many years to come.

Once the dishes were cleared George asked that Feng and the others to quiet down and pay attention. Before he could say anything Charles spoke up. "So what's this story you have for us, George? It's getting late, so please go on—if you're ever going to tell us about it."

"Well, it's Xiao Ping's story really. I can only say it's one hell of a tale. If it's even half-true, we have a decision to make as to what we will do about it."

Xiao Ping leaned forward and opened her hands on the table, as if to welcome them to some different world and time before exclaiming, "There's no half-truth, George! Yes, Ma Jun was dying; yes, he thought I was his wife; but no, he was not delusional. Definitely not! We need to go back and follow up on this; if you won't, then I will!"

George was shocked by Xiao Ping's little outburst. Whether she said it for effect or not he wasn't used to sharp words between them in front of the team.

Arthur broke the momentary silence between them. " Okay, folks, I'm not too tired to hear the story. Let's hear all about it; you never know where it might take us."

George glanced sheepishly around the table; Xiao Ping had everyone's attention!

CHAPTER 5

◡

XIAO PING NEVER EXPECTED THAT Ma's story would be so fascinating to the team and hold them captive until the early hours of the morning. There would be no question of a brief overview for any of them. They all wanted as much detail as she could recollect.

She had begun as concisely as she could, first explaining how Ma Jun had thought he was talking to his late wife. George interrupted to explain that old photos showed the remarkable resemblance of Xiao Ping to Ma's wife.

Xiao Ping continued. "It seems Ma Jun's inability to extend the family lineage left him no alternative but to pass along details of this family oath and secret to someone other than the son they could never raise. He pleaded with me in his dying hours to find someone to carry on this tradition, now and on into the future. From what he told me their forbears had somehow become guardians of certain scripts, writings of some kind dating back before the earliest emperors of China."

"There was no explanation as to how these originally came under the guardianship of the Ma family?" asked Feng.

"No, that seems to be far back in time, but he told me that I must support the maintenance of the scripts. He also said a treasure of some kind had been provided for the family."

"A treasure, Xiao Ping? Now we're getting somewhere!" muttered Feng.

"For us I think the scripts, or whatever they are, may be the important thing," noted George.

Xiao Ping could sense George's irritation with Feng.

"Did Ma say anything more about the writings or Feng's treasure?" asked Charles.

"No, he claimed he'd seen the treasure itself only that once with his father, Ma Yu. It was to be used in extreme circumstances to protect the scripts and support the guardians. I suspect he wasn't entirely truthful on that point; some of it must have been used to acquire the fine antiques none of you, except George, got to see."

Xiao Ping paused, waiting for other comments before going on. She pulled some hastily scribbled notes out of her small bag and rearranged them quickly. "There's a lot in here, I didn't want to forget anything."

She explained how Ma Jun's father, Ma Yu, and his father before him told how someone would return in the distant future for the treasures; at that point the guardians would be rewarded beyond their wildest dreams. If they were found to have failed in their original oaths to safeguard the scripts, they would face retribution. The terrible consequences would somehow reach back to the ancestral members of their family lineage. "I don't know how that could be, but Ma Jun looked terrified as he told me."

She looked quickly over the first pages of her notes, before glancing back at the expectant faces. She noticed George glance at his watch and the others around the table; no one else seemed ready to go to bed.

"Do you really believe all this, Xiao Ping?" Feng asked. "Surely this is just a story. Every school kid learns about the Taiping Rebellion; it's only one of several in our long history. It began in 1850 and lasted till 1864 when it was crushed by the Qing government. We all know about it."

"Indeed, we're all familiar with it, Zhao Feng," George said. "But should we pursue this more it will help us to know as much of the timeline as we can. If none of you wants to leave at this point, let her go on. I'm still skeptical, but as you can tell Xiao Ping is convinced this is for real In fairness, we've heard a lot more fanciful tales in our work together."

As soon as Xiao Ping repeated Ma's stories of jadeite and other treasures, Zhao Feng leapt to his feet, startling George as the chair crashed to the concrete floor.

"Aiyoo, Xiao Ping, I can't believe this!" Feng said. "Stones of heaven, jewels, gold! George, we must go back. For China we must do this!"

"For China or for you, Feng?" George scowled at Feng.

" But, George, jadeite from Kachin? That's the finest of Burmese jade. You all must know that the emperors of China throughout the dynasties have prized this stone. Even in modern times this "Stone of Heaven" is more valuable than diamonds or gold. This stuff is truly the most precious. Now I know why Xiao Ping wants to go back!"

George slammed his hand on the table, not a gesture the team was used to seeing from him. "That's enough, Feng! We're not in this business for profit. We're uncovering a treasure more important than that, perhaps a trove of history no one has heard or seen before. We aren't even through listening to Xiao Ping. And remember, we have other obligations ahead of us that we're already late for."

Feng quickly apologized for his interruption.

George was becoming more irritated but noticed that his wife was patiently listening to the exchange. He knew what she was up to. The others were being hooked on the story and gradually being reeled in to support her desire to investigate it. Now she spoke up.

"In any case, everyone, this is not the end of the story. When I'm finished you will understand that verifying it won't be easy." With that Xiao Ping told them the next part of Ma Jun's story, how the rest of that night father and son talked about the legend handed from father to son through the years. They had all faithfully determined to honor their family obligations and protect the treasure as best they could, despite what was happening around them. They also understood they did not have much time. She explained how the father took five pieces of the jadeite stone and with his son carefully repacked the writings and precious items along with the rest of the contents including the letter they had found. They sealed the treasures again and determined to find a hiding place they could use for the caskets until a safer time.

"So, George, do we know where this place is?" Charles asked, then looked around the table. "Anyone?"

"Not me, but perhaps Xiao Ping and Zhao Feng do. Either of you been there?"

"No, George," Feng said. "And sorry again about my outburst . . . but the place does exist. I'm not sure about this resting pavilion, or whatever it is, but the temple is certainly there. It's not the original from the Tang Dynasty. That was burned down a long time ago. Today, though, there's a cable car that goes to the top of the mountain. I doubt that many people walk up there anymore, but it should be easy to find. Don't you agree, Xiao Ping?"

"Of course, Feng, as soon as we get there." She smiled broadly and George shook his head.

"All right," George said, sighing. "Let's not get ahead of ourselves here. Please go on with the story, dear."

"Well, Ma had little difficulty finding separate buyers for each of the individual pieces; he traveled to separate jade factories to avoid questions about how someone of his standing came to possess the rare jadeite. He was able to acquire ample funds to buy property, which he planned to farm, and to fulfill his promise to fund the temple.

"He found a landowner in the area south of Mount Tianmen who was anxious to move. The man's children had left the farming business and he was growing too old to keep up with it. Ma made an offer for the land and the man accepted it; he'd had no other offers due to concerns over the Taiping Rebellion and people's fears for their future. Ma, however, believed that the tide was turning and he was fortunate. He didn't have to go into heavy debt as so many farmers did during those difficult times."

" So, George, if Xiao Ping does want to go back it should be pretty straight forward to check the story," Arthur said. "We head to the mountain, go up to this temple or pavilion—whatever it is—and check for a slab with a horse chiseled on it. Won't that clear this up quickly? Surely it wouldn't take all of us to do that."

"Sorry, Arthur; it's not quite so easy. Please let Xiao Ping go on."

"Sounds straightforward to me too," Feng said.

"It would have been more straightforward if not for the Cultural Revolution getting in the way. Ma Jun's area was like the rest of China in that ten-year period beginning in '66. There was much damage done to their cultural heritage by groups of those so-called Red Guards."

"Please go on, Xiao Ping," George said. "Tell them what Ma Jun said happened next."

Xiao Ping confirmed George's comment that during this time the family of Ma Ping; his son, Ma Yu; and grandson, Ma Jun, witnessed much destruction around them. They had been luckier than those in many other parts of China, in terms of the oppression of the landowner class. Their region had remained somewhat calm; however, Ma Jun became increasingly concerned when he saw a local Red Guard brigade, formed in his neighborhood, systematically attacking fellow landlords as well as sacking buildings and homes for items that they considered should be destroyed.

"In addition, the system of land ownership and landlords was under great upheaval. Following what was deemed to be years of abuse of the people by landowners and the feudal system in agriculture, many area landowners were finally brought to task and suffered great abuse and loss of their properties. Some deservedly so; others, however, were simply caught up in the whirlwind of tragic events that swept the land, and many of them were killed."

Charles edged forward in his chair. "So the treasure or whatever is still there? Did he tell you more?"

"Not much more, I'm afraid; he was failing fast at that point. I stayed with him for a good many hours but he barely spoke again. I think he was relieved somehow to have finally told someone the story. It seems that all the Ma family efforts to evade the Red Guard troubles were to some degree wasted. Other locally formed guards had begun fighting with Red Guards in many of the regions, causing them to be spared to some degree. While their landholdings were eventually redistributed, they still remained safe; they were able to use the treasure stones to quietly reestablish a portion of their holdings and live well."

"So did he say if any of the stones were still left, or did he use them all?" Feng wanted to know.

"They kept the stones they'd taken from the casket in a safe place, unknown even to Ma Jun's wife, in case of any other mishap. They lived comfortably for many years, but the story of where their money came from was why they always kept to themselves. As we all know, by '76 the Red Guard turmoil was so far out of control the government and Chairman Mao finally put an end to the misery and restored some semblance of normalcy to the nation.

"So that was it; he told me he had not been back to the caskets. And thinking I was Wan Yan, he begged my forgiveness for never raising their son. Huang, the village leader, confirmed to me that Wan Yan was younger than Ma. We could see that in his photos. Apparently, when she passed away years earlier she was in fact giving birth to their only child. After that Ma went into a great depression. According to Huang the child was male, but lived for only three years; the child passed away from a mysterious disease that swept the region. Ma's own father, Ma Yu, passed away in 1990, and in all the time up to our visit to the village, Ma Jun claims neither he nor his father ever said anything of what happened to anyone, nor made any effort to move the caskets."

The evening ended very late. Xiao Ping answered everyone's questions as best she could. Then, looking around the table at them, she asked what they should do with this story. All of them concurred that it would be best to retire to their rooms and get some well-earned rest; they would talk about it again in the morning. George had no doubts that sleeping on it wouldn't change Xiao Ping's mind; she knew exactly what she planned to do.

ONCE GEORGE AND XIAO PING reached their room he managed to quell Xiao Ping's excitement while they undressed and cleaned up before going to bed.

The room itself was not too small. It had a clean bathroom and reasonable furniture that, while showing its age, was kept in good order. Of great relief was to find the hotel provided nice hot water for showering, a clean toilet and bath tub, something George found much less of an issue than it used to be years ago in China. The one nice thing for him was the hard bed. After living in China for so long a firm bed was just the thing for his back, and helped him sleep well.

"This bed's good for me; the damn beds in those new hotels are getting softer all the time," he said. "Thank goodness this is nice and firm. I'm really beat after today. The evening took longer than I thought. I need to get some sleep, and so do you. We can lie in tomorrow but not too long; we really do need to get a move on. The folks in Changsha are expecting us."

George told Xiao Ping to say no more about their discussions until the morning. Begrudgingly, Xiao Ping did some quick laundry in the sink using the small package of powder for cleaning clothes she always carried with her. After washing the items, she hung them to dry overnight above the tub. The bed was not king-size or queen-size either; it was comfortable width-wise, but being quite tall George's feet stuck out the bottom.

Once in bed George began putting together a few notes about their recent visit, something he always did at night before sleeping. It seemed to calm him from the day's activities and helped him unwind. He had resisted overdoing his intake of the hotel manager's local baijiu, so his head was relatively clear as he jotted down the key areas covered by Xiao Ping. When he finished his notes and turned to say goodnight to her she was already fast asleep, not surprising to him after the events of the past few days. He had no doubt the next day, when Xiao Ping was awake and refreshed, she would plead with him—and the rest of the team—to add this to their list of projects. He did not anticipate just how passionate or determined Xiao Ping was about to become.

The morning came sooner than George had expected, with the noise of Xiao Ping rising early as usual ahead of him and getting ready for the day. He sleepily swung his body over the side of the bed. Finding the slippers that all Chinese hotels provide, he shuffled over to the bathroom to express his usual morning's greetings and shave before taking over the shower. Within an hour they were both ready and headed off to join the team for breakfast.

George brushed off Xiao Ping's "Well, what do you think?" and numerous "What shall we do?" queries with his own comments regarding at least getting breakfast and coffee into them before discussing anything work related.

Once they had all gathered in the restaurant area of the hotel and finished breakfast, the talk immediately turned again to the stories of Ma Jun, and to Xiao Ping's desire to hear their opinions on investigating this further. Charles and Arthur told Xiao Ping they basically loved the story but were looking forward to the next project they were committed to. Zhao Feng seemed to be as excited as Xiao Ping, and, while George said he found the story very intriguing, as team leader he was more concerned with getting to the next scheduled stopover in the year's itinerary. George could see Xiao Ping's irritation.

"George, can't you see how exciting this is? We really must get involved right away. It's such a potentially staggering opportunity to prove this story out and find the coffins and their contents."

He felt Xiao Ping's eyes bore into him while out the corner of his eye he could see Charles and Arthur smile slightly, as if they were waiting to see if he was going to give in or continue to fight her. "Look, the best I can figure is that we'll be finished with the current projects in around six months. We can certainly look at this further then, assuming our university colleagues agree it's worth pursuing."

Charles and Arthur agreed that George's approach was logical; it would be quite useful to line up the university to do some investigating on their behalf in the interim, and then try to fit it in later in the year.

Xiao Ping remained calm for a while, but George could see the color in her neck gradually redden, her voice become more agitated and louder, her hands and arms start flying in all directions in front of her, mostly directed at him! Clearly she was on a mission and she wanted to be sure he could see where she was headed. He knew she was not going to take no for an answer on the subject. She finally glared at him, and he felt her stance stiffening.

"I am not moving anywhere and I've decided to head back and follow this story to its end . . . with or without you, George!"

Arthur nudged Charles as if acknowledging that George had already lost and would have to figure out a solution to their predicament.

"Okay, enough already, Xiao Ping! Look, everyone, we can't change the schedule set by the university—and ourselves—some time ago. Too many arrangements are in place, and if we don't show up the people involved will be very unhappy. This won't do our reputations much good when we want to work in other locations.

"The only way to pacify my lovely wife and stay on schedule is for Xiao Ping and me to head back. Charles and Arthur can take Feng with them to Changsha where we can all meet later. I still suspect we'll find this just a great story passed amongst the Ma families for all this time. In the end, that's all it will be, a good story!"

Feng said he didn't want to continue on to Changsha. He preferred that George go on and let him and Xiao Ping do the detective work. He was quick to voice his views on that but George told him that with Charles and Arthur's Mandarin skills somewhat limited there was no option; Feng had to go with them. They discussed advising Professor Cai Levee of the situation and their change in plans, but Arthur confirmed Xiao Ping's reaction that this was too early to bring it up; in all likelihood Cai would press them all to go on and come back later. They decided it better to say that George and his wife needed a few days' break before continuing. The couple had not had one for a long time and recent weeks of travel had been grueling.

So the decision was made, much to George's wife's satisfaction. Since she was the proponent of staying, George left her the task of calling Cai and letting him know their plans. While not happy about the senior team leader not going to Changsha, Professor Cai finally asked that they at least join the others as soon as they could, and finally to enjoy their break, especially in such a magical part of China around Zhangjiajie.

After settling the hotel bill for the night, the group left with much fanfare. The hotel manager and key staff gathered around to bid everyone good-bye; they would be welcome back anytime. George had Xiao Ping phone Mr. Huang, the village leader, that they were heading back for a few days to take some leave. George was a little surprised when Huang suggested to Xiao Ping that they stay at Ma Jun's vacant home while it was decided what should be done with it.

All Ma Jun's possessions were still there. Huang said they could stay in one of the other rooms away from where Ma had slept, laughing a little if they were worried about ancestral spirits. Xiao Ping was not enthusiastic about the idea, but George thought they might come across something in the house useful in their quest. Without being disrespectful to Ma's belongings, George hoped they might find something to help them unravel the story and determine what parts of the tale were true. Xiao Ping had spent many hours there and knew the home well so staying there would be relatively easy. George on his part certainly never had any phobias or fears of the spirit world.

Xiao Ping finally agreed with George it was a reasonable idea, and so they took the smallest vehicle, the Mitsubishi Pajero, and a minimal amount of luggage and equipment and headed back in the direction of the village of Ma Jun. Charles and Arthur with Feng at the wheel headed off to Changsha in the larger truck with their main supplies, including recorders, computers, and movie cameras.

George had planned how he and Xiao Ping would approach the next few days. First they would fully understand the lay of the land in the region, map out the different spots in Ma's story, and discuss with close friends and neighbors some parts of the story to see if there was anyone else familiar with any of the Ma family. They would not, however, reveal important details of the story itself and risk having hordes of locals around them, either following their every move or thinking that, indeed, there was a great treasure waiting to be grabbed.

Huang welcomed them back with open arms and led the couple down the narrow lane to Ma's home. As he unlocked the doors he told them everything was ready for them. Ma's bedroom door was closed but not locked and the rest of the house had been thoroughly cleaned for them by Huang's wife and two ladies from the village. Huang insisted they join him for dinner that night and would not take no for an answer. George would have liked to rest but could not say no; he hoped Huang would keep the toasting to a minimum and the drinks to beer only, rather than the local brand of baijiu liquor that could bring him to his knees.

Dinner that evening turned into yet another banquet. Huang had invited other village elders. As always, none of the wives appeared and Xiao Ping was the only female at dinner, the women servers bringing out dish after dish until the visitors begged them to stop. It was a little awkward trying to explain to the group why they had come back, so they decided to tell them Xiao Ping was interested in writing about Ma's family, and life in the village, a story to run alongside their earlier meetings in the village. They asked if they could be pointed to a couple of the villagers who were closest to the family and asked Huang to arrange for them to come to the house the next day to meet them.

By the time the many dishes were finished and the last bottle of baijiu emptied, the evening came to an abrupt ending at around 9 p.m. George enjoyed the customs surrounding the dining experience in China, especially the predictability of the ending of the evening. No matter how much food had or had not been consumed, or liquor drunk, there was a finite time for the meal. After two to three hours, the evening would end with everyone suddenly jumping up; there would be a flurry of farewell hugs amidst great laughter, murmurs of friendship forever, and so on. Of course, occasionally the evening did go on; fortunately, this night ended at a reasonable hour and George's head was clear. It would not have taken too many more farewell toasts to necessitate some help to walk him back to Ma's home.

The first villager to show up the next morning was a Mr. Zhang, one of the oldest people in the village but still going strong. Short in stature and bent over from years of working the fields, he had a dark tanned leathery skin with wrinkles that left no part of his face smooth. A wispy white beard gave him an appearance George had seen in many old Chinese paintings but saw less and less these days; Xiao Ping asked if he minded being photographed, which caused the old man to smile broadly, revealing a mouth missing a few teeth. Zhang was ninety-four years old but looked about ten years younger. Asked the secret to his long life, he quickly replied that plenty of wives, hard work, and his daily glass of baijiu were, in his mind, the main reasons.

When asked about Ma Jun and how long he had known him Zhang said he had known Ma from the very day of his arrival. In his strong and forceful voice he told them he remembered the first time Ma appeared in the village. He was the only one to see Ma, as it was quite early in the morning. He said that fog was hanging low around the village and most of the villagers were still sleeping. Zhang said the only reason he actually saw the man, whom he later knew as Ma Jun, was the noise of the rattle of an old cart passing his house, unusual at that time of the day. He also noticed the cart was loaded with something, but he could not tell if they were belongings or maybe goods to sell in the next village.

"It was some time later that Ma again reappeared in the village with his father, Ma Yu. They were looking for a place to start over; as Ma told our village chief, he and his father had lost almost everything. It was always a bit of a mystery to many of us how the Mas ended up with their home and some land to cultivate. Not too many people liked to ask at the time, but there were rumors a large amount of money must have changed hands.

"We always noticed that Ma Jun lived comfortably but they kept to themselves by and large, not that they wouldn't help us in the village if additional hands were needed. Ma Jun seemed to form no particular friendships and for many years there were rumors, which both Mas denied, that they were hiding from someone or something. My old lady always thought there was something suspicious there, but I was not one to gossip in the village."

Zhang took a while to think and then continued. "After about a year Ma met Wan Yan. She was something of an outsider, not a direct descendant of anyone in the village. Her family also moved into the village during the years of turmoil. She was quite a local beauty—oh yes, quite the one—but somewhat reclusive, thanks to the antics of her brother, Wan Haibo. Ai yo, he was notorious in the area, a bad seed that one was. Haibo was the local Red Guard fanatic. Fortunately for most of us he spent his time away in larger towns trying to climb the guard ranks and establish a reputation there.

"As for Wan Yan, the men all steered clear of her. Haibo was known for his violent temper. Although other Red Guard brigades passed through our area they knew Haibo's reputation and the family was left in peace."

George learned that Zhang, on the other hand, suffered miserably; he had been a large landowner in the area in early years. It was actually through him that Ma and Wan Yan met in the first place. Zhang's voice sank slightly as he related one particular story. A chilling darkness came over his face; George could see it was still a painful memory for him.

He told them he had already suffered a number of humiliating denouncements at the hands of the guards; his landholdings were taken from him and pieced out to other families and workers, but this particular event had been unusually harsh. George knew the history of those times. Though instances like this raged through China before and during the Cultural Revolution, it seemed from what Zhang said their village had not suffered as much as other areas to that point. People there were humiliated and beaten so badly that deaths resulted. In any event, on this particular day outsider guards moved into the village. Old Zhang's voice shook as he told them more.

"Those demons denounced me as a capitalist landowner! They went way beyond name-calling and chanting slogans with the crowds. The guards screamed out for my blood and started beating me mercilessly. Haibo not only joined in the effort but to demonstrate his importance in the region led the attacks on me. Me! A man who fished with him as a boy, gave candies and fruit to him for school, and never did any harm to him at all. Can you believe it?

"They dragged me into a stable area while most of the villagers, my friends and family, left the stable in disgust for the open area outside. They were either afraid for themselves or the brutal attacks on me. I never knew why. But this Ma Jun, who had been watching from a distance, apparently did not leave. I thought later that perhaps something snapped inside him. Whether this same thing happened to his father or not I never found out, but I heard later how Ma ran into the stable grabbing an iron pitchfork and made his way to the side door of the stable.

"About the same time Wan Yan, who had only returned to the village that afternoon and been told what was going on, also rushed to the stable. She may have been small, but by the gods, she had the tenacity of a lion. She headed straight for her brother standing over me. I tell you I was ready to die, the pain was almost unbearable."

According to Zhang she literally lunged at her brother's throat screaming at Haibo to get out and never come back.

"Oh, he was in shock for sure at what she did, and right there in front of the other guards! I can still hear them laughing at him even today. The two argued more, which made things worse, but then Haibo struck his sister violently across the head. She crumpled to the floor like a lifeless sack of potatoes on our farm, right next to me! Even the others must have been surprised; after all, she was his sister, his family. How could he do such a thing to her? It was then I finally saw Ma out of the corner of my eye push through the group. You should have seen him pin Haibo against a stable beam with the pitchfork across his neck. He threatened to squeeze the very life out of the man. Ma gave Haibo the choice of taking his troop away from the village right then and never returning, or told him it was going to be the last time Haibo was going to see another day alive.

"I could see Haibo looking around for help from his fellow guards. I remember the shock on his face when he saw a crowd of our villagers standing behind the guards with whatever tool they had been able to lay their hands on. They had scythes, axes, and other pitchforks we used in the fields. That was a sight, let me tell you.

"Haibo could see the situation was hopeless. He nodded his agreement to Ma Jun signaling to others they needed to leave. He rubbed his throat and gave Ma Jun one of the cruelest looks I've ever seen. In the voice of the devil from below he told everyone they would be back. But Ma just stood there, never moved. He stared him down and warned the others that the next time, if they ever came again to the village, Haibo would wish his end was coming from a pitchfork rather than what Ma would have in store for them. At that, the villagers apparently joined in the abuse and the Red Guards left with their tails between their legs."

Zhang's expression changed as he carried on his story, stressing his admiration for what Ma did that day.

"Many of our villagers came to help lift me up from the floor and tend to my wounds. They all begged my forgiveness and expressed their sorrow that it had gone so far that time. I could not stand so they brought me a chair. Ma Jun gently raised Wan Yan from the floor, wiped the blood from the deep cut on her face, and carried her out of the stable."

Zhang told them how this was also the story of his role as match-maker, because after this incident Ma and Wan Yan grew to be friends and more. They finally married some time after the Cultural Revolution was over and real peace reigned over the countryside. That would have been around '79, Zhang guessed. He said the couple tried hard for a family but Wan Yan died at childbirth, just as Huang had told George and Xiao Ping. The tragedy deepened when the son lived only three years before dying of tuberculosis. Indeed, he said, Ma never got over losing them and not having a son. He fell into a great depression, which he never seemed to come out of. He pretty much kept to himself from that point on, although Zhang would still see him occasionally.

Zhang felt he owed his life to him and did what he could to give him some company. Beyond all that he had not much more to add for George. He commented that Ma's father, Yu, a nice old gentleman, had passed away quietly about twenty years ago but also kept to himself. He acknowledged again the Ma family was not from around there, but he had no idea what drove them to come there. They had never talked about their past. Zhang did say that the villagers always respected the Ma family; they were always ready to help their neighbors. Wan Yan's family also appreciated Ma Jun after that, even though it was the last time they ever saw Haibo.

George and Xiao Ping met with three other villagers that knew Ma, but learned little more. Old Zhang had at least recalled Ma passing through the village with his cart, a small point indeed. So far this was one of the few hints that anything Ma had told Xiao Ping was true; of course, for Xiao Ping this was an important comment. They had about given up the idea of any more discussions when a young woman stopped by to see them. She had heard there was a foreigner with a Chinese wife visiting the village asking about Ma and she wanted to see them. Her name was Wang Huiping and she had known the Ma family while growing up. They apparently took some interest in her, as her parents had been quite poor and it had looked like she would not be able to continue her schooling.

Wang Huiping was twelve at the time and apparently quite the little artist, which surprised her parents as no other family member had ever shown any aptitude in that area. Working the land and supporting the family home were the skills left to the Wang family members, male and female alike. Whatever had sparked the talent in Huiping it was a surprise to George when she mentioned that Ma Jun had been a big influence in her life and really inspired her to bigger things. More importantly, she said that, until the death of Wan Yan and his son, Ma had been quite the artist too. This also surprised them.

When George and Xiao Ping had toured the Ma's home originally there was no sign of canvasses in progress nor paints, brushes, or any typical artist supplies. Huiping confirmed Ma had thrown them all out except for some pieces he had given her. In any event, she told them to open their eyes and look around at the paintings on the walls; Ma did half of them.

Ma apparently helped Huiping so much she had been able to secure a position in Beijing helping in the artist district known as "798," an artists' commune in an old electrical manufacturing facility built in the 1960s; it had since grown to become quite a tourist attraction for art. Huiping initially worked for a well-known artist who helped her to become one in her own right. She now had her own gallery, was quite successful, and lived very comfortably with a fellow artist, but they were not yet married. It was only by chance that she was here today in the village to see her parents, gathering some ideas for an upcoming exhibition in which she intended to feature her past and local village life.

Xiao Ping suddenly stiffened and a surprised look came over her face, "Oh, shit!" she muttered, then excused herself and disappeared into the house, after which George heard several doors banging, a period of silence, another outburst of "Yes! Yes!" shortly after which she came back. She was red in the face. When George asked what was wrong, she murmured, "Nothing, nothing, please go on!"

They talked for another hour but it was a little embarrassing for George; Xiao Ping seemed quite distracted from their conversations.

It was clear when Huiping got up to leave she had known Ma better than anyone, even old Zhang. She knew how Ma met Wan Yan and she'd been directly involved with him, albeit through art, and gave them much more insight into his character. Her description of Ma Jun left George the impression that he certainly was not one to make up stories and appeared to be honest to the core. Something Xiao Ping had always said about the man.

Huiping apologized to them saying it was time for her to leave; she had to drive back to Zhangjiajie for a meeting with one of her art dealers, then fly back the next morning to Beijing. She gave George her card with the phone number and gallery address and suggested when they did get back to Beijing she would love to have the couple visit the gallery and have lunch or dinner with her. With that she gathered up her things. They walked her to the door and into the narrow lane thanking her very much for the information, saying that if there were anything else needed they would give her a call.

As soon as they were back in the house and the door locked (likely no one in the village ever locked their front doors) Xiao Ping grabbed George's arm and he was dragged to Ma's bedroom as she yelled, "Come on, come on!" Inside the dark and quiet room she quickly flung open all the curtains on the two large windows that opened onto the courtyard.

"Look, look around you!" she exclaimed as the room flooded with light.

"Well, I never . . . I missed that completely! Ai yo, look at that, my god! Just look at that! Why didn't I see these before?"

Around the room were five works of art that Xiao Ping confirmed had Ma's signature chops, images that further reflected parts of Ma's story. They both rushed from picture to picture, one showing the resting temple, one a view of the mountain showing the side of the mountain with the pathway visible, one showing a fork in a path—with no marker off of it—that showed some unique-looking rock structures.

"The paintings themselves are so detailed and exquisitely painted, certainly of a quality I would love to be able to purchase for us, Xiao Ping. Do you think I should ask Huang in the village if they can find relatives of Ma's? I would like to know if they're interested in selling any? I would gladly buy all of them."

George could see Xiao Ping was elated with her discoveries, which all seemed to strengthen Ma's story. But no matter how much George liked them, even to the point of wanting to buy some, he still cautioned her the paintings could simply be a reinforcement of a story—a fictional story. He told her again that perhaps the paintings were just that, and nothing more.

After dinner that evening they pulled out their photographic equipment, tripod, and lights to photograph the paintings in detail. If there was going to be any truth to this story they thought the paintings might contain detail to help further their quest. That evening before going to bed George downloaded the photos onto his computer and also summarized the day's activities. He would have to e-mail the review to the others once back in Zhangjiajie; there was no connection in the village to the internet, only one shared phone at the local store where villagers could line up to call the outside world. Huang had told George that this situation was about to change; the local "party" had designated the village an area for upgrade and investment. One of the first efforts was to bring the modern world of communications to them.

In the morning they gathered up their things, having decided the next step would be to check out the area around Tianmen Mountain. First of all, though, they needed to do a little more research on the place and what they might need to take with them. George was not saying to his wife that he was now fully on board with the story even with the new information, but he certainly felt there was enough to warrant further investigation. He had assumed their visit back to the village would not turn up anything, which would dampen his wife's obsession with it. George knew now that was not to be; she seemed even more excited and certain of Ma Jun's story than ever!

The couple said their good-byes yet again to Huang and thanked him for his arrangements. George left him his phone number and address in case there was ever a chance to purchase any of Ma's art-work. They again headed out of the village, not sure of what they were going to achieve, but anxious to see whether anything would come of this effort.

CHAPTER 7

~~~~~

THE JOURNEY THAT MA ORIGINALLY took through the village must have taken quite some time with a cart and donkey in those years; the roads were little more than dusty tracks back then. He would have no doubt avoided the main travel routes so as not to encounter any of the gangs on the road, nor expose his cargo to too many prying eyes.

For George and Xiao Ping the journey was relatively fast but it did take a little more time than anticipated finding a place to stay. The hotel, or lodging house, was more of a backpackers' nightly stopover than a hotel. They did, however, have a nice tidy room in the back of the hotel on the top floor, which looked out onto the mountain where their search would begin.

The first thing Xiao Ping did, after entering the room and verifying that the small, single-person bathroom was nice and clean, was to fling open the picture windows and fire up her laptop to review the photos of Ma's paintings. While the paintings were clearly of the mountain situated before them, they were definitely not from the perspective of where they were staying. This meant that if they were going to trace the steps in Ma's story there would be more work ahead to locate the trails he took.

The lodge provided basic food for its guests within a kitchen area, where the owner and his family prepared a few dishes that were laid out buffet style. There was hot water, which could be used alone or along with the tea bags or jars of instant coffee that sat along a shelf above the food. Feeling quite hungry they decided to eat in. They helped themselves to bowls of noodles and some freshly stir-fried vegetables, which George found well made and quite tasty. He thought it a pleasant change to sit down with steaming hot tea without having to suffer through rounds of baijiu drinking, although there was local beer available in a locked cooler for sale if one needed it.

The kitchen had about twelve small tables and an atmosphere that was quite lively, with both Chinese and foreigners; most had been out hiking during the day and were sharing stories about their adventures. Furthermore, a number of children from the different groups were all getting along famously in a corner area of the kitchen that seemed made for them.

As the evening wore on everyone got to know each other, as travelers like this always seem to do. George therefore decided it might be fun to show these people the pictures and see if anyone would recognize the side of the mountain and at least get them started in the right direction. This caught everyone's attention and within a half hour they had everyone coming by their table and giving ideas as to where these views were from. The opinions were remarkably very varied; one Chinese hiker even suggested it may in fact be a different mountain.

After about an hour the owner of the hotel and his wife came by to say hello to the guests and make sure all had eaten enough. They were personable and outgoing, and they got along famously with everyone. They had been backpackers and hikers themselves, which led them to establishing their small but seemingly thriving lodge. When the owner, who called himself Sam to make it easier for foreigners, heard what was going on he came over too. He introduced himself first to Xiao Ping formally in Chinese, then slapped George on the back in a heavily American accented English to welcome both to the area and his hotel. He had hiked the mountains in the area for years and claimed to know the region like the "top of his hand," which George duly corrected for him to the "back of his hand," causing laughter all around.

George showed Sam and his wife the photos, and the couple immediately and almost in unison said, "Oh yes, of course, that's the old trail we used to use ourselves! It's not used much these days as most of the tourists use the cable car to get to the temple. The old trail can be difficult in parts now."

Sam told them he had started his business originally eight years earlier but hiked the region for close to twenty. He did not go out much anymore; business had improved to where they were quite busy taking care of everything; besides, he had developed arthritis in his right knee and hip making it hard to hike for any distance. He still got out occasionally because he loved the mountains and the land so much, but it was becoming less and less frequent. His wife, on the other hand, whom he originally met while hiking, was as sprightly as ever. She still managed most of the lodge's tour guiding service when asked.

George watched Xiao Ping's eyes light up as she pulled out the photo of the painting showing the resting temple alongside a pathway heading up the mountain; she asked the couple about it. Sam was surprised to see the picture and pointed at it with his finger. "This painting is really special; whoever has done it was a fine artist indeed.

"I know exactly where this place is! It's a pity but it's fallen into disrepair. You know, so few travelers use the route these days. I'll say this: these paintings must have been done some twenty or thirty years ago. Of course I could be off a few years."

When Xiao Ping asked if his wife would be able to take them there Sam readily agreed. "Unfortunately, you will have to wait until day after tomorrow; my wife has an all-day guided trip planned for tomorrow. It was prepaid so we can't change it."

George told Sam they understood and would appreciate her help. "We will gladly pay for her time but we only need her to get us there, and then leave us for the day."

Sam said that would work fine for his wife, if George and Xiao Ping went early enough in the morning; his wife could then be back to the lodge and squeeze in one of her short afternoon trips. With that, George felt they had made some progress and decided to call it a day.

George could tell Xiao Ping was excited but frustrated that they would not be headed out right away. The couple set off to their room and together gazed out at the mountain, which was shrouded in darkness until the odd lights began to flicker in the distance. They wondered aloud what the day after next would reveal after all they had learned that evening.

Now they had another day to fill since they couldn't leave until the following day. George was impatient but figured they could actually relax after breakfast, take a short walk, then spend the afternoon reviewing their notes and planning.

One thing Sam did have in his lodge was a basic phone line and internet connection, so they were able to call their colleagues. They also e-mailed the photos and update of their investigation to Charles, Arthur, and Feng.

Charles told George the Changsha visit was going well. He said both George and Xiao Ping were missed but, according to Charles, Arthur had really charmed the people they were working with. Feng, however, had received bad news from home; his father was ill. Feng had left promising to be back as soon as he could. His father, at eighty-eight years old, was apparently quite frail and Feng had already lost his mother two years earlier. In any event Charles told George to do what he needed to in furthering the quest, but asked that he and Xiao Ping be on their way to join the meetings there as soon as possible.

After the call they decided to talk over the entire situation concerning Ma Jun. They would go over all their notes to see if anything was missed, review the photos of the paintings, and just generally talk out where they were in readiness for the outing with Sam's wife. George was meticulous as always in documenting everything. Xiao Ping did her best to develop a timeline of events in Ma Jun's story while he laid out the ancestry details. George checked stories of the Taiping Rebellion in the area, and whatever existed on the internet relating to the Cultural Revolution and Red Guard activities.

"Look at this, Xiao Ping, this is interesting. One source here described an incident in Changsha back then where factional Red Guard brigades fought each other as occurred in other parts of China. It says here a group was able to get their hands on weapons after breaking in to a PLA army ordinance warehouse. They apparently decimated their opponents in a street battle. And, guess what, Xiao Ping? It mentions that the leader of the losing guard brigade was none other than Haibo, Wan Yan's brother!"

"Let me see! Let me see!" Xiao Ping almost tore the laptop from George to look at the article herself. George looked on as she scanned it quickly. "So it looks like he really did not return to the village but stayed in Changsha. The account of the fighting seems to indicate that Haibo's body was never found; he appears to have been the only survivor. I'm not surprised. I'll bet he was a coward and left everyone there to save his own skin."

As they worked their way together through the entire story George detected a slightly puzzled look come across Xiao Ping's face. He repeatedly asked her if there was anything else she could remember Ma saying, perhaps something that was not in the notes. She mused for some time then murmured, "No, no, I don't think so, no" with one of her gazes into the distance, which told George something really was lurking in that little head of hers.

"Well, Xiao Ping, what is it? Just tell me!" It was then she told him that she did recall some of Ma's last words, but had not bothered with them too much because they didn't really mean anything.

Since George was always meticulous in his research of stories and recorded every single thing he pressed her to remember what Ma had said.

"Well, okay, it was something he shouted out before he slipped away."

"Tell me what it was, as closely as you can."

"I can tell you verbatim what he said, darling. He shouted, 'Wan Yan, there is something you must remember always, always. I am my father's son, I am my father's son. Remember, I am my father's son, I am my father's son.' You don't think it means anything, do you, George?"

All George could say was he was glad she remembered these words and would file them away for future reference, agreeing with Xiao Ping it seemed of little help in the task ahead.

Later that afternoon, they received a call from their new friend Huang at the village with some information. He had personally been involved in gathering and boxing up Ma's things in the house to keep everything safe for possible relatives who might be found. He thought that perhaps in Ma's papers some relative's name would show up. In the end they had not been able to find anything really helpful; most of the papers were bills and receipts. There was, however, one strange item—a receipt for two small specially made coffins from a funeral company in Zhangjiajie.

Xiao Ping, listening on the cell phone speaker to the conversation, immediately brightened and signaled to George with a thumb up, as if to point out more proof of the story. When George probed for more details on the receipt Huang said there were no indications of any family involved, simply a specification of the construction (something plain, simple, and of cheap pine to keep the cost low).

George could see from Xiao Ping's expression that her mind was closing in on the fact that the coffins were ordered from Zhangjiajie and not the local village. Not a real issue, but if Ma's story was correct, there was never time to order and procure coffins that far away from Ma's original village. George next asked Huang what the date on the receipt was; Huang could not remember the exact date but he did recall it was some month in 1987.

After thanking Huang for calling they sat together on the bed looking at each other in silence for a while. They looked at each other with this latest news. This threw a whole new level of doubt. The pictures relating to the story had altered George's view but this news brought back his original suspicions that this was indeed one of Ma's stories developed in his loneliness.

This new information on the coffins put everything in a new light; the timing just would not fit in at all. After a further hour of sitting in the room, George reading one of his books, Xiao Ping reading through her notes all over again she managed to convince herself that everything fit too well despite George pointing out the anomaly of the coffins.

"Look, George, the story Ma thought he was telling to his beloved Wan Yan was simply too clear. I just can't see any reason for Ma to fabricate anything for a wife he seemingly loved so deeply. I think it's simply that the coffins must have deteriorated and Ma replaced the original ones to avoid any damage to the so-called treasures."

"Really, Xiao Ping, I find that a little farfetched. But since we are here, and of course for my own peace to keep you happy and avoid weeks of misery, we will still visit the mountain. But I won't leave Charles and Arthur handling our commitments alone. We really must head off within the next couple of days to join them."

Although he could see she wasn't happy, she clearly appreciated his concession to check out the mountain and the pictures. George knew if he had not agreed to go she would have insisted on staying behind anyway and headed up there on her own, and he would have worried about the possibility of an accident while she was rummaging around, perhaps slipping or falling and breaking something.

They ventured out of the lodge to eat that evening, away from the nightly buffet or snack area and searched for something more substantial. They passed one small restaurant that looked extremely busy. George guessed it must be good, but it turned out to be a donkey meat restaurant. In the end they settled on a dumpling and noodle restaurant that seemed popular and at the same time looked clean throughout. George ordered wide noodles with vegetables and asked for a little spice, while Xiao Ping tackled a fiery noodle dish on the menu from Sichuan province. After being prodded several times to try them he did, to his regret. The beer he was drinking disappeared very quickly as he tried to cool the burning in his throat and mouth, much to his wife's amusement.

They finished the meal, which cost an unbelievably small amount, and walked back to the hotel. It was now dark and the roads were finally quiet. They talked again about what if anything they would find the next day. George tried to convince her to keep her expectations in check; he could see how excited and desperate she was that the trip to the mountain would more than support Ma's stories.

They rose early the next morning, headed to the breakfast area, and waited for Sam's wife, a really nice person who had adopted the name of Ivy for their foreign guests. She used the name so much now that even for Chinese guests she referred to herself as Ivy, which sometimes to George sounded more like "Herve." She was an attractive woman, petite but clearly very tough and fit, her skin well tanned. For a Chinese woman her voice was powerful, with the many sounds that one often hears coming from a long-time smoker. When George asked her politely if she smoked, she laughed and quickly told them she was a fully reformed smoker, thank goodness, and doubted that even with her hiking and climbing she would not have remained in good physical condition had she not stopped—under

Sam's pressure—three years earlier. Xiao Ping and George had never smoked; he tried a pipe earlier in his professorial career. Having been lucky to obtain tenure at an early age he felt it gave him a more elderly presence and an added air of "experience." He gave it up when he managed to burn a nice hole in one of his favorite and most expensive jackets.

All their tools for the day's trip were packed in large backpacks. They asked Ivy to drop them at the closest point she could to any of the places she recognized from their paintings, and they arranged it so that she would pick them up at 6 p.m. The lodge prepared their "hiker kit" for the day; for them it consisted of a ham and some kind of sauce sandwich, some strange-looking chips, fruit, and a bottle of water; a few candy bars were thrown in for energy. It was nothing special, but for what they were planning to do it would be more than adequate.

En route to the mountain as new guests Ivy asked them a number of questions; she appeared to be trying to figure out why they were so interested in the mountain and this particular spot when it was off the regular tourist route. They told her it was just that those paintings she had seen photos of came through their work, and they wanted to see them in the flesh so to speak since they were in the area. When she asked how long they would stay Xiao Ping blurted out "one week"; at the same time George said "two days," to which Ivy commented she hoped they would stay for the longer period as the lodge appreciated the business.

Ivy said there was much more to see in the area than Tianmen Mountain. She also offered to Xiao Ping, not realizing George had a Chinese driving license, to rent them an old four-wheel drive Beijing jeep they could use during their stay. To help they could rent it for the week at half price; they would only need to pay for the gas, with no restriction on kilometers. Xiao Ping said that might be a good idea but George only said maybe, depending on how the visit went that day and if they decided to stay the week.

The journey to the mountain was pleasant enough; Ivy was a great conversationalist, switching between Chinese and English depending on the subject and whether or not George was part of it.

They arrived at an almost empty parking lot that obviously dated back to a time when this mountain route was popular. They still had to pay a small entry and parking fee, but the area was largely vacant; a couple of sorry-looking vehicles and a worn out electric guest cart were parked off to one corner, the cart sitting on blocks with all the wheels gone. The two cars covered in dust confirmed they could not have been used for years.

For the purpose of their visit the situation was ideal; the fewer people there were in the area the easier time they would have scouting around. The road that climbed up to this parking area had been a little winding. George had the feeling it followed in parts what could have been the trail mentioned in Ma's story. Ivy told them in older times the journey by foot would have taken longer but this initial ride to the parking area took a lot of time off the journey. They would not be too far from the resting temple remains, once they had parked and set off on foot up the trail.

After unloading backpacks from the car, they assured Ivy they were fine and that her directions were clear, not to worry herself about their safety until the 6 p.m. pick-up. Ivy left the parking area and headed back down the road, away from the mountain toward the lodge and the next group of hikers awaiting her help. With that they began to walk up the trail hoping that well before lunch they would reach the so-called resting temple to determine what remained of the facility after years of neglect. George could not help but see the obvious sense of urgency in Xiao Ping as she tried to get him to climb the trail at a faster pace. He hoped for her sake they would indeed find something but he remained inwardly pessimistic that they would ever discover anything new at all.

CHAPTER 8

AFTER AN HOUR OF HIKING what seemed a magical area, they could see in the distance a structure emerging; whether it was what they were seeking remained to be seen. They arrived at a large clearing as the last of the morning fog lifted off the mountain. The building lay before them, empty and dilapidated but quite serene in its own way. Much of the small pavilion had fallen in, but some parts of the structure remained intact. It was not as big as they had imagined from the story; George thought it looked larger in the painting. Xiao Ping quickly withdrew a file from her backpack holding photos of the paintings. It became clear even to untrained eyes that, while this temple had seriously deteriorated from the picture Ma had painted, the outline was far too close for this not to be the place in Ma's story.

George persuaded Xiao Ping that before they started rummaging around it would be good to eat and drink something, regretting he had not packed a thermos of good hot coffee to accompany their lunch. They spread the food out on a large rock away from the temple and settled in to eat. They were a little surprised at a rustling noise, or more of a shuffling sound, coming down the trail and around the corner to their left. The slight buzzing gradually increased in volume, and soon into sight came an old Buddhist monk chanting some words among which George recognized "Nomo Amitabh a, Nomo Amitabh a." The monk glanced in their direction, smiled briefly, waved, then bowed his head. He continued to shuffle down the trail, increasing slightly the pace and volume of his chanting giving George the feeling their presence had interrupted his daily praying and meditation on a normally deserted trail.

Looking again at the temple they noticed some parts of the roof had collapsed while others remained in good shape. Sturdy round pillars that had long since lost their smooth coverings and reddish colorings held up the remaining portions. The roof tiles, where there was still roofing, appeared to be in good shape in one corner of the building. Elsewhere, either tile was missing, or tufts of weeds and even the odd small sapling sprouted from the roof remnants.

As they began to look around the monk returned, this time not chanting to himself but approaching with a broad smile. George struggled to understand what he was saying. Xiao Ping managed quite well as he confirmed being originally from Hunan province; he apologized for his local dialect and asked where they were from.

They were anxious to get started on their search but the monk seemed delighted to have foreigners on his trail to talk to. George's slight irritation with him quickly melted away when he told them how he began his Buddhist journey here on the mountain some forty years ago; he was clearly an expert on the history of the region. He was primarily a devotee of the temple on top of the mountain origi-nally built during the Tang Dynasty. It too had fallen into ruin over the years but was replaced with a more recent construction fully in accordance with the Tang architectural design.

He explained that now there was little human traffic on this pathway as the French, years before, had built a cableway to the top of the mountain; it was over 7000 meters long and rose to a height of 1,279 meters.

He rattled off many more facts at length. In addition to his re-ligious duties George thought he must also have been the temple's historian and tour guide. He also talked about the Tianmen cave, a large cave high up the mountain with a roof height of 130 meters in-side, adding that there was a vegetarian restaurant at the temple too with stupendous views. The couple understood why the new route and cable car would be more popular and make for a less harrowing ride up to the temple, just from their own short walk up to this point.

George could sense the monk looking over the resting temple with some kind of sadness in his eyes as he reminisced about the building's past. It seemed to have become his special project from all those years ago when worshippers and tourists struggled up the mountain to reach the temple. His suggestion to rebuild the stop-over where people could relax, rest, and pray a little had been well received by the temple leader; however, the funding was such that approval was given only on the basis that new funds, over and above those for the main temple, could be found. He and three of his brother monks had thus toured the region, sometimes far from the area, seeking support for funding of the construction.

About this time a gentle rain began to fall and the monk suggested taking cover, asking them to follow him quickly—straight into the resting temple. As they moved into the rear of what must have been the main building they were startled to find a corner about ten meters by ten meters that was in good condition. It had some basic seating, its walls and woodwork painted with a number of Buddha scenes. There was nothing too elaborate but faces of the Buddha provided a calming influence. Seeing the surprised reaction on the visitors' faces the monk asked them to be seated. He smiled and told a short story from a couple of years before.

"At that time I was coming down the mountain and encountered a foreigner looking around this temple. We fell into a discussion that lasted the whole day and ended with us praying together. I remember the American's name was 'Shtott." George politely corrected the monk that in English the pronunciation was likely Scott.

"Of course, yes, Shtott, exactly. He was visiting the area and also walked the trail only to find this sadly dilapidated resting temple. He said he'd worked in China for several years. In his early time in Beijing he was introduced to a number of temples by a good friend and found great solace and peace in them as I hope you two do. His friend helped him to understand some of the basics of Buddhism, although he admitted there was still much to learn, as there is for all of us.

"At the end of our simple prayers the foreigner impressed me so much with his sincerity I took off a very old jade Buddha, suspended on a worn leather strap around this old neck of mine for some thirty years, and gave it to Shtott. The American was surprised by what he saw as generosity and asked where he could write to me when he returned home. He said he would like to return this honorable favor. I wrote an address on a slip of paper for him but told him the greatest return favor for me and for Buddha would be for him to continue his journey on the path to enlightenment. I hoped he would come back and visit someday."

The monk described how three months later a letter arrived from some place in the USA called Asheville. In it was a letter of thanks for the monk. The necklace the monk had given him turned out to be quite old and extremely rare, so for him to have been given this was indeed a great honor. Anyway, from their day together Scott understood how much the resting temple meant to the monk. He had enclosed a bank draft for ten thousand dollars to be used as the monk saw fit in helping with his dream to restore the temple stop to its original condition. With that the monk swept his hand around this protected corner of the temple and said, "This I dedicated to Shtott and also Ma Jun."

At that remark George and Xiao Ping sat bolt upright. "Ma Jun? You knew Ma Jun?" Xiao Ping said.

"But of course," the monk replied. "Who do you think painted these walls? Ma Cai the great, great grandfather of Ma Jun, contributed to the original construction. Ma Jun and his father, Ma Yu, were later contributors to the funding of the building. I visited the Ma family several times collecting small amounts for the building costs.

"Yes, during its early construction the Mas visited the temple and I'm told offered an especially large contribution to enable the temple to be finished, not as grand as originally envisioned, but certainly enough to finish the work. So sad what the Red Guards did here, especially after Ma Jun created some really beautiful paintings for us."

Xiao Ping immediately blurted out "And the burial of the Ma children?" This drew a surprised expression from the monk, questioning how they would ever know that.

George immediately jumped in to say they had come from the village where Ma Jun just passed away after telling them of this burial, saying no more to the monk about treasures. A great sadness seemed to come over the monk, who commented how sorry he was to hear this sad news. He would initiate prayers and ceremonies for Ma Jun as soon as he could; he would also try to arrange for Ma Jun, his father, and the original Ma Cai to be honored in a main temple ceremony. He told them the family had done much for the temple over the years and, of course, the children were still buried there. When George touched again on the subject of the Cultural Revolution and the Red Guards he clearly bristled at the mention of them.

"Much of the destruction you see was indeed caused by the Red Guards and their fanaticism; they even threatened to blow this place off the mountain. They never did, but still they caused considerable damage. May Buddha forgive them when they meet their destiny, as all of us will."

Xiao Ping casually asked where the children had been buried so they could all say a prayer over them for Ma. The monk led them to another area, protected from the rain but not the wind and dust. He grabbed a brush nearby and began sweeping the floor area. He told them every day he would, if no one were around, sweep the floor clear of debris and dust, especially around this section of the floor. The other monks would have simply left the temple there to crumble, but this monk had too much of a personal connection to let it go completely.

When he finished sweeping, the first thing that jumped out to George and Xiao Ping was one particular floor slab. On the corner chiseled deep in the surface was the Chinese character for the horse, or Ma, just as in the story. Likewise, the next slab to it had a flaw across one corner. The monk told them that a similar mark had been there, but somehow it had repaired or replaced. His suspicion was the slab may have been damaged and then repaired by Ma; he recalled being gone for several months to avoid the troubles and coming back to find the floor as they were seeing it that day.

George finally looked at his watch and noticed the time had flown by. It was 4:30 p.m., and they needed to get back to the parking area to meet Ivy.

They thanked the monk profusely and told him they would be back the next day, giving the reason for their interest in the area to be for the background material of a book they were developing. It would follow the lives of a number of Chinese families from ancient to current times, which in this case was partially true as far as George was concerned.

By the time they reached the car park area Ivy was already waiting. They headed straight back to the lodge, along the way accepting her offer of renting the old Beijing jeep. They had decided to stay longer and knew they could not expect her to abandon all her other guests just for them. They both thanked her profusely for showing them the way to exactly where they needed to go, and for the use of the jeep in the following days.

Ivy warned that the vehicle was very "basic"; they might have trouble getting it started. "Don't give up," she said, laughing, "and don't crank the windows or they will never go back up again!"

She indicated where the jeep would be waiting in the morning; she or her husband would fill it with gas and leave keys inside the ignition. She parked back at the hotel, and then left for her office saying not to worry about the jeep being stolen with the keys left in it; once George saw the jeep he understood why. Ivy also strongly advised them not to drive it at night.

That night, after eating downstairs at the buffet with other hikers and having quite an enjoyable evening, they both sat down to compare notes and thoughts on the day's events. So much had fit in with the story told to Xiao Ping, but perhaps with a little different viewpoint; the story only proved that the Ma family indeed supported this resting pavilion on the mountain and that two caskets were buried there. The only remaining piece of the puzzle for tomorrow was to track down the small cave entry in which Ma had supposedly placed the coffins and see what that would bring. George wondered if they would find the trail and infamous marker in the story.

They called their colleagues that night for an update; Charles and Arthur reported that things were going well. The new interpreter they were using for the local dialects was good, apparently very attractive, to the point they jokingly commented that Zhao Feng could take a lot longer before coming back. They had tried to call Feng on his mobile but there was no reply. Charles still had a home number for Feng's father from one of the Spring Festival trips he had made previously. Xiao Ping tried calling there too so she could update him directly but there was no answer. She determined to call him in the morning. Hopefully he had not taken his father, who already had one stroke a year before, back to the hospital again.

They decided to leave even earlier the next morning for the mountain. George was still anxious to get back to the team, even though they were doing fine. He felt guilty that his colleagues were working hard while he was not there leading the effort. He and Xiao Ping asked Sam to put a lunch box together for 6 a.m. and leave it in the communal fridge for pick-up. He would have none of that;

he would be up and have it freshly made for them. Sam promised to rustle up a large thermos for George saying he would fill it up with his finest imported coffee, likely Nescafe instant.

—⌒—

George could tell Xiao Ping was even more excited the next morning as she rushed to get ready, shouting at George to get out of bed, shower, shave, and dress so they could be on their way. Sam insisted on making a quick breakfast for them; he would not allow them out of the lodge for a day's hiking without something warm inside. No one else was around so they sat in the kitchen chatting with Sam while he cooked. He deposited two steaming dishes on the table for the couple, together with a hot pot of green tea for Xiao Ping and his "imported" coffee for George. The couple ate quickly; Xiao Ping seemed in no mood for a leisurely breakfast. She had already packed a few basic things in her backpack in addition to the lunch; she included her cameras and a battery-powered lamp in case she needed added light for photographs.

George decided to let her drive the jeep that morning, a sorrier piece of an excuse for a vehicle than he had ever seen before. Neither could get it started, so it was back to the lodge to ask Sam if he could help unravel the mysteries of the vehicle. He gladly came out and guided them through a starting sequence that seemed completely illogical and included hitting the dashboard three times. To George's disbelief, when Sam went through the routine she fired up like a baby. When he shut her down and said it was George's turn to try, he got most of it right but missed hitting the dashboard three times. It stalled and he gave up. When Xiao Ping had everything in the correct sequence the jeep fired up right away for her too.

They finally sped off to the mountain site with Sam yelling out not to worry about the gearbox clunks and grinds. By the time they arrived at the parking area on the trail George was glad to get out of the bone-shaking vehicle. At least they were now free to explore on their own, without an onlooker trying to figure out what they were up to. They headed up to the resting temple and looked around more than they had been able to the day before while talking to the monk, although in many ways they had been fortunate to run into him. They needed to keep an eye out for him, but they hoped since it was early they'd have some time before he might show up.

Ma's story indicated walking the main trail to look for an out-of-use side pathway that would have a marker beside it. Expecting the area to be overgrown, they determined to walk together, one behind the other, to check both sides of the trail. George was not sure if the side pathway was headed off to the left or right of the main trail. Maybe Ma forgot to mention it or Xiao Ping missed hearing it.

The couple had a frustrating morning, walking up and down two or three times to no avail. There were a number of side paths in disrepair, which made it very difficult finding the right one. Despite all efforts, and with no visible marker, they still could not locate the right path.

CHAPTER 9

AT LUNCH THEY SAT DOWN in the temple to rest and eat Sam's packed lunch. They were quite pleased to hear the shuffling of feet and chanting sounds coming closer. The monk appeared happy to see them again sitting below Ma's paintings in the renovated rear of the temple. He accepted their invitation to join them once assured this was indeed a vegetarian luncheon. Sam had packed plenty of food, enough it seemed for three people.

As they talked more about the paintings and the sad passing of Ma, George decided to see if he could narrow the search down without giving too much away.

"Old friend, is this trail you walk daily the only one you and your fellow monks took over the years before the new cable route was developed?"

"Why, yes. This was the main route to the temple in past times but there were side paths in earlier years our monks would take alone. There we would meditate, of course, sometimes remaining in the elements for days alone as part of our search for enlightenment."

George thought for a moment before commenting. "As we walked the trail we noticed quite a few of those pathways your fellow monks must have taken."

"Oh no. There was only one main route most of us monks took in those days. All the other markings of pathways you have seen are what my brothers called the 'picnic trails' of tourists. They used to come here often, before the cable car was installed on the other side of the mountain."

Xiao Ping's eyes brightened; she asked if he, or any of the monks, still went there, but he indicated the practice had subsided over the years. He told her he was too old now to continue doing it, as it could be dangerous.

"This area was famous for its many caves too you know. For safety reasons the local government tried not to have tourists wondering off the main trails. They visited our temple several times and asked for our assistance in discouraging devoted followers from seeking out those caves where statues of the Buddha were once placed."

George acknowledged he had also seen a number of old signs in Chinese that said not to leave the main trails and beware of falling rocks, etcetera. He asked if the monk might show them the path he used to take; they wanted to take some photographs for their article as related to the history of the mountain. The monk readily agreed, advising that it was no more than 100 yards or so down the trail from there, but he was not surprised they missed it now that it was overgrown.

As soon as George and Xiao Ping were shown the pathway they almost kicked themselves; they had passed it at least three times. Slightly overgrown, it traversed the main trail and one side seemed like it might have been used more often. When George commented to the monk how the one side looked more traveled than the other, he agreed. He affirmed it was also the side he always used. The other side had not been so popular because the views were less spectacular. George thanked him for showing them where it was and told him they would take a walk along his old pathway, which drew a few warnings from him to be very careful; the path was dangerous in some spots, with rock falls over the years.

The monk said he was happy to have seen them again, and he wished them well. Xiao Ping told him they expected to be back the next day and would again welcome him in joining them for lunch.

The two went to the pathway and looked around some more. Although it was overgrown they could see some disturbance but no markings as such. They had just started down the path when Xiao Ping stumbled over some loose rocks and fell right across George's path. Fortunately he was able to catch her and was pleased she wasn't hurt in any way. Other than a scrape on her forehead he sensed that her pride as the experienced mountain hiker was a little tarnished as she mumbled an excuse for the fall. As George looked around he finally saw the weathered marker they had been looking for; it was clearly a crudely chiseled outline of a horse, just as Ma had told Xiao Ping his father Ma Yu had carved.

Feeling more settled they walked the path, continuing to look for the place where Ma supposedly entombed the coffins after removing them from the temple. It was clear to George, looking at the slight damage to the pathway, that someone had definitely taken the trail earlier—not too long ago.

After walking some distance George heard Xiao Ping yell for him to come quickly. On the right was a narrow entryway that had been hastily filled in but was by no means invisible. Whatever brush had been pulled over it must have moved in the strong winds of the night. If someone was not looking for anything like this, as they were, they would have easily passed by and not paid any attention to the area. They went over to the entryway and George removed some of the materials that were meant to hide it.

"Well, look at that!" was about all George could say when he looked down where the rocks he removed were falling. Right there under the loosened pile of rocks was the tip of a slab buried in the ground with the symbol of a horse chiseled into the corner.

"Look at this, Xiao Ping. Whoever was here tried to remove the marker but couldn't. Either the rock has bedded in with the weather extremes over the years or they never had time to pull it out. We should definitely ask the monk tomorrow if anyone else has been by here recently. But who could it have been? Someone from the village? A relative we don't know about? The girl who studied with Ma?"

Xiao Ping just shook her head, her brow furrowed. George continued to pull smaller rocks down from the top. The opening was about five feet high and quite narrow. Widening it enough for George would be difficult; all they could do was open it from the top. Whoever had been there before had stopped bothering to pull away rocks about halfway down and must have crawled in; that told them the individual was small.

They both had the same concern, that Ma had told someone else the story in the village. Someone had definitely been inside recently. While George continued trying to enlarge the opening, Xiao Ping decided to slide in the same way someone else had. She grabbed the large lamp from her backpack and slid in with it.

It took George some time to squeeze through; removing some of his outer clothing helped slim him down a little but it was a struggle getting in. Xiao Ping was already standing there ahead of him, the narrow entry, barely wide enough for any coffin to slide through in fact had opened up into a small cave; she was piecing papers together while around her lay the broken remains of two open children's coffins.

George gasped. "My god, Xiao Ping, it's true!"

"*I* never doubted it, never," she replied a bit sarcastically. "But look at the mess here; there's a problem, George." The papers she was piecing together had been scattered across the area. Someone must have read them, ripped them up in disgust, and thrown them aside.

"What do they say?"

They sat down together on the edge of a rock jutting out from the inside of the cave while she translated the Chinese for him. The letter was elegantly written in a calligraphy that was quite beautiful and easy to read.

"Does it say who wrote it?"

"Oh, yes. It's from Ma, all right. It's awkward piecing it together but listen here: 'To those who have returned for the treasure, on behalf of the Ma family and the generations who have guarded its secrets and treasures, I regret to the bottom of my soul and of my ancestors' souls, I have failed the oaths made since the beginning of time by successive Ma elders and their sons. Not only am I the first Ma not to raise a son to this world, I am the one who squandered treasures such that finally there is no more. It was said that upon your return to this land if the treasures were depleted, a great curse would fall on all our ancestors, and for that I am deeply ashamed. The events of recent years in our lands have resulted in great tragedies, death and destruction. I used this treasure to keep from starvation and gave much to others that were in need. Today I take out the last remaining piece that will help a friend and prepare for the day I pass from this world to the next. To my father Ma Yu, Ma Ping, and all the fathers before, I beg forgiveness. I go to my resting place expecting to be tormented in the afterlife.' It's signed, 'Ma Jun.'"

George sat there for some time gazing around the cave, looking again and again at the letter to determine if this was some fake to throw them off the trail, that someone had already taken the treasures away. Xiao Ping looked despondent to George; she seemed convinced the letter was authentic. George was not so sure; the one thing he had noticed was the ground inside the cave and outside on the trail. If indeed the letter was not a fake, and the so-called treasures already taken out, then he figured the pathway would have been much more disturbed than it was.

After they climbed out of the entryway with the torn pieces of the letter in hand they placed the rocks back, not for any reason they needed to, just out of respect for what may have been Ma's last act in connection to the treasure and its guardianship.

Xiao Ping had been convinced of a successful outcome after finding the temple, talking to the monk, locating the marker, and finding the entry. George could tell she was crushed by the contents of the letter and the empty coffins. And she was angry that someone, neither could guess who, had been there before them.

They made their way wearily down the path to the jeep. It took several attempts to get it going; they were so dazed by their finding on the mountain that they kept forgetting the starting sequence. Fortunately, when Xiao Ping got really angry at the jeep and started to cry the thing fired up. George drove back deciding she was in no mental state to drive. He remained convinced it was still just a great story, but certainly had to admit to himself the visit revealed more truthful elements than he'd expected.

About all George could do to calm his wife down was to tell her all of this had ended too neatly and perhaps there was more to the story. The best thing they could do was to get some food and drink, clean up, and go over all the events again—and document everything as they always did.

Once back in the room they called Charles and Arthur to advise them they would be staying part of the next day and then head out to meet them. Their colleagues were happy to hear that. Charles told them that Zhao Feng too would be traveling back the next day; his father had pulled through and was in good condition.

Xiao Ping was pretty miserable but said she needed to talk with someone from a Chinese view. George could hear her phoning to Feng's father's home to talk to Feng before he left for Changsha in the morning. Charles and Arthur expressed their regrets the search had ended the way it did, pointing out how close villagers were; they assumed Ma must have related the story earlier to a close friend.

Xiao Ping sat glumly in bed reading a book to try to keep her mind off what they found, other than muttering to George that she supposed they would be heading off to Changsha in the morning. All he could say was he guessed that was all they could do. George pored over both their notes again and thought about the sequence of events, applying the same thought principles he always used in these cases.

He tried to divorce himself from the personal involvement between Ma and Xiao Ping. He poured a glass of wine bought from Sam's "wine cellar," a bottle of Great Wall Five-Star Cabernet Sauvignon. He thought the wine actually tasted quite good. As he sipped from his glass he thought of how wine's popularity in China had grown by leaps and bounds. A far cry from his first experience in the eighties when locals would put lemon and ice in the wine, a time that Chinese wine and vinegar seemed to be closer relatives than they were supposed to be.

As he ran through the pages in front of him, it suddenly hit him like a bolt of lightning. He yelled out to Xiao Ping asking to confirm what Ma said about a number of things. She confirmed what was written in her notes and no more. He sat there grinning from ear to ear, with her questioning what he was looking so smug about.

"We're not going to Changsha in the morning; we are definitely going back to the resting temple!" She leapt out of bed and ran over, grabbed him by the shoulders as if to try to shake the smile off his face, shouting loudly at him.

"George Mathers, what have you found?" And again, "What have you found? Tell me right now!"

He asked her to sit next to him and shared his thoughts. The key, if correct, was the coffin's invoice itself—and, possibly, some of Ma's final words.

"Okay, here me out on this. I could be way off base. Anyway, try this: We have proof two coffins were purchased somewhat recently. It's dawned on me that, while we assumed the cave we found was empty, this was perhaps simply a decoy set by Ma. Remember the story of how the cave entry was supposed to be two hundred paces along the trail? Think about it; we didn't measure it out, but as far as I'm now guessing now I bet we were only 150 or so paces along the trail, depending on the size of Ma's stride. "His comment about being his father's son likely related to the time Ma Cai's father fooled the Taiping, and then Ma Yu and Ma Jun tried to safeguard the treasure by moving it again from the temple. My guess is, the coffins we saw are indeed the original ones, and the new ones are in another location, moved there for safety. Think about it, those coffins were definitely not new, even though the cave had kept them in pretty good condition.

"Did he perhaps tell someone his story, regret it, and then need to protect the coffins' contents from the person he'd confided in? Were his ramblings to you a repeat of what he told Wan Yan before she died? Did Wan Yan pass the information along to someone, her rogue brother perhaps?"

Although George's words elevated her excitement, he warned her again he could be completely wrong. They would visit the area one more time, and if they found nothing, they would abandon any further search. George still suspected that in the end all he could do was determine this was indeed a great story with some facts woven around it, but a story all the same.

Xiao Ping managed to contact Feng before he boarded his flight to Changsha. It was a quick call and George overheard little of the conversation before she hung up. A worried look appeared on her face. When George asked what was wrong she responded it was nothing; she would talk to him later about it. He did notice her troubled expression but didn't press her further.

CHAPTER 10

THEY FOLLOWED THE SAME ROUTINE as the day before but left a little later as their conversation the night before had lasted until around 1 a.m. The jeep started first time thanks to George's skills in following the startup routine. They bounced out of the pothole-ridden parking area on what Xiao Ping told George she hoped would be a decisive day in their quest.

After hiking up the trail they ran into the monk, out earlier than normal but with a bounce in his step. He smiled broadly as he approached them. After morning pleasantries and comments on the weather, George apologized profusely for having spent so much time together without even asking his name.

"My son, to know the name and not the person means nothing, but to know the person and then the name means everything. To my fellow monks I am simply "Master" but my real name is Jing Kong. The name in Chinese means clean and empty, something that nicely links my meditation efforts to clear the mind and being of all worldly matters."

He seemed most happy to tell the couple of an exciting development. The previous day he had received a call from Beijing and the caller was none other than Scott Ramey, the American who donated the money to fix part of the temple. He wanted to travel down the next day and meet the monk again along with a fellow Chinese traveler.

Jing had told Scott another foreigner was in the area and gave him the name of Sam's lodge as a convenient place to stay. He told Scott he was sure George and Xiao Ping, if still in the area, would happily give him and his Chinese friend a ride to the resting temple. Scott said he hoped the couple would not consider it a nuisance to take them along.

George looked at Xiao Ping with quizzical eyes; being married for so long they could often read each other's mind. This seemed to George very weird. Were this Scott Ramey and his friend involved in what seemed to be going on, or it just a happy coincidence?

The monk seemed overjoyed to have this visitor return; his generous donation had enabled much-needed repairs to be done on his beloved temple. Once the monk finally wandered back to his walk, cheerfully shouting good-bye, they heard a renewed enthusiasm in his daily chanting. They smiled at each other and commented he was indeed a human who was happy with his lot in life.

They headed to the trail and turned off the pathway as they had the day before, the marker clearly visible now. George began to pace out the distance properly this time. He told Xiao Ping to stop counting her steps; being much shorter than him, her steps would be nowhere near the specified distance. As they walked Xiao Ping kept looking around her. When George asked what was bothering her she simply replied there was nothing, she was just taking in the surroundings.

Eventually they came across the cave access and noted it undisturbed from their activities the day before. Passing by the entrance, they headed along the path, which became more treacherous the farther they went. It looked as if they were the first people to pass that way in a very long time. At about a hundred twenty or so yards from the main trail the path seemed to dead end. They carefully scanned the area for signs of a hidden cave entrance but found nothing. George decided they would retrace their steps and double-check every nook and cranny between the two locations. Neither could turn up a hint of a hidden entryway.

At this point George spread out the lunch Sam had packed for them. Xiao Ping was anxious to keep looking but George insisted she eat. He told her it would relax them and clear the mind. Staring at the dead end of the path it occurred to him that maybe it was not the end of the trail. The monk had told them there had been numerous rockslides in the area; he looked carefully at the coloring and texture of the land around the area. To his eye it seemed they were indeed looking at a rockslide, not a dead end. He told Xiao Ping they would finish lunch and then do a little careful climbing over the area.

Xiao Ping would have nothing of his suggestion and told him he should leave any of that to her; she was younger and more agile. She preferred George relax with another cup of Sam's gourmet coffee while she investigated. As she clambered over the rocks George could see how skilled she was; he was somehow relieved she was looking for a way over first. She was gone about fifteen minutes before her face appeared over the rocks with a big smile, and she confirmed that George had been right. It was definitely a rockslide. The path continued on the other side as it curved around. She also commented, while breathing heavily, that the view was spectacular. "No wonder the monks used this route to meditate alone," she said.

They loaded everything on their backs and Xiao Ping led George over the rockslide and onto the trail again; this portion was even less traveled than the first part. They had to estimate where the 200-pace mark would be due to the rockslide. George figured just by eye they could be plus or minus ten paces off so it might take a little time. He wondered if maybe the so-called 200-pace marker was also some kind of false measure to throw people off finding it.

They spent two hours scouring the path, their spirits waning; they could find no hidden cave or entryway. There was only the sign of an area where a rock, shaped like a seat, jutted out from the mountainside. An area at the back had obviously been where the monks prayed; carved into the rock was the upper part of the Buddha, but the statue had been defaced. Xiao Ping said it was most likely due to Red Guards, who did so much damage in their time to religious objects. It had not been an elaborate carving. It would have added to the atmosphere, though, for any monk dedicating himself to hours of prayer and meditation, while gazing out on the incredible scenery below.

As George wandered farther down the path, beyond the 200-paces mark, a clump of trees smaller than their neighbors alongside the path caught his eye. Not only were they smaller but a different species, though perhaps from the same family. Standing there for a while he noticed a different smell in the area. Gazing up he saw a small entry-way that looked more like some kind of animal access; perhaps the smell was coming from something inside. He kicked at the lower part of the dirt packed around the base soil and a small group of stones started to show; they were carefully stacked, not naturally placed. He kicked around the dirt harder to reveal more of the stone and then yelled out to Xiao Ping to come right away! Once she was there it was apparent he had found another filled-in entryway to a cave. George wondered if this was the answer to their search or simply one more entry filled in for safety.

George knew what Xiao Ping hoped it would be and started to carefully uncover the rocks sealing the entry to create an opening. This effort took a long time; it was a far more solid construction than the other entry. It still seemed more like an effort to disguise it than to just be there for safety. They finally cleared the mud and soil from parts of the packed stones and rock sealing the entry.

By then it was getting a little late in the day. Unless they wanted to work in the dark they needed to head back and return the next day. Xiao Ping was all for staying but the last thing George needed was to fall over the rocks climbing back to the trail. She suggested they at least peel a few more stones away and get a peek in the cave. They managed to excavate a few of the small rocks away from the top for an opening about the size of a man's head and shoulders to look into.

Xiao Ping took out her camera with an optic light and flexible lens from her pack and snaked it into the opening. She wiggled it back and forth for about ten minutes with George repeatedly saying they should get going, that everything could be opened up the next day. Finally she pulled the extension out, her face beaming. "Guess what? A coffin!"

"Not two?" George asked.

Xiao Ping ho-hummed a little, then said that with the small opening she could only see one. With that they put the rocks loosely back to cover up the hole and packed for the journey back. George had to admit he was now almost as excited as Xiao Ping; clearly they would be extending their stay and seeing more of their friendly monk!

On the way back to the hotel they talked excitedly about the day's events, George of course taking great pride in having figured out what had happened. He could not wait to tell their colleagues. As soon as he mentioned that, Xiao Ping snapped at him. "Absolutely not! I was going to tell you something earlier but I didn't. We are saying nothing to Charles or Arthur about this yet—especially not Zhao Feng!" George was stunned by the remarks and by the serious look on her face.

"Look, George, I would have said something earlier but I wasn't sure until now. I didn't want to get you started on something that turned out to be a mistake on my part."

"What the heck are you talking about? What's the problem with Zhao Feng? You know he had to leave for his father. Are you angry because he left Charles and Arthur high and dry?"

"Not at all. You know I called Zhao Feng yesterday, right?"

"Yes, of course . . . I remember you looked a little strange afterwards."

"Exactly. When I called him on his cell about his father the first thing he asked me was if we had found anything yet in the cave. Not how we were or anything else. He told me he was at his father's house, but flying out the next day to Changsha. He said his father was out of the hospital and back home."

"So what's wrong with that, Xiao Ping?"

"Well, he didn't know I had his father's number and already called him there a couple of times. The first time there was no answer. I assumed he was at the hospital and didn't think any more of it. The second time though, before I finally got hold of him, a relative answered. She told me Zhao Feng was away working in Changsha, that his father was not there."

"Really, that's strange!"

"Yes, she said he was on vacation with Zhao Feng's sister and would be gone for the month. When I asked how his father was, she said he was in excellent health and fully recovered from his stroke a year earlier. When I talked to Charles and Arthur about what we found, they also hadn't been able to get in touch with Zhao Feng. Therefore, as far as I'm concerned, the only way he could have known about everything was that he was the person or with the persons that opened the first entryway."

"And you haven't said anything about this to anyone?"

"Once we were in Changsha I planned to confront him about it and get the truth out of him. In the meantime we need to say nothing to anyone. If Charles and Arthur ask, we are simply going to take a side trip and have decided to meet them at the next assignment near Wuhan."

George's mind raced. Why, he wondered, hadn't she mentioned her discovery about Feng—and her concerns—before? Although he wasn't sure what to think at this point, he agreed to follow her suggestion for the time being.

"This is getting more serious than I thought; that is, if you're right about Zhao Feng. Who knows, maybe this guy Scott and his friend are somehow involved too. Tomorrow we'll make our way into the cave with plenty of time to look around. Then we might finally see what this so-called 'treasure' really is!"

CHAPTER 11

THEY ARRIVED AT THE LODGE a little late and feeling quite weary. Sam sought them out to say there were two new guests at the hotel asking for them; they were in the buffet area eating having just arrived from Beijing. He'd put a note under their door to call Room 31 or 32 once they returned. To get it over with, George and Xiao Ping decided to go directly to the buffet area, introduce themselves, then head to the room to clean up and rest.

The dining area was relatively empty, so spotting this Scott Ramey and colleague was easy. They strode up to their table and introduced themselves. Both visitors rose and apologized profusely if they were inconveniencing George and Xiao Ping. Scott Ramey said hello warmly, and the Chinese gentleman introduced himself as Diao Lijun, a director of the Antiquities Department of the Palace Museum in Beijing's Forbidden City. Scott said he was just a visitor who was happy to be back in China having retired at the end of the year before. The Chinese gentleman's stated profession brought a quick glance at George from Xiao Ping as if to say "What now?"

George indicated they would love to talk, but he and his wife really needed to clean up and get some rest. He did mention to Scott that they understood he was an old friend of the monk Jing Kong, and aware they might like a ride with them to the mountain to visit with the monk in the morning. Scott genuinely thanked them and said that would be perfect. While he would have liked to fill the couple in that night he felt they might as well all, including the monk, listen to the reason for the visit together if that was possible. George told him that might be difficult as some days the monk's walks were not always at the same time. Maybe he would not be there when they arrived.

Diao Lijun jumped in to say the monk had promised to be there early and would wait at the resting temple until they arrived; he had something special to show Scott. George decided to say no more; he guessed the monk was anxious to show Scott what his ten thousand dollar donation had been used for. Both men seemed extremely warm and in no way sinister, but Xiao Ping and George remained cautious about what they said to them. When warned of an early start in the morning both visitors laughed and said it was no problem. Scott was still on U.S. time and Diao Lijun had also recently traveled from the U.S.; their sleeping patterns were both messed up anyway.

Sam had everything ready for their trip the next morning: packed lunches and large flasks of coffee, with green tea for Diao Lijun and Xiao Ping. After a quick breakfast of eggs and some kind of pancake with pickles they all climbed into the jeep. The new guests laughed about the startup process for the venerable old piece of machinery and congratulated George when he fired up the beast.

Scott was particularly excited and remarked it was going to be a great day. He chose not to say much about his reason to visit so that everyone could enjoy what was going to happen.

When they finally arrived at the temple, Scott helped with the packs. The monk was already there and rushed out to welcome them, especially Scott. He threw his arms around him and thanked Buddha aloud for bringing them together again. The introduction to Diao was more formal and at that point nothing was said of Diao's role in the visit. In any event, Jing led Scott by the hand into the dilapidated resting temple to the corner area he had funded. There were flowers and candles lit. With a flourish the monk waved his arms around the area and thanked Scott so much for his generous offering, urging him to see what his money had done.

Diao went directly up to the paintings on the wall and commented that these were magnificent and asked who the artist was. Jing replied that a patron, a local man named Ma Jun—now passed away—had done them for a very special price. The monk commented to everyone how well the work Scott funded complemented them. Jing then asked everyone to pause to say special prayers there, to welcome his guests first and then to pray for the soul of Ma Jun.

When that was done Scott asked everyone to be seated as he had something to tell Jing. "I have spent a good many years in China but the most precious day was spent with my special friend here, who we all call Master. Since that eventful day in my life I have tried to live my life in ways the master talked to me about. I know he will be pleased to hear that I did as he suggested—study the Buddha's life and his principles."

"Schott, I am so pleased to hear that; you make me happy man today. One opened pearl in a sea of oysters closed to the fisher's knife is a just reward for one's efforts."

"Master, I never forgot how at the end of our day together you took the jade Buddha from around your neck and gave it to me without any reservation, a necklace you had worn for so many years."

The master interrupted the story briefly at that point, looking at Xiao Ping. "Do you know who gave me the necklace? It was Ma Yu, the father of Ma Jun, on one of my fund-raising travels; such a kind and generous man he was."

Scott told the group how he loved the jade Buddha and its color, which seemed to set it apart from other jade pieces he had seen. One day in Asheville, North Carolina, he visited an old flea market (George had to explain to Master and Diao what a flea market was) where he came across a large jade piece stuck way back in the corner of a so-called "just arrived" section. The seller had just brought in a number of Asian objects, part of her father's old collection from travels to Europe years ago. The family was in financial trouble and needed money quickly. Her father had passed away and she was anxious to give him a decent funeral.

Of all the pieces there a jade statue caught Scott's eye. It was again of Buddha and quite heavy, but what struck him most was the coloring that was similar to the jade in his necklace. He made a good offer, in her eyes, paid in cash, and left the store pleased with his purchase. For some reason he decided to see what it might be worth, and his wife suggested putting it out on a popular website called Craig's List to see what would happen.

"I was shocked; I had four calls within an hour from people in different parts of the country interested in the piece. They wanted to know right away how much I would take for it and if anyone else was interested. I asked all of them to call back in a couple of days. I decided I'd better take it to an appraiser first before responding. I thought there was no way it could be any normal piece of jade."

With a smile he turned to Diao, then to the monk. "This is where Diao Lijun comes into my story." A big smile appeared on Diao's face as Scott pointed his way. "Just one day later there was a knock on my front door and this fine gentleman was standing there. Turns out he too saw my picture.

"He introduced himself as a curator from the Forbidden City Palace Museum, and asked me where my piece came from; he said it might have been stolen when the Summer Palace was looted in the 1800s. I explained how it came into my possession, and that I'd been attracted to the piece because it was similar in color to the necklace you gave me, Master.

Diao then jumped in. "Yes, that is true," he said. "The minute I saw the necklace I knew it was quite old, a very rare piece indeed." Diao laughed. "I told Scott he'd better insure it right away. He told me no problem; he had his wife's jewelry insured for over $50,000, that's 300,000 Chinese yuan, Master. When I told him he better add a million or more dollars to that figure he almost fainted.

"I explained to him that the necklace and the jade statue were made from the most precious jadeite, a passion of the Chinese emperors. It likely came from Burma but was carved in China during the late Ming dynasty.

"Scott's wife, Rebecca, joined our conversation and my next statement to Scott and Rebecca was that I was there on behalf of the Chinese government. Part of my work, George, is to seek out treasure plundered from China and to secure its return to our homeland. I told them if they would sell to no one else and enter into a direct agreement with the Palace Museum for this piece, we would pay $750,000."

Diao grinned as he described Scott's wife almost passing out on the spot, especially when she was also told the jade around her husband's neck was also worth a cool quarter of a million dollars.

"Of course, I wanted the name of the lady who sold him his piece, just to see if there were any more pieces and to perhaps discover where her family had acquired the statue. After considering my offer Scott said he couldn't accept it, but he had another proposal in mind. I can tell you now I could even have paid up to one million dollars if needed, but I asked what he had in mind."

At that point Diao stopped talking and Scott took over again. "From my time in China and what I knew about its history I always felt ashamed by the treatment of the Chinese by the foreign troops and the plundering of so many Chinese treasures from the Old Summer Palace and the Forbidden City.

"I told Diao I would accept his proposal with a slight modification. First, I would accept $500,000 directly, and second, the Chinese government would have to invite me at their expense to visit China with my wife, Rebecca. She is in Beijing as we speak. But third, $250,000 must be provided directly to Master Jing for the complete renovation of the resting temple."

"Of course," Diao said, "on behalf of our government I agreed right away to Scott's proposal."

Master Jing looked shocked and was visibly shaking as Scott and Diao presented him with a formal document signed by the national and regional authorities agreeing to indeed spend up to 1,500,000 yuan, the equivalent of $250,000, for reconstruction of the pavilion—at the direction of Master Jing. Any amount left over would be retained for the temple's ongoing upkeep.

With tears streaming down both Jing and Scott's eyes, they embraced. George could see Xiao Ping getting emotional too. Diao Lijun smiled from ear to ear, and George felt a lump well up in his throat. A little later Scott reached into his shirt. He took off the jade necklace with its new leather strap, saying that Jing's old one had finally failed some months earlier. He tried to return it to the master but Jing would have nothing of it and pushed it back to Scott.

"There is no need; it is yours now. I never knew its real value anyway; in any event my gift has been returned to me in ways I never imagined. You must keep it, dear friend, and learn from it."

Xiao Ping and George strolled outside the temple while the three of them talked before bursting out laughing. "What a turn of events!" George said. "There I was thinking this was all connected with finding the treasure and it was nothing of the sort."

They went back into the pavilion and George suggested they all get together for dinner that night. If Scott did not mind, however, they needed to get other things done. The problem was that if they drove all the way to the lodge and back, they would lose much of the day.

Diao said it was not a problem; he already had his cell out and was calling a taxi service. They would continue talking with Jing before heading down the mountain for the taxi. The master would walk with them to the park but would not be able to join the rest of them for dinner. Master Jing hoped Scott would visit him the next day and take the cable car to the top of the mountain to meet all his colleagues. They would have a special reception for him; the monk wanted to provide a temple blessing for Scott and his wife. George and his wife would be more than welcome too if they were able.

Diao was still smiling broadly, and Xiao Ping said they would be delighted to travel to the main temple as she had heard the views were spectacular.

As Diao wandered out with George and Xiao Ping he told them that Scott was a good friend to China, an honorable man indeed. Scott had told Diao how the next day after his visit a collector from the U.S. had called him and offered him $1.5 million for the jade; Scott told him it was sold. The only thing he asked of Diao was under no circumstances to tell his wife about the offer. That was when Diao invited his wife on the trip, telling Scott she would receive a very special gift on her visit. When Xiao Ping asked what that would be, Diao said it was to be a solid gold lady's watch encrusted with diamonds. They planned to give it to her at their farewell banquet next week.

Leaving the group behind, George and his wife headed off down the trail, having checked to make sure no one was following them. They quickly turned off onto "their path," and down to their discovery of the day before, getting to their final destination in much less time.

Once at the site they headed to the area behind the shrubbery and started where they left off, taking great care to stack the stones as they took them down. They had determined that regardless of what they discovered, they would have to close the cave back up and leave it just as they'd found it.

It took them far less time than expected to get an opening wide enough to get into the cave. They wanted a reasonable opening to let in light, even though they had brought several camping lamps between them. The large backpacks, which appeared full when they arrived, only held some basic tools and photographic equipment. They had actually stuffed them with paper so that no one would think they had gained any contents along the way. They—especially Xiao Ping—were starting to get a little paranoid that someone might be watching them.

Xiao Ping was the first through the opening; George followed gingerly. The gap was a tight squeeze for him and he had visions of nasty crawling creatures awaiting him on the inside. As it happened, the cave while small at the entry, opened up as one went farther in and was of course much darker toward the rear. The cave was dry, a good sign depending on what was there to protect. There were obvious signs of the presence of a large population of bats living there but something seemed to have driven them out of the cave.

This time they moved about much more carefully and Xiao Ping began photographing the area before they touched anything. They were a little surprised to find only one coffin in this part of the cave, so they set about searching the rest of the cave to find the other one. After about ten minutes neither could find another one. George thought it was strange; maybe Ma had taken one away. But why? The cave seemed an ideal place, both temperature and humidity-wise.

After covering every nook and cranny in the cave George looked at Xiao Ping and pointed to the coffin. "Shall we?"

"Should we fetch Diao Lijun and the master to join us?"

"If there is anything of value there—historically or otherwise— Diao will whisk them away. Do we want that?"

They had talked about advising the authorities before, but knew once they did, whatever contents were there would be taken away and that would be it for them. Likely they would be in trouble anyway coming this far in the search without advising anyone. George was unsure if they would have been believed anyway. At this point, they decided to see for themselves what was in the coffin and wrestle with what to do afterwards.

George dragged it away from the wall and lifted one end to see if it was heavy and if anything moved inside. The box was clearly full of something, but not so heavy that whatever was inside could not be moved downhill between them. It did seem too heavy for skeletal remains. The likelihood of it being an actual child's coffin and having Xiao Ping scream her lungs out when the top came off was remote.

The coffin was secured by simple nailing around the lid, nothing exotic or intricate, so George set about carefully raising the nail heads and extracting each one individually. Xiao Ping looked on, her eyes wide. The top was a nice tight fit but came off after a fair bit of wiggling by both of them. When it finally pulled open the contents were shrouded in what looked like very old cloth, dark brown and definitely not the kind of cloth either of them had ever seen.

This was the moment they had been waiting for. Both let loose a series of "You open it!" then, "No, you open it," until George finally said, "Look, Xiao Ping, once and for all it was your story; you open it!"

She started to peel back the layers of cloth gently, since the cloth might hold clues as to its origin. They both knew not to disturb any of the evidence in terms of what they were finding. The contents were tightly packed and would have to be handled with great care. If the stories of this so-called treasure went back generations, it could disintegrate when open to the elements, depending on what it was. George was thinking of the terracotta excavations in Xian where the Emperor Qin's burial mound still had not been excavated. Scientists feared exposure to the air would damage whatever was there. Already the unearthed soldiers had rapidly faded in color.

When the covers were finally peeled back what sat before them was quite astonishing—no jade, no gold, no silver, no artifacts, just a mass of dark brown shapes covering the entire surface. George decided to lift one out gently; perhaps this was another kind of covering; however, below that piece was more of the same. They quickly realized the whole coffin was filled with layer upon layer of them.

George took a pair of white gloves used for handling precious objects out of his backpack to examine the object more closely. Xiao Ping donned a pair of her own and began photographing what George was doing.

Their reaction to the first piece George held was that it was perhaps a part of the shell of a giant sea turtle, but upon closer inspection they determined it was not. It was about the size of an oval plate, not very thin, nor too thick. They planned to measure and weigh them later, perhaps using part of one for carbon dating and testing. So far the treasure was looking pretty strange; that is, until the objects were turned over. Their undersides were creamy in color. They were flatter than a turtle shell but still with a slight curvature, full of strange markings very finely done and quite small. The unusual symbols covered almost every part of them, giving the impression this was some kind of writing, perhaps a form of ancient script or hieroglyphics.

The writing was nothing like Xiao Ping or her husband had ever seen, if indeed it was a form of writing. They gently turned over what they began referring to as "the shells." Every one—some small, some a bit larger—was covered with thousands of symbols. They both sat down and looked at each other in amazement.

"Xiao Ping, this is truly a kind of treasure. Even without studying this further, it's certainly a spectacular find. There seems no way we can avoid advising the authorities now of what we've found."

"Darling, let's not to be too hasty. We've come this far and verified at least a part of Ma's story. Why not unravel it all first if we can?"

While George was sympathetic to her, the sheer number of shells would take years to interpret if they could even break the code.

"Perhaps we should talk to our new friend, Diao Lijun," Xiao Ping suggested.

George thought for a while. "I suggest we say nothing about what we've found to anyone just yet. We can close up the coffin and the cave entry, then head back to the lodge. I'd like to phone Cai at the university; he's only person I think we can trust. I'll try to persuade him to fly down to Zhangjiajie right away; we can tell him the entire story and seek his advice."

Xiao Ping was not completely onboard with the plan but had no better idea. It seemed to George that her first reaction, to simply carry away the contents and work on them alone, would never work in the long run.

It took some time to close up the coffin before leaving. Xiao Ping carefully wrapped a few shells in cloth and placed them in her pack. She was nervous about leaving everything behind, despite George's confidence that, since no one had come across this cave in years, the likelihood of someone finding it now was remote.

Xiao Ping had continued to develop conspiracy theories, what with the issue of Zhao Feng and then the strange appearance of Scott and Diao Lijun. Perhaps their difference was a result of Eastern versus Western thinking!

They covered the entry as best they could and placed more tree branches over the area. By the time they left, the entryway was as well concealed as before, if not better, but in a way that could be accessed quickly the next time.

They walked back down the trail, clambered over the rockslide, down the other side, and made their way to the car. Along the way George could see his wife anxiously looking around in every direction, seemingly convinced someone was lurking out there and watching their every move.

Back at the lodge a message awaited them advising that Scott and Diao had gone back to Beijing—Diao on official business. Scott also was anxious to return to accompany his wife on another day of touring with the assigned welcome guides. George decided to call

Cai before eating dinner. He tried the office at the university but with no success. Fortunately he had Cai's cell phone number; on the fourth ring Cai answered.

George had known Cai for years; in addition to collaborating together he considered Cai his best friend in China. He respected him and trusted him with his life. He therefore simply told Cai he needed him to fly to Zhangjiajie right away; they had discovered some amazing items and before doing anything would like him to see them. Despite Cai's many questions George declined to tell him more. "Just trust me, Cai," he said. "I need for you to come. Xiao Ping and I will pick you up at the airport and fill you in."

George advised Cai to dress comfortably and be ready to do a little mountain hiking right away. "Also, Cai, please come without telling anyone. It would be better if you can tell your colleagues you're just taking a few days off. Believe me, your visit will be worthwhile."

Cai said he'd see what he could arrange and would get back to him as soon as possible; after just forty-five minutes he called back. "This is really unusual coming from you," he told George. "I have to say, I'm intrigued. I wouldn't do this for anyone other than you or Xiao Ping." He went on to say that he was taking sick leave for the rest of the week; he'd be on the first morning flight from Beijing. "This better be well worth it." George assured him it would be something spectacular.

They spent the rest of the evening looking at the few shells Xiao Ping had brought with her and the writings covering them. They wondered what secrets they might reveal, what they really were, and who had written them. This truly was a treasure, though nothing that the Mas could have lived on. Then again, these artifacts had clearly been around a very, very long time.

That night they spent many hours trying to find some clue as to what language they were looking at. If it was not a form of written language, was it a form of pictograms, hieroglyphics, or something no one had ever seen? George's hope was that somehow Cai might throw a light on it. They slept poorly in anticipation of their colleague's arrival. Whenever George did finally fall asleep, Xiao Ping would wake him to tell him of her continuing nightmares. They were always the same. Someone was in the cave stealing the coffin.

CHAPTER 12

THE NEXT MORNING THEY WERE up early and headed to the airport in Zhangjiajie. George was nervous driving the jeep into a large city. What if they were stopped and the vehicle checked for roadworthiness? On the other hand, this was not exactly Beijing. Xiao Ping told him she doubted there would be anything to worry about other than breaking down; certainly Cai was going to have a shock when he saw the stylish ride in store for him. They would be waiting outside the exit for him rather than inside the airport.

Once at the airport George decided not to shut the jeep down and risk the thing not starting as had happened on occasion, despite following the starting instructions to the letter. When Cai finally appeared with a large bag over his shoulder, Xiao Ping jumped out of the waiting crowd and ran to collect him; they chattered as they made their way to the jeep. Cai struggled to climb into the rickety back seat. George smiled noticing that Cai, who always dressed well, even looked smart in the hiking attire he must have bought hastily for the trip.

Before giving George a brotherly slap on the back Cai said, "Da Ger Ger (Older Brother), this better be good!" With that, they completed greeting each other. Once George had told Cai they really did have a story for him, he left Xiao Ping to give Cai all of the details of their journey to date, from beginning to end. George interjected the odd comment if he thought she'd missed something important.

Cai asked numerous questions and tried to poke holes in the story where he could, as much a test of the story as anything before admitting the pair certainly had his attention. As they'd warned Cai earlier they did not go to the hotel but headed straight for the mountain. Cai knew the region quite well as he had spent one summer in the area and visited Tianmen Mountain via the cable car. He had no knowledge, however, of the older route and resting temple.

When George told him they had reserved a room in a backpackers' lodge for a couple of nights, they could see his disappointment. Cai appreciated the finer things in life (the jeep certainly was a letdown from his own Mercedes), and George guessed he was looking forward to an evening of fine wine and dining in some five-star hotel in the heart of Zhangjiajie.

One part of their story that held up with Cai was the reference to the visit by Diao Lijun. He confirmed that Diao was indeed who he claimed to be, noting that he was a unique individual in his field in terms of honesty and devotion to duty. "Diao's a rare bird these days, George; he hasn't been tarnished like others by corruption or double-dealings and is held in high regard.

"You'd be surprised to know he's a full party member. He's not averse to criticizing excesses of the past either, especially the damage done during the Cultural Revolution to the historical relics of China. While Diao will tell you he holds foreign powers in low regard for pillaging the country, he will admit if they had not done this perhaps even more of China's greatest artifacts would have been destroyed during that period. On the other hand, he feels strongly that governments should return plundered items and if necessary put copies in their place."

"I guess I'm not overly surprised to hear that," George said. "The short time we spent with him impressed both of us, but I wouldn't have guessed he was a party member."

They headed up the mountain to the resting temple and would work through the story from there. Their famous monk was nowhere to be seen on the trail; George expected he would be disappointed to hear Scott and Diao had returned to Beijing so quickly. When they arrived at the temple there was a stranger walking around taking photographs and making notes. Xiao Ping and George looked at each other with a little alarm in their eyes before they said hello.

They were quickly relieved to learn he was from the local building preservation department in Zhangjiajie, which specialized in restorations. The authorities in Beijing were footing the expense of renovating the temple as funded by Scott Ramey; the architect was assigned to work directly with Master Monk Jing. The monk had already outlined what work the Buddhist monastery would like to have undertaken and left for the day. The architect would prepare sketches and finally develop a work plan; under local regulations they would have three contractors bid on the work.

The good thing was, they only used respected and professional restorers for this kind of work. Fortunately for them, the architect would not be back for at least a week to meet the monk and present his ideas, and it would be at least three months before approvals and contracts would allow work to begin.

Since the architect was still hovering there, they just walked around the building remains themselves. George showed Cai the only finished area. When they stepped over the slab with the Ma symbol George simply smiled and pointed it out to Cai without saying anything out loud. He was getting as paranoid as his wife!

They headed down the side trail afterwards, making sure they were not followed. Xiao Ping showed Cai the turnoff marker with the Ma symbol. They stopped briefly by the first cave area but did not attempt to go in since there was nothing there but two empty coffins.

Climbing over the rockslide they made their way to the second cave, looking carefully for any signs that someone had been there after they left. An avid reader of detective stories, Xiao Ping had placed a number of twigs across the pathway, very thin and unobtrusive, that would have broken or moved if anyone passed by. They were all still in place.

Cai remarked on the beauty of the location when they arrived at the cave area gazing out at the views of the mountains and valleys around them. Before going in George asked him to spot its location. They felt quite good about their amateur camouflaging efforts when he could not immediately find it. They all laughed about it, and then headed to the shrub area to remove the scrub and other branches they had laid behind the growth and over the entry. They took down the stones that blocked the cave entry, and Xiao Ping set the lights in place as Cai climbed carefully into and around the cave before he looked at the coffin.

The coffin was not so old, he noted. George pointed out that the two in the other cave area were certainly very old. He said Ma Jun must have switched the contents so that whoever came across the decoy cave would note the empty coffins were indeed very old. The fact there was only one coffin and not two in this cave was a little mystery of its own. They told Cai they had searched the area for other caves to check if Ma had split his so-called treasures into two, but found nothing.

They had not shown Cai any of the shells to this point; they wanted his reaction on seeing them for the first time. Clearly Cai was peeved at not being told in the car what was in the coffin, but George had enjoyed making him wait to see the shells.

Cai donned a spare pair of gloves and a facemask (George had not thought to wear a mask) and peeled the covering cloths back carefully. "It's lucky this cave remained dark and cool," he said, "and the contents have suffered no inundation from the rains or snow." He let out a slow whistle in awe as he saw the shell-like objects laid before him. "These are definitely from no animal I've ever come across." He slowly turned the first shell over to its underside and sat down directly on the floor to scrutinize what was in his hand. Picking up a few others he noted that they were all completely different.

"We think these are some kind of ancient writing tablets," George said. "Maybe the shells are from some type of giant turtle we haven't come across before. I think they're amazing and so does Xiao Ping."

"It's incredible! I have to agree with you; this is some form of very ancient writing but I have to admit I've never seen anything like it in my career, nor as beautifully done. If indeed the coffin is full of these shells, and they are all covered with writing like this, the amount of information they contain must be huge. I wonder if this could even be a lost history of the earliest inhabitants of China, something we might at least be able to date from carbon analysis."

Carefully they reexamined the coffin as best they could without removing all the shells. They satisfied themselves that the coffin was indeed crammed with them; there were hundreds of them, each shell's surface decorated with this strange script.

"How do you think we should proceed, Cai?" Xiao Ping asked.

After thinking about it for some time he finally answered. "Look, to be frank with you both, in China these kinds of discoveries are unusual and difficult to manage. I foresee a huge fight developing for possession of these artifacts between the local authorities, the provincial authorities, and even the national bureaucrats—and that's not even considering the Buddhist monks. They might claim them to be sutras from ancient times."

"I never thought about that," George said. "They're really nothing like the writings I saw and worked with in the Dunhuang Buddhist caves in western China."

Cai nodded. "To be honest, I agree with Xiao Ping's comments in the jeep coming up here. We should try to unravel this mystery ourselves but it needs to be contained to a small group until we can decipher the writings. Then we can publish our findings and apologize for not having reported them from the start."

Although Xiao Ping said she thought this a good idea, George was not so sure. Cai assured him he could protect everyone from any troubles, pointing out his biggest concern—that the relics could be mishandled, some even sold off, or disappear as different parties got involved.

George reluctantly agreed to Cai's suggestion under pressure from Xiao Ping as well. They proceeded to gently remove the shells and place them carefully into the two large backpacks and an extra oversize one brought along for Cai. Finally they closed the lid; if someone came by they would simply find an empty coffin, just like in the first cave.

As they'd packed the shells Xiao Ping made an interesting discovery, a blank shell with no markings. Cai was particularly pleased to see it. He said this was one he could take to his expert colleagues to ask them what animal it came from and its age, without revealing the graphics on them to anyone. They discussed keeping the circle of people knowing about this to a minimum. George mentioned that Charles was absolutely trustworthy, but Xiao Ping immediately told Cai about her suspicions regarding Zhao Feng. He smiled and said no problem, to leave it to him and give him half an hour to check into it. He picked up the phone and stepped outside the cave.

George and Xiao Ping could hear him talking to an obvious confidant about Zhao Feng before ending the call and thanking the other party.

"That was my brother," Cai said, stepping back into the cave. "He's a special investigator. Works with the Beijing central police department. Normally his activities revolve around monitoring foreign visitors to China, especially certain countries' diplomats, people he won't tell me about."

By the time they'd reached the parking area, Cai had received his call-back.

Within fifteen minutes he received another call and asked Xiao Ping to confirm Feng's cell phone number. After listening for several more minutes he thanked his brother again profusely, telling him the information was very useful and added, "You know how it is, Didi (younger brother), some employees just do take time off and claim they are sick these days."

Cai turned to Xiao Ping and began reeling off precise details concerning Zhao Feng's travels while they were at the lodge. "Didn't take my brother long, did it? Quite a guy, he is, bit scary at times though. Anyway, he says Feng did fly four days ago, but not to his father's home as he told you. He was in fact on an Air China flight to Zhangjiajie. He checked in to the Kempinski five-star hotel at noon, rented a car and driver for three days, paid in cash, and traveled, according to the desk clerk, to the Tianmen Mountain area. How about that?"

It was immediately obvious to George and Xiao Ping that Zhao Feng had flown back from there the day before they found the first cave; then he'd headed to Changsha to check into the hotel. They looked at each other with raised eyebrows, not just at how quickly Cai had gained this important information, but how they had misjudged Zhao Feng for the last few years. Xiao Ping blurted out the need to fire him right away.

"No, not yet," George said. "My recommendation is we not rush back and fire him, as I know you'd like to do. We need him to think for a while that we found nothing and that's the end of it. Let's finish our work here, entrust the shells to Cai to transport to Beijing, and then fly on to Wuhan and meet the others. We can watch Zhao Feng closely in the coming weeks until we have a better plan to deal with him."

Cai spoke before Xiao Ping. "I think you're right for now. We need to handle these artifacts with great care and in secrecy. Within the university there's an area I'm responsible for. It's a large storage room and lab with good lighting and lots of space I can make available. It can be locked, with access limited to whomever we all agree is to be part of our team. The lab's wired for internet and phone. It's ideal for our work; we need to figure out what these shells are and try to decipher them."

Xiao Ping and George did not have a better idea. Cai was right in the middle of this venture now; they could either put their trust in him or not. Of course, they could simply report their findings to the local authorities, but they were sure their involvement would quickly end. Xiao Ping said she felt it was her obligation to Ma Jun to carry on as if she was Wan Yan, staying with the story for as long as possible. Everyone agreed and they headed for the lodge.

Back in George and Xiao Ping's room, they discussed their next steps and overall game plan. Cai would take the backpacks to Zhangjiajie and transfer the contents into sturdy but nondescript suitcases. To be sure that nothing went amiss he would take the overnight train to Beijing with the cases to avoid any loss, mishandling of the contents, or trouble if someone wanted to check the contents. He would then lock them in the lab. The place he'd told them about was an old strong-room used in the days when biologists were studying different viruses. The storeroom had been used to secure dangerous specimens and cultures. The whole activity had moved three years earlier to a new, modern facility outside of Beijing. There was a sign on the outside of the lab area still warning of danger and the risk to anyone entering. Cai promised to clean it out and add another sign saying access was strictly limited and to contact Departmental Director Cai Levee for more information. George liked the idea; at least they'd get some warning if they were about to be exposed.

They were anxious to get started but concerned that the team's already scheduled work would tie them up for another six months. Cai asked how they felt about waiting, starting once they had finished their last commitment in inner Mongolia, not far from Hohot. A local Mongol legend was to be investigated. Yet another claim of records of the real location of the burial tomb of Genghis Khan had come to the group's attention. The tomb to this day has eluded all seekers. For Xiao Ping there was no question where her priorities lay; George had mixed feelings. He was excited about their find, but Cai was even more passionate about what he had held and seen. In the end, the consensus was that this discovery really was the chance of a lifetime. Whatever the writings revealed might rival anything the world of antiquity had seen.

Cai held an important position with the university and was involved with the cultural activities going on between the U.S. and China. In this regard he had a suggestion if everyone agreed. "Why don't I head back to Beijing as we've discussed. You two travel to Wuhan, meet with Zhao Feng and the others to complete the work there. Tell Charles and Arthur, as well as Zhao Feng, the entire story up to the discovery of the empty coffins; nothing more than that.

"We'll keep the coffin contents and the lab project secret for a while. Xiao Ping will need to watch Zhao Feng closely. As long as he believes you too came across the same empty coffins and there's no more to the story, then all will be well. The question is whether or not this was just a case of Zhao Feng seeing his one opportunity for financial gain or not. Will he do it again? Or will he have guilty feelings and this incident never be repeated?"

George expressed the view, which Xiao Ping backed up right away, that he'd turned out to be a rotten apple and they needed to get rid of him as soon as they were in Wuhan and could confront him. Cai, however, took a very Chinese view of the situation. He did not want to create an enemy just yet; he just wanted to neutralize him. He suggested a whole new approach that George admitted was quite clever.

They would complete their project in Wuhan. It would take at least one more month; then Cai, on behalf of the University of Beijing and the cultural exchange with the U.S., would announce that due to certain budget matters the next project was being put on hold. He would obtain a nice position for Zhao Feng in a prestigious university far away from Zhangjiajie and Beijing, something he could not turn down. Also, to make things seem real, they would give Arthur notice that he would be retained until year end; if the budget constraints continued he too might have to leave.

When George became alarmed about Arthur, Cai motioned him to calm down; it would never happen, but the story had to fit for Zhao Feng. He knew Charles was due for an extended break; he would be going back to Danville, Virginia, for three months. His family had a small farm there and a couple of the old tobacco barns were on the verge of collapsing. His wife was concerned about the safety of them and wanted them taken down and restored. They would let him go as if he was being furloughed pending budget renewal. Then, last but not least, Professor Mathers would be retained to assist the university in preparing a special collection of the team's work over the past few years. As for Xiao Ping, she was to simply remain with her husband. If funds were adequate, she would provide some part-time support in Beijing; however, travel would be severely restricted due to the so-called budget constraints.

They made a few refinements to the planned story but after discussing all the options came back to agreeing the plan was as good as it could be. George agreed with Cai's thinking about Zhao Feng, and he managed to convince his wife that firing Zhao Feng at this stage could create some unwanted problems.

After assuring Cai the couple had one hundred percent trust in Charles and Arthur—and had no problem bringing them into the picture eventually—George suggested they break the so-called budget news in a week or so to the team. They would not tell Charles or Arthur what was really going on right away. They needed to be genuinely surprised and shocked by the turn of events. If Charles and Arthur were told ahead of time, George was convinced that Zhao Feng would sense something was going on.

George glanced at the clock and was surprised to see it was 1 a.m. Other than finishing off the two bottles of Argentinean Malbec wine, which Cai had brought along with him, they finally called it a night. Cai would head to Zhangjiajie with the three backpacks to switch into cases, the others to Wuhan to meet with the team there.

They all had one last look at the treasure trove of shell-like objects and hugged each other. George laughed as Cai looked at both of them and tried to put on a Sherlock Holmes impression. Cai said, "My good friends, the game is afoot!" With that they agreed to meet early for breakfast, check out, call their colleagues, and set their plan in motion. Cai assured George that canceling planned meetings after Wuhan was nothing to worry about. He would tell the people involved that the program was simply being delayed for a year due to budget constraints, and that the activities would resume at a future date.

⎯⎯ᵕ⎯⎯

THEY WERE ALL UP EARLY the next morning, but only Cai had slept well. George and Xiao Ping tossed and turned with little sleep as they told each other their concerns about what lay ahead and the trouble they could have if they were not careful. And not the least of their worries was about Cai. They were able to leave China at any time, but Cai was more vulnerable and could get into real trouble. When George brought this up to Cai one more time before they left, he just laughed, appreciated their concerns but added that his university life had become too routine and boring anyway. He finally felt truly energized by the situation. He was grateful they both trusted and thought enough of him like a brother to bring him into their confidence.

They had a great breakfast with Sam and Ivy that morning. Sam offered to run them to Zhangjiajie in their only nice car after everyone reminisced about the fun of driving the old Beijing jeep. Sam thanked them profusely for all the business the visit had generated, laughing heartily when he told them that before their arrival the jeep had been sitting there for months unused. He told them his story of how to start it up had actually been a joke, especially banging the dashboard three times. He had been shocked himself when it actually worked. They all had a good laugh over that.

They settled accounts for the vehicle use, rooms, and food in a process that involved so much paperwork that George asked Sam if he had ever heard of something called a computer program for it. Ivy laughed. She said getting Sam to use a cell phone had been a technological advance for him, and she was indeed working towards the goal of not having to use all the different carbon copies and files. Credit cards were a challenge to Sam though. She said if it were not essential for the times, her husband would gladly have a "cash only" sign above reception.

Ivy would not let Sam drive their guests and insisted, for everyone's safety, she would take them. Cai would stay at an airport hotel before leaving the next day. They added a nice amount to the bill to cover her round trip to the airport. After hugs all around, the bags were loaded in the car.

They left Sam's lodge, promising that the next visit might be when the renovation of the resting temple was completed. The monastery planned to eventually inaugurate the renovated temple in a very special ceremony. Scott Ramey was invited to be its guest of honor and Diao Lijun would be welcomed too. Master Monk Jing had cordially invited George and Xiao Ping since they had all been there at the same time. It was viewed as a wonderful development; the continued thread that connected everyone through the Ma family was strong enough that the Master thought they should be there too.

They said their good-byes at the airport in Zhangjiajie, Xiao Ping and George heading to the ticket area to get a flight to Wuhan. There was no flight out until later in the afternoon so the pair headed to one of the executive waiting lounges where for 100 yuan ($17) they could enter without a club card and use the facilities. At least they were able to relax in more comfortable seating until the flight time. George set about calling Charles and Arthur to tell them they were headed to Wuhan and to make sure they had reservations for them. He filled them in on the story of finding the two empty coffins in the cave and nothing more, telling them that both he and Xiao Ping considered it the end of the story. George emphasized it was still a nice tale, one that would make a good article in the future.

He handed the phone to Xiao Ping so she could tell Zhao Feng about the events in Chinese. Feng expressed his regret they had found nothing; he told them it was a real disappointment. Feng, of course, was not told about Ma Jun purchasing two coffins in recent years. He was sorry to hear how it ended, saying he too had been a great believer of the story relayed to George's wife. He also seemed to appreciate greatly Xiao Ping asking him how his father was. He said his trip had been very opportune, claiming his father had to be rushed to the hospital right away. They'd feared it was a more serious stroke with potential damage to his right side. Happily, his father's condition was caught quickly enough that he made a speedy recovery.

Xiao Ping confided to George later that his lies made her blood boil. Zhao Feng said he was pleased to be back to work and looked forward to the upcoming efforts in Wuhan. He had missed both of them but was glad to be back working with Charles and Arthur again.

George and his wife arrived in Wuhan shortly after six p.m. Charles was there to meet them with Zhao Feng alongside. After shaking hands and quick welcoming hugs for Xiao Ping, they headed off to the hotel the team had selected. Once again it was only a small hotel on the outskirts of Wuhan where they would plan the meetings scheduled in the area.

At dinner that night they went through the results of the visit to Zhangjiajie again in person—the search for the cave, how the torn note was found in the cave, and the empty coffins. George thought they did an excellent job of presenting the sequence of events and their disappointment when they finally ran into a dead end. They both paid particular attention to Zhao Feng's reaction. Feng did a good job in George's view of not giving anything away in his expression, although George noticed his eyes flicker a whole lot more when they came to discussing the discovery of the trail and the cave.

The general consensus was that someone must have discovered the cave ahead of them, tore up the letter from Ma in frustration, and left empty-handed, but no one knew when that might have happened. George could not tell Charles and Arthur at that point about his flash of brilliance, which he continued to rub in to his wife as they traveled, or exactly how they found the second cave. For now, at least, their plan was in motion. Two weeks later Cai would send George an official document from the university outlining the suspension and by then have used his connections to come up with a job offer for Zhao Feng. At some later date they would make sure he was terminated when the time was right and he could do no harm to their project.

Cai checked into the Marriott Hotel at the airport in Zhangjiajie the day after George and Xiao Ping left and took a cab downtown to seek out sturdy and lockable suitcases. Cai's purchase before leaving Zhangjiajie was a typical Chinese negotiation of the kind George had no real patience for. Not Cai though; for him it was a great sport securing what he wanted for the lowest price possible. It took him a solid half hour of haggling, walking away, and the seller crying that the price was less than his cost, before both parties felt they had a good deal, shook hands, and became instant friends forever. Cai left the store happy that he had good suitcases for the right price. The seller likely rushed to his neighbor's store to tell him he had just taken this guy from Beijing for a nice profit; typically everyone was happy this way! As George would often point out to his American visitors, this selling process in China between seller and buyer has gone on for centuries. Anyone visiting China and places like the silk or pearl markets in Beijing knew the dance very well, but Cai knew George had tired of it over the years.

That evening after a good dinner Cai transferred the shells from the backpacks to the cases. He took several hotel towels from a maid's cart in the hallway to help pack them, instead of using the original cover, which he did not want to damage any further. He had sized the cases to accommodate the shells so that in the end everything set snugly in the cases; they were both sturdy and had two good locking clasps, which he also bought heavy combination locks for.

The next evening he boarded the overnight train for Beijing traveling first class where there was adequate space for the suitcases and he could keep a close watch on them. He had already called ahead for a van to meet him on arrival and help with the luggage.

When Cai reached the university the next morning he had a cart waiting for him to maneuver the cases around; he told the driver there was no need for him to help and to just go ahead and park the car. He made his way to his office on the second floor of the B block, gathered up the keys, and headed to the old lab. He managed to unlock the door, which clearly had not been used for some time, and wheeled the trunk through the strong-room door. He could not remember what was actually in that area and hoped it was going to be okay when he opened it. There were three keys to this door, all different, so it took time to open it. He guessed in its day maybe three managers had keys so no one manager could open the door on his own if there was anything dangerous in there, or any one person could take something dangerous out on his own. He would have to get more keys cut for the rest of the team in the future.

When he finally opened the door he was pleasantly surprised. It was larger than he'd remembered. The fluorescent lighting was good, still in place and working well. It was a little dusty but the room was nicely laid out with tables to work on and cupboards for storage. He would need to find some chairs though for those who worked inside. There were plenty of power sockets but internet outlets were outside the locked area; however, one of his predecessors had apparently installed a decent WIFI system in the main room two years before, so Cai figured they could get set up fairly quickly in the lab too.

Charles was the computer guru and Cai expected that once Charles got up to Beijing all that could be straightened out. He would not be able to provide the team with computers; the university was very tight in that regard. Any kind of tables, chairs, and cupboards were no problem to obtain, but phones and computers were treated like gold.

Cai had an assistant called Liu Tao who had been with him a long time; he trusted him completely. He would not tell Liu Tao what was really going on but that in a few weeks Xiao Ping and George Mathers would be coming in to work with Cai on writing up their projects. They would need to be uninterrupted for some months to come. Liu Tao was to help with anything needed. In the meantime Cai asked that he clean the rooms and stack some tables and chairs in the outer room along with three comfortable easy chairs—if they could be found.

Cai winked at Liu Tao as he often did and asked him to say nothing about the arrangement. The area was to be out of bounds to anyone who Cai did not authorize, which drew a puzzled look from Liu Tao. He had maintained a lot of confidential documents and information for Cai over the years, but this was different and a foreigner was involved. Cai told him, chuckling, that there was no problem. They were working on something that would be great for the university when completed, but if they told everyone about the research planned the dean of the university would say they had too much else to do.

That was all Liu needed to hear; he nodded his assent and confirmed to Cai his special project was safe with him. Cai had no choice but to involve someone in his little scheme and so Liu fit the bill; other faculty members would be far more inquisitive. For them the story would be that Professor Mathers and his team were there to spend the next year documenting their activities. They would be preparing a series of books to be published in association with the university. It was a long-term project and they would be left to their own devices but allowed access to the university. Cai told Liu he would be monitoring the progress, but he expected this would take quite some time to assemble.

In phone conversations later the next day George told Cai that it was dangerous for them not to be seen to generate anything during their stay. He felt the team had enough materials from their travels over the years to really put together a couple of volumes on Chinese myths and fables. These could be interwoven with an updated history of China that was sure to please the university leaders. They would therefore organize themselves such that work was always continuing on this "official" project.

Cai agreed with George's idea and told him he visualized having the official work laid out in the outer room for all to see and the "shell game" to be hidden behind the strong-room door. He would claim that the keys to the room had been long lost and it would be too expensive to try to unlock it, a pointless exercise anyway since that lab storeroom was no longer needed.

In Wuhan, Xiao Ping and George were anxious to get the month over with and move on to Beijing to begin unraveling whatever secrets were contained in the shells. More interesting events, however, were evolving in Beijing, which George would learn about later!

Cai had taken the plain shell that he found to a colleague, Professor Ding; he was a leading anthropologist who had done extensive studies on both humans and non-primates in the biological, evolutionary, and demographic studies of species in China. Cai asked Ding which animal this shell could have come from. Cai said he thought it was *not* from a giant sea turtle, as the fellow who sold it to him had claimed. He was wondering what the professor thought, flattering him that if anyone knew it would be him.

Ding sat down and turned the shell over many times, took it over to one of his lab desks, placed it under a large microscope, and peered into the lens. He went over to his computer, fired up the main menu, and spent the next half hour searching through new and old files alike. He seemed eager to help. Cai imagined that he was hoping to bolster his renowned university position as the leading anthropologist in Chinese academic circles!

After a half hour or more, while Cai sat patiently sipping a large glass of green tea, Ding came back over and said he regretted to say he was stumped. "This is a good one, my friend, a really good one! I do agree with you that this is no giant sea turtle shell. I did think for a minute it might have come from a rhino of bygone times, maybe from a huge crocodile of some sort, but I cannot be sure. I really need to know how old it is. Have you had it carbon dated? Has the structure of the material it was composed of been examined? Is it even animal?"

"Ai yo, Professor Ding, if my expert old friend is that uncertain I will have it further examined. Is there anyone here specialized enough within the university complex to take a quick look at it?"

Ding took pen to paper. "Here, Cai, take this note to my colleague. He owes his friend Ding a favor; he will examine the shell for us."

When Cai said how disappointed he was that Ding could not give him a clue about the creature and its origin, Ding could not let Cai leave without a more educated response. "Little brother, depending on the carbon dating, in my professional opinion this so called 'shell' is from no known creature in any records, dinosaurs or other long extinct animals included. But I would hypothesize it *is* prehistoric. While I do need the dating, I believe this is definitely not manmade."

He asked Cai again where he'd obtained it. Cai told him about his stop at the Panjiayuan antique market in Beijing. Ding had suggested he go back and get more, asking Cai if he could give him the seller's booth name too. Cai said the fellow had no more, could get no more, and was not one of the usual sellers. The old guy had spread these things on a blanket and seemed to be about ready to travel back home to the northeast of China. He was in Beijing visiting his daughter and had brought a few things along with him to help cover some of his costs. He wanted 2000 yuan ($340) for the item but in the end had taken only 200 yuan ($34), which was what Cai paid. Cai amazed himself at how easily he wove this little story for Ding.

"Well, if you find more see me," Ding had said. "And as soon as you get the dating information please come back." Cai said he would and jokingly apologized for stumping the erstwhile professor.

"Not stumped, my little brother! Not stumped at all! I would wager 10,000 yuan ($1600), depending on the dating, that says it's prehistoric. Get me more and I can tell you if it walked, swam, or flew! The money will be mine, of that I am sure!"

The next day Cai was able to track down the associate professor in Ding's note. He specialized in dating all kinds of things, animal and other, and was extremely busy. At first he brushed aside Cai's request to date his sample but on reading the comments in Ding's letter shrugged his shoulders and congratulated Cai on stumping the old man for once. He told Cai he would examine the piece only to get back at Ding; he would need at least a week. Cai had no choice but to leave it with him and his staff. As he headed out the door with the team looking at him, the professor declared he should not worry.

"We're the best lab in China, and we will solve poor old Ding's problem for him. Of that I'm sure. You tell him I said that when you see him. Stumped he may be but I'm sure we won't be!"

Before Cai left he was asked yet again where he actually found this item. He repeated the story he made up for Ding.

"Well, I can tell you one thing," the professor said, "it is definitely not manmade and a fake something or other! That's about all you get these days at the Panjiayuan market. Thank heavens for foreigners; they will buy anything, especially if someone tells them it is genuine Ming dynasty. Hah! Everything in that market was likely fired in some kiln the Tuesday before, of course."

A week later Cai went back to the lab and waited for the professor to show himself. When he appeared he seemed somewhat nervous. Cai became alarmed when the professor confessed he did not have the piece. He apologized profusely and assured him he would get it back, questioning why Cai thought it was so important to know about such an inexpensive piece. Cai brushed the question aside and tried to appear calm, though he wondered what the team would say when he told them. The professor did proceed to tell Cai he had no clue what the age of the thing was.

"We've tried every known method we can think of to determine the composition, but we drew a blank. The whole lab's amazed at its properties; we couldn't cut it, nor drill it. It wouldn't shatter when we froze it to the lowest temperature. We even tried to see at what high temperature it might soften—to no avail. We haven't been able to put a scratch on it!"

Cai was a bit alarmed at the tests they had tried on the piece as he thought about what he had just been told. What if they had destroyed it? When he told the professor he was sorry they could not help and would try elsewhere, the professor became more agitated. He asked Cai again to confirm if he really did buy it at Panjiayuan market and truly had no idea who the vendor was. Cai said yes, then asked again politely to let him have the piece back.

"I'm afraid I can't give it back to you right now," the professor said. Cai noticed him looking over his shoulder at one of his staff before going on. "Cai, I regret to report our young Li over there tried to help by involving his brother, hoping his lab could find the answer and put one over our Professor Ding."

"And?" Cai said, raising his voice a bit.

Stammering, the professor explained that Li's brother worked for the Chinese People's Liberation Army (PLA), and in particular in the weapons development area, specializing in materials and armored vehicle protection. Li had taken the piece to his brother, told him what they had seen, and asked him to take a look at it. The piece had not come back, but the military had recently sent a representative to their lab to find out what they had done to this material and where it had come from.

Cai's heart pounded in his chest as the professor continued to apologize, then admitted he'd told them the whole story of how it came into Cai's possession. He had also showed them Ding's letter. He provided them Cai's information and where they could find him.

"No one has contacted me," Cai said, feigning an air of indifference. He said that if the piece was gone it was gone, that poor old Ding would never have an answer to his question, and that he himself was only out 200 yuan for something he'd planned only to hang on his wall.

Cai left the building and headed back to his office, kicking himself all the way for taking the shell to someone he didn't know. Then, as he thought about what the professor said his team had tried to do to the piece and failed, it dawned on him why the military would be interested. Something that light with those properties would make incredible body armor or light cover for vehicles. He knew right then there was definitely a visit coming his way . . . before that, he would have to update the rest of the team on these developments.

The next day Cai was not surprised to find Liu Tao at his door with three gentlemen standing behind him. Liu appeared quite nervous and after bringing them in left abruptly, closing the door behind him. The three men standing before him looked quite serious, one clearly military, an officer dressed in full uniform, the other two in similar dark suits. One looked sinister while the one with glasses had a nervous habit of removing them every few minutes and cleaning them. After inviting them to sit down Cai sat back and asked what he could do for them. The only person that did any talking was the officer who introduced himself.

"My name is Major Yi of the People's Liberation Army, special intelligence unit. To get straight to the point, Cai Levee, where did you acquire this unusual shell material which found its way to our military labs for testing?"

Cai was put off by the directness of the man; there were no pleasantries of any kind and the two men with him remained stern-faced. He went through the same story he gave to Professor Ding knowing full well the three had already talked to the professor and his lab people. They went over the story a dozen times with the same questions over and over.

"Who was the seller? Where was his stall in the market? We need precise information from you!"

"Look, I've told you several times already, this was just a migrant seller who was in a side area where the sellers lay out their goods on blankets. They sell what they can and disappear if any of the market management come by to ask them for fees. I paid 200 yuan for it, and only because it looked interesting."

"Were you there alone or with anyone who could vouch for you?"

" No, as I said before, no one was with me. I often go there alone on a Saturday morning; my wife refuses to go with me. She finds it boring and thinks half the so-called artifacts at the market are fakes."

The officer added a comment that it was more like 80 percent.

At that point Yi pulled out a file and gave a photograph to Cai; it showed him at the market with a small fat package of brown paper, about the size of the shell, walking by the sellers and looking down at their things. Cai confirmed it was indeed a photo of him; he was stunned as he realized they already had photos of him at the market via CCTV. Fortunately the date and time matched the story he had just given the major.

When asked again if he knew where there was any more of this material around, Cai said he had no idea. Asked if he could identify the seller he replied that he doubted it. He said he hadn't paid much attention to the man, even though they haggled the price down from 2000 yuan to 200 yuan.

With that the three men got up to leave. As they walked to the door Cai asked if he would be getting his property back at all.

The major turned to him. "Absolutely not; it is now the property of the state. You can donate it to the nation or, if you prefer, I can give you 200 yuan and a bill of sale."

In response to Yi's comment and the smirk on his face, Cai smiled. "That's not necessary. I am glad to donate it and if I have forgotten anything that might help I'll call you."

Yi quickly gave him a plain white card with only his name and a cell number on it.

Liu Tao came back in after they left, still looking very nervous. He told Cai they had shown him a photo and wanted him to confirm it was indeed Cai, which he had. He asked Cai if there was a problem, but Cai assured him it was not a big deal and he need not worry about it. After the mysterious visitors and Liu Tao were gone, Cai left the building to call Mathers. Cai could tell George was badly shaken by the latest news but he assured him it was okay, that fortunately on the day of the photo he had bought a small painting about the same size, so the image in the photo backed up his story. He told George the painting, meanwhile, sat on his credenza in the office.

George got more anxious after Cai called back later and told him it would be better for a few days not to talk to each other too much, that George should buy a cheap phone and a call card for it as he planned to do. That way they could talk to each other privately. He again insisted there was nothing to worry about; it was simply prudent to be a little more careful for a while.

Later, George related all of this to Xiao Ping, but she was not quite as concerned as he was. She told him to go ahead and get both of them a cheap phone. She said she still had faith that Cai knew what he was doing. George was beginning to panic and wished she felt the same way.

CHAPTER 14

YI AND HIS TWO ASSOCIATES left the university without speaking to each other; they climbed into their black Audi A6 with darkened windows and headed back to their headquarters. The A6, a popular car among government and state-owned enterprises, sped through the streets of Beijing. The new government was promoting local Chinese vehicles to replace them, but this was still the dominant vehicle on the roads.

The black Audi was back at its headquarters in short order. The mechanical safety barrier slid open while heavily armed soldiers saluted as they went in without even stopping to show the occupants' passes or paperwork. Outside the building there was no signage, national flag, or insignia to indicate what the building was for. The locals had their own ideas of what went on inside, but it was conspicuously plain and unassuming in its position and style.

The three men left the underground parking lot, nodding to the driver as they headed for the elevator. Yi slid his security card in the slot and punched the sixth floor button to ascend for their meeting. They walked into the anteroom of their leader, General Zhu. His adjutant was waiting there patiently to take them in.

Zhu was infamous in the intelligence community within the PLA (People's Liberation Army), which had served the Communist Party well since its earliest days. The story was well known in the ranks; Zhu was a career officer from humble beginnings in the city of Datong in Shanxi Province, a heavy coal-mining city where his father and grandfather had worked the mines all their lives. He had worked his way up in the military—to avoid mining—from being a simple foot soldier to his current position. He earned a strong reputation for being tough when needed, but also as a leader who took care of his men and followed the rule of law.

Zhu was often confused by some to be a relative of the great Communist leader Zhu De, who at Mao's side played a key role leading the fight against the Guomindang Nationalists; he'd traveled with Mao on the Long March as well as being part of the government after the founding of the PRC in 1949. Zhu had admitted to using the name similarity to his advantage on occasion. While never claiming to be a direct relative it added to the aura around him. Major Yi knew that for all the good things said of Zhu he was not a leader to be on the wrong side of.

Motioning the three men to sit down, Zhu asked Yi how it went. The other two men remained silent. Yi cleared his throat before outlining the discussions with Professor Ding, the university lab professor, the meeting with Cai's adjutant, and then the conversations with Cai Levee.

"In summary, General, everything checked out with what we were told by this Professor Ding in terms of where the material in question originated. The surveillance photos that are time stamped show Cai where he claimed to be, along with the package in hand."

Zhu then turned to a younger man sitting to his right and asked him what he thought. No one had even said who he was to that point. Zhu apologized to Yi for the secrecy and told him this was Ouyang from the psychology department on the third floor; the other gentleman to his left worked for Ouyang. He proceeded to ask Ouyang what he thought. This irritated Yi, but he kept quiet as Ouyang took his glasses off for the fifth time and started cleaning them. He finally answered Zhu. "Based on my observation of Cai's eye movements, his eyelid motions, the directions his eyes moved as he spoke, and certain key body movements, I am 100 percent certain this Cai Levee is lying."

Yi sat up straight.

"Imagine you are a university professor, sir. Three men walk in unannounced and question you. One is clearly a senior military leader, two meters tall, built like an ox—no offense, Major Yi—and the two others are dressed in dark suits and ties. The two say nothing. I ask you all, would a normal person in that situation trot out verbatim a story given to two others that is word for word the same, and show no surprise or emotion?" Ouyang repeated this to Zhu for emphasis, then went on. "No, sir, not in my field; and believe me I have worked with the best, or worst, whichever is your view."

"What about you?" Zhu said as he looked at the third member of the team, not even mentioning his name. Yi glanced at the individual, who was sitting there like a stone statue. The man pursed his lips slightly, then turned towards Ouyang, and muttered, "I agree with him."

With that, Zhu thanked all three and asked Yi to stay while he ushered the other two out of his room.

Yi was perspiring slightly as Zhu returned to his seat and told Yi to relax, they were just getting started on this project but he needed to fill him in more on the situation. Zhu told Yi this whole matter was now of national importance and had moved into the highest levels of the military and the government.

"Hell," he said to Yi, "you will never guess what our crazy scientists have done this week. They've tried every tool in their arsenal to dissect this shell thing. Diamond wheels . . . failed! Oxy acetylene lances . . . failed! Ovens . . . failed! They took an army tank, fitted the shell into a frame that they mounted on its 8 cm. armored steel frame, put it in an enclosed concrete bunker to contain it, brought our latest and greatest shoulder-mounted missile and laser-guided it at the shell."

"And?" asked Yi. He noticed Zhu looking down into his desk drawer and reaching into it.

"They blew the shit out of the tank, Yi. It took fifteen guys to sift through the debris and guess what they found?"

Yi said he had no idea.

Zhu described the miserable remnants of the tank, telling him the tank looked like it had been put through a meat grinder. He pulled something out of the desk and threw it at Yi; it was the shell.

"Look at it, Yi, not a damned scratch on it!"

Yi let out a low whistle as Zhu commented that he had no idea if this material was from the Americans or the Russians. " If either of them have it and they start using this in their weapons or for soldiers' combat protection we could be screwed in any future conflict. Yi, this situation is as big as our past effort to obtain nuclear technology. We have to get to the bottom of it. Do you understand now the seriousness of the situation?"

"I do, sir. This is of grave concern for the future."

"Do you feel up to the task of continuing this investigation on the ground under my leadership?"

Yi apologized for his judgment about Cai, but assured Zhu he was ready. Zhu told Yi to redouble his efforts, that the minister was now directly involved, and that their group had carte blanche to do whatever it needed with whatever resources, using whatever methods it chose to get to the bottom of this.

"You will take sixty people, pull them off their current projects, and put them full-time on this. Anything you need you will have. You must report in every day and come back in a week's time to report to the joint committee of military and ministerial top-level personnel. We'll want to hear you've made concrete progress on our quest."

"Of course, General, you can rely on me and my men."

"All leave is canceled for those assigned to the task, and secrecy is imperative, Yi. Cai Levee and his family are not to be approached again directly in case suspicions are aroused that he is under surveillance. I am assigning another of my officers to your team to feed back to me all updates so that you can get on with your work. If you need Ouyang again you have only to ask and he will be made available."

Yi shifted slightly in his chair, thinking that Ouyang would be the last person he would call on; something about him made Yi uncomfortable.

"What kind of budget will be at my disposal?" Yi asked.

"It's bottomless! Use it wisely."

Yi left Zhu's office with Zhu patting him on the shoulder. "You have my full confidence and support, Major. If anyone throws up any kind of refusal to cooperate or give you what you need, then use my name and they can call me direct!"

Yi knew, of course, that anyone who did call Zhu would do so at his or her own peril.

When Yi got back he was highly energized, calling in his immediate reports to set everything in motion. He outlined their tasks pointing out that secrecy was vital, including not divulging anything to colleagues, friends, and families. All leave was canceled; they would work twenty-four hours a day if needed and were to drop every case they were working on to focus on this. The only real information Yi gave them on the shells was that they were looking for some secret material the Americans had developed that had somehow shown up in China.

They were to break up into four separate teams of fifteen persons with specific projects to focus on. He asked his assistant to put fifteen beds in one of the large recreational areas and stock the kitchen with food and drinks so teams could eat and sleep at the office if necessary in the coming week. He then listed his action items for the group, left them to pick whomever they wanted on their teams, and told them if they had any problems with department heads to have them call him.

Yi wanted teams operational within two hours of this meeting. He wanted files prepared on Levee and all his contacts for the last two or three weeks—where he had been, everything possible. For emphasis he told them he wanted to know the kind of toilet paper Cai Levee was using down to how many times he used it. He wanted around-the-clock surveillance on Levee. He wanted names of anyone he talked to, his family information, hotels checked, airlines, cars rented. He wanted all computers hacked and as many bugs in Cai's office and home as the investigators thought necessary. The team leaders were to keep him informed of all progress.

Their target was to find out as much as they could about what was going on for his meeting with Zhu next week. He advised them to especially look for any American or Russian contacts Cai may have had and to make sure those leads were fully covered, but to take great care with those, they did not need any international interest aroused at this time. If a foreign power was involved they did not want them to know an investigation was in progress. Before he released his direct reports he asked the group if there were any questions. No one said a word, simply looked at each other; that their next seven days were going to be grueling showed on all their faces.

Yi's surveillance specialist finally commented that bugging Cai's office was going to be easy; he had no doubt they could get that done within a few hours, though his home might take longer. Yi told him to have it done by the next morning, or just call him from his new assignment in some forlorn part of Xinjiang in the far west of China. The remark drew smiles and snickers from the rest of the men sitting near him.

Yi glanced toward an ominous-looking stranger in the back of the room; clearly he was one of Zhu's men. He asked if his "guest" had any other suggestions but the man simply shook his head and said nothing.

With that Yi got up, and his men snapped to attention. "Get moving," he said. "I'll be back in three hours to check the third floor of the building on the east end. I expect to see sixty people in place, desks set up along team lines with leaders sitting with them, not in some distant office. I want to see the fifteen beds already in place. This evening we all eat together in the office and discuss everyone's activities.

"Call your families to pack what you need; tell them you are on special assignment and likely will not be home for a week, maybe longer. All leave is canceled. Now get moving!"

As everyone left the meeting Yi could hear the murmuring amongst them. They were clearly not a happy group but they'd received the message loud and clear from him. He did not particularly care how they felt; this was a high priority investigation with no time to lose.

All was running smoothly for the team in Wuhan. George and Xiao Ping had not told the team everything that had happened in Zhangjiajie, other than the discovery of the first coffin. She and George tried to keep their concerns hidden from the team. George was becoming increasingly nervous about the whole situation after Cai's phone call, trying not to let Xiao Ping see his concern. They buried themselves in work.

Xiao Ping told George she was convinced it was going to blow over and they would soon be back in Beijing, working in the lab to figure out what the shells really were.

Cai's phone calls became less frequent and they only used the non-registered cell phones when they talked, yet they were still careful about what they said. It seemed that, since the visit to his office by the military guys, Cai had received no further calls and things were quiet for the time being. The lab in Beijing would be ready for the team by the time they finished in Wuhan.

George was finally able to advise the team of the budget situation and planned changes. Zhao Feng was not happy with his situation; however, there was not much George could do about it. He was pleased that they at least had a good situation to go to.

When Cai came to his office two days after the visit by Yi he became suspicious right away that someone had been in his room. He noticed one of the artifacts on his credenza was slightly out of position and examined it closely. Cai was very fastidious with the collection of artifacts on his shelves; the cleaning staff knew this after years of taking care of him as he'd instructed them to never clean those shelves. He dusted them personally every morning, a reminder of the pollution in Beijing that affected everyone's homes and offices throughout the city.

Cai could see that whoever had been inside the office did a very professional job in putting everything back in its place. He knew that without his little fetish about his collection a normal person would never have detected the intrusion. He understood right away his office had been searched and that likely both his office and computers were now bugged. He would have to be even more careful in the days ahead. He also decided not to tell Xiao Ping or George what was happening, as he suspected they were becoming more worried by the day.

A week later an exhausted team of people were thanked and told to rest for the day while Yi headed off to meet with Zhu and present his first week's report. He was joined by Zhu's "special guest," as well as Ouyang, in the lobby. One of Yi's assistants came running out with a bunch of files and a computer, assuring him everything they talked about was there, that his presentation was ready to go.

Yi was a bit surprised to see so many people at the meeting in the conference room. He counted twelve people around the main table and eight more seated along the perimeter of the room. Yi and Ouyang were directed to sit at the main table while Zhu's adjutant sat by the door as expressionless as ever. Yi busied himself setting up the computer, the projector, and his files, trying his best not to look nervous.

Zhu advised Yi that around the table were leaders from the military and the government, as well as certain party observers, Yi did not need to know any names. Yi listened as Zhu introduced him and Ouyang to everyone else at the meeting. Yi was told to present his findings over the last week, then leave the group so they might review whatever Yi had uncovered. He should return at 3 p.m. that day for instructions from Zhu as to further actions.

Yi noticed at one point that Zhu was looking toward the back of the room directly at his man; he saw clearly Zhu giving him a quizzical look as if to ask if the presentation would be okay. He was relieved to see the stone-faced look of the officer ease to a slight smile and his facial movements tell Zhu it was going to be just fine. Yi's nerves calmed slightly.

Yi then led the audience through the complete story of Ma Jun, as they knew it and had pieced together. He guided them through charts showing the relationship between the Mathers team and the university, as well as documents covering the special cultural projects they were involved in—all the way through to the empty coffins found on Mount Tianmen. His charts showed all the dates of the visits to Sam's hikers' lodge, the visit by Cai Levee, as well as the meetings with Scott Ramey and Diao Lijun.

Yi added his own hypothesis that the shell claimed to have been bought at the market was somehow tied into this story of Ma Jun and the empty coffin. When he finished his report and sat down there was complete silence and looks of disbelief in the audience, particularly when he commented that as yet he had no idea if more of the shells existed.

When asked if there were any questions, the group began to pepper Yi with a number of them, particularly how his team had managed to put together this fanciful story in such a short time.

"Who is this American Ramey? Is he connected with the CIA?" asked one of the scientists.

Yi smiled slightly. "No, Ramey seems clean; we checked him out both here and in the U.S. He is known to be a good friend of China." He explained what he had done with Diao Lijun. One of the ministers interrupted him.

"I can vouch for Diao Lijun; I know him well from the Forbidden City Palace Commission. He is beyond reproach and has returned a great number of stolen treasures to our homeland."

Yi nodded and continued. "Mathers too has a clean sheet, although an American passport holder, he is originally from England. Again, another cleared individual, married to a Chinese. They have worked here for many years and are highly respected in their field."

"What about our own, this Cai Levee from Tsinghua University? What about him?"

"I am not sure about him yet; I suspect he is somehow driving what is going on. Not that anything has been said directly, but I have that impression from the voice recordings and transcripts of certain conversations."

One of the people at the table at that point interrupted him. "Major Yi, everything we have heard today is frankly ridiculous. This is without doubt an American game we are being sucked into. Why? I do not know, but this story of Ma and coffins and all is utter nonsense."

One of the scientists blurted out that maybe this shell thing simply came off a space vehicle, or rocket that circled over China. He thought it was perhaps some kind of heat shield. "Based on what we've learned today, I believe it has to be American. They are further ahead on material development than our Soviet friends. It is critical we get our hands on more of this material."

Yi was relieved when Zhu finally called the meeting to order at that point, but again asked Yi to explain where all this information came from in such short order.

Yi then explained to the group how they had an early break in their investigation when they found out Cai's brother was also a special investigator in the government sector. They hacked into his system and found a file that was set up a short time ago with flight, hotel, and car rental details for a Zhao Feng traveling to Zhangjiajie. This rang alarm bells because it tied in with the information that Cai and Mather's team had been there, as had Ramey and Diao, all too circumstantial not to merit careful follow up. They decided to take a little more aggressive action on this and picked Zhao Feng out for special attention.

"Three days ago we flew overnight to Wuhan and at 11 p.m. removed him from his hotel, took him to one of our safe houses, where he was blindfolded and cuffed throughout his stay. We left him there for one hour and at Mr. Ouyang's suggestion we played some tapes over the speaker system so he would think he was in a rather nasty prison; a few extra screams added to the atmosphere we had created."

A couple of the military guys snickered at that point but one minister looked slightly alarmed. Yi confirmed quickly that at no point in their interrogation did they physically harm him. "When we went back an hour later and removed his hood Zhao Feng was in a state of panic. He'd filled his trousers completely and been sick down his shirt. He was so terrified that he readily told us everything he could, including how he tried to get ahead of Mathers and his wife in hopes of finding some kind of treasure, but he found that the coffins were empty. He confirmed he had ripped up the note from this Ma Jun character in his anger."

Zhu turned to Ouyang and asked for his comments on the interrogation. Ouyang again nervously removed his glasses, cleaned them, and began outlining his background to the audience—his career in psychological and physical interrogation over the years, how he had assisted in the interrogation of Zhao Feng. "It is of course my opinion that Feng was telling the absolute truth, as he knew it," he said.

Yi then confirmed that a team from Wuhan had also flown to Zhangjiajie and visited the lodge and mountain, interviewed the monk, visited the cave, retrieved the empty coffins for analysis; so far everything in Feng's story panned out. There was one exception in that Feng had no knowledge of the visit by Cai Levee and had not been told much about the meeting with Scott Ramey and Diao Lijun. As far as Feng knew, no one was aware of what he had done. He had told the team he was visiting his father at that time. Since then things were normal at Wuhan and nobody had challenged his story.

"The interrogation was completed by 5 a.m.," Yi said. "Feng was returned to the hotel after being cleaned up and given something by Ouyang here to calm him down."

"Will he talk?" Ouyang was asked. Both he and Yi smiled. Yi stated that there was no chance of that; the man was warned of the consequences of revealing any of these events and assured that his next visit from them would not be so pleasant.

Yi had seen the fear in Zhao Feng's eyes firsthand, and also noticed how much more fearful the man was of Ouyang than himself. He knew at that point there was no risk of Zhao Feng talking to anyone, not even his mother!

Zhu thanked Yi and his team for their excellent progress, told them to keep up the effort, and to leave the group to consider the information. They were to be back by 3 p.m. sharp. He told the group he was still unconvinced of the connection between what Cai supposedly purchased and the search for treasure with Mathers, but every lead had to be followed to its conclusion.

Zhu later described to Yi how once the three men were gone, the meeting erupted into a number of heated discussions, some treating the story as a complete fantasy hiding an entirely sophisticated espionage effort by the Americans. Others thought this was indeed the result of something falling off a space rocket or missile over China. Whatever it was, the scientists and military specialists were scared about what would happen if this material were out there and in the hands of their enemies; it needed to be found if it existed and its composition figured out at all costs.

At 3:00 p.m. Yi arrived for a meeting with Zhu and was quite surprised to see him dressed in casual clothes in his office, and a suitcase sitting by the door. Zhu smiled and asked Yi to sit down and take notes. "After you left the meeting this morning I told the group I had a proposal to make to them. I asked them to allow me to get out of this office and back into the field for one week and let others handle my departmental activities. I told them if they allowed me to do whatever I felt was needed that by the following week I would either know if any more existed, where any more of this material was, or have it sitting on the conference table. I didn't say what my plans were. I never fully trust a large group like that with confidential information. The last thing we need is the Americans alerted if they are involved! I plan to start focusing on this right away. I already have a stand-in proposed."

Yi was floored by Zhu's decision to become directly involved. Trying to seem sincere he said, "I hope they agreed to your request; your involvement would be welcomed by the team."

"Don't flatter me, Yi, I've been in your shoes. I can guess how you really feel, but don't take it personally. Anyway, yes, the group readily agreed, although one of the ministers spoke up right away emphasizing there was to be no international incident arising from any actions we take. The nation's laws need to be upheld and human rights respected. Of course that comment drew a few snickers from our senior military friends at the table. I gave them my full assurance on that point and then brought the meeting to a close."

Zhu told Yi how he finally placed the shell on the table for effect, turned toward the scientists, and told them he was returning it to their care. He had invited everyone to look at it, leaving the two scientists to tell the group what they had tried to do to this odd-looking material, whatever it was. He'd had enough of all those people and headed back to his apartment to pack.

Yi listened carefully as Zhu explained what he had in mind next, though he wasn't happy with the situation; nevertheless, at least now Zhu's neck would be further out than his, should anything go wrong.

CHAPTER 15

CAI HEADED OUT FOR A coffee break. The drinks at the university café were pretty awful but a café just off campus served premium stuff. It was a small place opened by two former students trying to catch the wave of growth in coffee drinking among the Chinese, especially students. They took their business seriously and imported the very best beans from overseas, freshly roasting their coffees in the café. The exotic aromas filled the rooms, drawing in real drinkers who had no qualms about dropping 35 yuan ($5.50) for a cappuccino, quite a lot for students especially. The owners knew Cai well; he was a regular and they supplied him with ground coffee beans for his use at home.

They always knew exactly what he needed when they saw him through their window crossing the street from the university entrance and usually had it ready by the time he arrived. Cai chatted with the pair while sipping his coffee for a good half hour before leaving. Once he was out of sight of the café, a large black van suddenly stopped alongside him and two hooded men grabbed him. A third man pulled a bag over his head as they bundled him inside and sped off. It happened very quickly.

Inside the van Cai's arms were pulled behind him and cuffs placed on his wrists as he was forced to the floor. Nothing was said to him nor was there any talk among his abductors. There was nothing he could do.

One of the abductors searched Cai's pockets and pulled out two cell phones, a fancy smart phone, an Apple 5, and a cheap locally made phone they would find he was using to call Mathers. Soon they would have access to all calls made on these phones. While they headed to the airport the phones were passed to a specialist, who hooked the smart phone to a computer to unlock it and send two text messages, one to Cai's assistant and one to his wife. The message said that Cai was sorry but a student was in difficulty and he had to travel to Xiamen to the young man's home, which he would explain later. They were not to worry. Of course, both recipients tried to call right back but every time they did the phone was busy.

Yi had told the men that, yes, this approach was clumsy but he had many other things to organize before the Wuhan flight with Zhu and his team.

After a time, someone grabbed Cai's arm and injected him; their captive gradually reacted to the drugging and his body became almost lifeless as the van turned a sharp corner, rolling him to the other side until one of his abductors grabbed him. The van passed through the security checkpoint at the airport after the long drive, and headed for a hangar where Zhu and Yi were pacing up and down.

When the team carried Cai out of the van toward the plane both leaders looked at each other in surprise. Zhu demanded to know who decided to drug him, as he wanted him awake. One of the abductors stepped forward and saluted. "Sorry, sir. I forgot to tell Wang; he always takes care of that part. He simply followed usual procedure."

Yi received an icy glare from General Zhu. "Please, Yi, no more mistakes like this!"

Despite Zhu's apparent calm Yi knew the instructions he gave to his team had been overly zealous but he said nothing. He felt Zhu's arm wrap around him, and his voice soften. "Oh well, at least we can talk freely on the plane now."

Once all the men and equipment were onboard the converted Boeing 737, the plane taxied onto the runway awaiting clearance. It was now getting late in the evening and they expected to be in the military's guest house by midnight. Cai would be taken to the safe house to be kept in one of the rooms, blindfolded and cuffed for the following day. Zhu wanted to have the day in Wuhan to prepare for the following evening and make sure everything in the safe house was to his liking, that his little stage was set. Although Zhu had not given details of his plan, Yi had a pretty good idea of what was about to happen, as did Ouyang, whose presence on the trip was likely a precursor to what was in store for George Mather and his colleagues.

Yi knew that Zhu had spent a considerable amount of time with interrogation services in his intelligence career. While others could be brutal in their techniques, Zhu was renowned for preferring to play with people's heads rather than using brute force. That was not to say he never resorted to physical torture when he had to; there were enough stories of those times amongst the troops, but they knew he always considered it his last resort.

Reportedly Zhu held no regard for the methods the Americans used in Afghanistan and Iraq. He was vaguely amused by the arguments going on in the U.S. about methods used against terrorists; he did hold, strangely enough, human rights to be important. Yi was told several times they were not to break the commitment he made in Beijing to avoid any violations since foreigners were involved. In any event, Zhu voiced confidence he could do what he needed without using any abusive force.

Prior to Yi leaving his office, Zhu had told him he needed psychological profiles and background information on all of Mathers' group, as well as Cai Levee, ready for him to read the next day while they were together in Wuhan. Ouyang was to be given copies of everything too. The time allocated to do this was very tight. One of the teams had been challenged to do the best they could and to talk to whomever they needed to, also to be very careful and avoid drawing their targets' attention to the fact they were being investigated. The team was told they did not need to bother with Zhao Feng; they already had a clear picture of him and his vulnerabilities. How they were going to handle the foreigner Mathers was trickier and politically more sensitive.

CHAPTER 16

GEORGE AND XIAO PING HAD a good day in Wuhan; they went to bed early that evening after writing up various pieces from the day's interviews. They were both a little edgy, and of late had begun to disagree more than usual. George put it down to the situation with the coffin contents and Cai's questioning by the military; he was becoming more paranoid by the day.

George decided to call Cai without Xiao Ping around and let him know that they should be talking directly to the authorities; this had gone too far now. He could not get a hold of him, however; every time he called, Cai's phones were busy. George finally called his office and was told that Cai had left for Xiamen, which seemed very strange. Other than saying it was university business, the guy on the line wasn't helpful. He said he was Liu Tao, but George thought the man did not sound like Liu Tao. He hoped it was just a bad line; if it wasn't, then something more serious could be going on.

After talking for some time with Xiao Ping he finally turned out the lights and was soon able to drop off to sleep. But his sleep was short-lived when powerful hands grabbed him and dragged him from his side of the bed; a bag was thrust over his head and a gag stuffed in his mouth. George heard a brief scream of surprise from Xiao Ping before she too went quiet. George could sense she was kicking and struggling as was he. Very strong arms held him tightly; there was little a completely out of shape academic like him could do, so he simply gave up the struggle. He could feel them being herded out of the room and down the hall to the fire exit.

There were obviously more attackers involved, and George guessed more victims. They all clattered down the back stairs with not a word from any of the captors. He was pretty certain who they were, but making sure Xiao Ping was okay was foremost in his mind. He suspected they were being transferred to a number of vehicles; he found himself in a van speeding off into the night. He figured it must have been close to one or two o'clock in the morning and wondered how long it would be before they were missed.

When they arrived at their final destination George was pushed into a room and the gag was wrenched from his mouth. Assuming his colleagues were experiencing the same fate he tried to persuade his captors to at least put Xiao Ping and himself in a room together. No one said a word in response, and the door slammed shut as he heard Xiao Ping screaming for him.

One other door closed during the night, and the lock clanged telling George there was one more victim. He remained blindfolded with his arms cuffed behind his back in a soft chair, which might have been comfortable except for his being restrained. He did not sleep at all, expecting some interrogator to drag him out for questioning; he shuddered at the thought that he might be beaten. All of this, to him, seemed clearly connected to the contents of their infamous coffins and Ma stories. He was not sure when this would end but was determined to put a stop to it, one way or another.

Yi reported to Zhu that his guests were all in place, and he was told not to disturb or talk to them, to keep everyone apart and in silence until 8 a.m.; then Zhu wanted them all brought in and sitting in the large interrogation room. Yi was to arrange for steaming hot coffee and whatever pastries he could find to be sitting on the table together with some fruit. There was no need for cigarettes; according to their profiles, no one smoked. Yi knew better than to complain to the general about why he was planning to make things so comfortable for their new guests.

Yi was to bring the four detainees in, put the American and his wife in the middle of the four of them, but also to put their two chairs close to each other. Zhu told Yi he wanted the couple to feel their bodies touching before talking to them. Also Yi was to instruct each one of them that if anyone spoke one word without being asked to speak they would be hauled back to their individual cell rooms.

With Zhu making all the arrangements, Ouyang looked at Zhu and, smiling, asked why he was even needed there. He was told to stay and observe. If Zhu did not get what he wanted, Yi and Ouyang were free to do anything they wanted in order to get them to talk. They all went off to bed to rest and be ready for the task ahead. Yi was hopeful Zhu's approach would fail and he could get his hands on the suspects to show both Zhu and Ouyang he knew how to make people talk.

After hours on end George finally heard the door open and someone come into his room. The man spoke like a senior level official, telling George he was being taken to his wife and others, but that under no circumstances was he to say any word whatsoever unless asked. If he did he would be taken away from the meeting and put back in the cell. George gathered this would be repeated almost verbatim to the others. At any rate he was ushered into a large room, helped onto a chair, a pleasant aroma of fresh coffee and some kind of baked goods filling his nostrils.

He was dying of thirst and starving at the same time. As soon as they sat him down, he sensed Xiao Ping and two others coming in. He was relieved to feel Xiao Ping's body close to his; they rubbed arms as if to say they were both okay. More footsteps followed with some whispering back and forth before the door clanged shut. George was dying to shout out, "What the hell's going on?" but did not want to go back to the cell. Finally he heard a chair scrape the floor as someone had sat down for a while then got up and walked around the table behind him. The man removed the cuffs and hood from George, then George heard the same thing happening to the others. They were then told to stay seated and to not speak.

After being blindfolded for so long it took some time for George's eyes to adjust to the light; after a while the shape in front of him came into full focus. Sitting across from him was a large and very determined-looking man, clearly military and definitely someone not to be messed with. Glancing left and right George saw Xiao Ping sitting next to him looking straight at him, totally petrified, and he did his best to calm her with the most comforting look he could muster. Zhao Feng to her left looked completely dejected. On George's right was Cai Levee, who was nervous as hell like the rest of them.

The man introduced himself as General Zhu and asked if any of them had heard of him; no one had. He welcomed them to this "voluntary discussion" and invited everyone to help themselves to coffee, tea, and bakery. He said he knew they had come a long way to the meeting and wanted them, his "guests," to be comfortable.

Weary and with added confusion all four grabbed some coffee and a little something to eat wondering what was next. George listened as Zhu proceeded to tell them who he was and that he was here to cause them no harm. He looked at George. "Professor, you come from a very advanced country. I can just imagine what you are thinking is going to happen here, but I must tell you that the interview techniques of others are abhorrent me. I am sure in our little meeting today there will be no need for any of that."

George waited while Zhu paused and pointed to the two other men in the room,

"However, there are others in this building with more experience than I have in that area." As he said that George could see Zhao Feng start to shake, Xiao Ping visibly tighten up, and Cai breathe in sharply. He sensed the fear permeating the room and this man had not touched them yet! For whatever reason, George found himself surprisingly calm; he had no idea why.

Zhu welcomed them by name and came over to shake each of their hands, apologizing if anyone had been injured during the journey. He outlined the purpose of these meetings in that he was there on behalf of the People's Republic of China—its military and political leaders—to obtain some lost articles.

He then went through the results of their inquiry in surprising detail, as well as some of their methods used. Zhao Feng was not mentioned as a source, but George guessed he was the main source of the Ma story and the search for the coffins. Zhu referred to two coffins standing in the rear of the room as having coming from the cave. While they contained something before, they now were empty, according to the story he had been given.

Zhu went over how his people had paid a visit to the mountain. They had followed up on both Ramey and Diao Lijun, who Mathers met on the Tianmen trail, and they had questioned the Master Monk. The general said the monk, however, knew little but spoke very highly of the professor and his wife. With that he sat on the chair directly opposite George, looking straight at him. George felt the glare of eyes that were both warm and sinister at the same time.

"Professor Mathers, I am not an unreasonable man compared to others that could be sitting where I am. I believe we can resolve our little problem here quite quickly with no one coming to any harm. I know you are an honest and honorable man, as well as a good friend to China." He tapped one of the files on the desk. "It is all in here. In fact, all of these files show me I am dealing with good men, except perhaps one or two misguided ones." He glanced at Cai and Feng.

"You are lucky too; you have a fine, smart, and pretty Chinese wife in Xiao Ping. I am sure you would agree, Mr. Mathers."

He paused for effect, then said, "However, you are all in a difficult situation now with the find that Mr. Cai here has delivered to us, not directly but through Professor Ding's efforts to figure out what the item is. People in both the government and military have charged me with finding the rest of the pieces, and I have instructions to do anything I have to do to find them. I would personally like to have us all leave this meeting in the next few days alive, healthy, and with this matter behind us."

George was surprised by the perfect English Zhu used; any thoughts that the general might not understand English disappeared.

"Shortly, I expect our police forces in Beijing and Wuhan will be receiving urgent calls regarding the fact that you are missing. We are expecting to receive them soon and the calls will all be directed to my team here to manage. If we do not resolve this matter then I cannot control the outcome." He pointed at each of them, one at a time, as he continued. "Four people here—one, two, three, four—can be found within twenty-four hours in two car accidents, and their bodies identified as yours. We would of course honor your religions closely and cremate the bodies quickly, in time sending our heartfelt sympathies from the nation to your families and embassy. Now we can continue in peace here discussing at great length what we can do to resolve my problem . . . until I decide enough is enough."

With that Zhu turned toward the door, speaking to George. "Professor, you are free to have your own meeting now; I will return in one hour so that you can tell me how you would prefer for us to continue. Of course, telling us the full story in this matter—and revealing the location of whatever else you might have found—will bring this matter to a speedy and, I hope, less painful conclusion. Let me know if you need me to freshen up the coffee."

He paused one more time before he left and looked over at Cai Levee. "Mr. Cai, you have a very nice display in your office. I hope you enjoyed knowing that my people visited your office that night. I do like, by the way, the nice little painting you bought at the Panjiayuan market, very similar taste to mine. I must say surprisingly close in size to the shell you supposedly bought." With that he closed the door leaving them to think about what he had said.

George suspected they were not alone; he had seen too many movies not to believe they were being watched and listened to from another room.

Outside, Yi was led by Zhu to the viewing room to join the others watching the detainees; Ouyang shook the general's hand, saying it was always a pleasure to watch one of his mentors at work. Yi wondered aloud if he should not go back inside and drag one of them out by the neck for a little effect, maybe Mathers' wife. Yi was quickly rebuked; Zhu told both of them to do no such thing, he expected this matter to be over quickly.

Over Yi's objections, Zhu told Ouyang that in his opinion the group was not made up of criminals or spies. He guessed they had by chance stumbled into this, and had clearly gone down the wrong path in trying to keep this for their own glory, or for whatever reason.

George's mind had been whirring the whole time Zhu was talking. He had an idea, which he whispered to the others, not telling them everything but saying that whether they liked it or not, that was what he was going to do right there and then. He stood up and addressed the door Zhu had left by; he could not see where the cameras were but said to Zhu in a loud voice, "General, I have a proposal for you, if you would care to save time by coming back now."

Zhu walked back to the interrogation room. "What is your proposal? I hope it's one that we can all sign up for. I have full authority to negotiate on behalf of my country."

"General, we can solve this quickly, but I have a specific request before we proceed with finalizing an arrangement. I believe it will give you what you are looking for and provide us some feeling of safety."

"I'm listening, Professor. If it is reasonable I will consider it."

"We would proceed to reveal the entire story, with nothing left out, and we will be in a position to deliver more of the items you are seeking; there is much more to the items than meets the eye. To do this I ask only three small things. First, that you contact Mr. Diao Lijun and arrange for him to be here for our negotiations, and second, until you can get him here, that you allow us to shower, sleep, and get a decent meal. Lastly, I would ask that my wife and I to be left with each other until we all get back together."

Zhu asked for a couple of minutes and stepped out of the room. George's colleagues looked at him quizzically. Zhao Feng appeared a little sheepish; George suspected he was wondering if someone was going to bring up his little act of treachery. Cai simply muttered that he hoped George knew what he was doing, while Xiao Ping was hugging her husband and telling him to be careful. George felt strangely calm about the whole thing.

CHAPTER 17

OUTSIDE THE INTERROGATION ROOM ZHU talked to Ouyang and Yi.
Yi wanted to quit fooling around and basically beat the hell out of
George with his wife watching. Yi watched Ouyang simply nod to
Zhu, as if he already fully approved of Zhu's approach and likely
guessed what he was going to do.

"Yi, you are to immediately contact Beijing," Zhu directed. "Get
a message to Diao Lijun and have him in Wuhan and this facility in
the shortest time, today if possible. I want to lose no momentum."

Yi mumbled loud enough for Zhu to hear that maybe they should
get a rocket or something.

"That's not such a stupid idea, Yi, although I think Diao might
enjoy a ride in one of China's newest jet fighter planes at the base."
Yi's face dropped when Zhu added that he was not joking, to get it
done.

George stiffened when Zhu walked back into the meeting and
straight over to shake his hand. "Professor, we have a deal. We are
going to try to track Diao down as soon as we can. We are all reasonable people here and I hope we will all have a good outcome
from our discussions. I am agreeable to you and your wife staying
together. You will be confined to your rooms where you can sleep

or relax. I've requested new clothes be bought for you, a gift from military intelligence of course."

When George asked if he needed their sizes Zhu laughed and turned to leave. "Professor Mathers, we know more than you can imagine!"

George and his wife, along with the others, received a call in the early evening to assemble for a meeting in the interrogation room. They were again escorted there, this time without handcuffs or their heads covered. They all wore fresh clothing and had been allowed in sequence to shower. Xiao Ping had been taken care of by a female officer, who had provided her with toiletries and makeup.

Entering the room, they were all surprised to see both Zhu and Diao waiting for them. George couldn't fathom how they had gotten Diao there so quickly—in a matter of hours, really.

Zhu re-introduced all of them to each other and then held the palms of his hands towards George. "Okay, Professor, my part of the agreement is complete. May I hear yours?"

At that point the female officer who had helped Xiao Ping came in smiling and sat down with both a keyboard and tape recorder.

George went through the story for both men. He outlined how he and Xiao Ping discovered the second cave and the single coffin inside based on the two hundred paces in Ma Jun's story versus where the first cave was. George could see Zhao Feng's eyebrows rise in surprise. He left out two parts of the story, however. One part was the Ma Jun's last words about being his father's son, and the second that they knew Ma Jun in recent years had purchased two coffins. Even though they had only found one, that part still bothered George. He then proposed a deal to Zhu and Diao, indicating that he had no interest in the coffin's contents other than for historical and archeological research.

George pointedly told Diao the shells were likely some kind of historical record that they hoped dating would identify; so far they had been unable to decipher them. George could see that Diao in particular was most excited at the description given of the artifacts.

George said, "As far as I'm concerned the pieces are of historical value and belong to the Chinese people. What we request is permission and support to continue to investigate the pieces with computer technology, photographic records, etcetera, to attempt to translate what is on the shells. Furthermore, we should all be absolved of any criminal charges and any transgressions we might have committed in our efforts to protect them.

"Our activities are to be forgiven without fear of penalty or retribution, as we had no malicious intent. If the Chinese government chooses to restrict the physical study of them to military research and use, it is their prerogative. I urge Mr. Diao Lijun, however, to look at them himself and give his opinion to General Zhu."

George finished his proposal commenting how he too was baffled by the failure of labs to identify the shell's material or possible origin. "All of this testing to date leaves me completely mystified as to how the markings or writings covering the backs of all these shells were done when the labs cannot even get a mark on them."

Diao, who appeared intrigued as he listened to the entire tale, turned to Zhu. "General," he said leaning toward Zhu, "on behalf of the academic world I would fully support this team trying to interpret these works. We might even fund the endeavor. I am anxious to see these objects as soon as possible, but I do, of course, understand that this must all be decided at the highest level. I am concerned about destroying these items for military purposes, as perhaps others might be, but if the party chooses that route then so be it."

Diao asked everyone how long the shells would be needed before turning them over to the military such that the group had sufficient information to continue its work. George chatted quietly with the others, briefly talking about the digital mapping of each shell and the care they would have to take. George guessed at least two months of initial work was needed before they could feel comfortable letting the shells out of their hands. Zhu thanked George for finally telling him the truth at least, but added he needed to discuss further with Diao and a couple of key ministers whether or not they could agree to his proposed terms. They both left the room to call their superiors and discuss the offer further. The group, instructed by Yi not to talk further on this matter, sat around for almost an hour before Zhu and Diao returned.

Right away, Zhu reported that the Chinese authorities would agree to George's proposal but on several conditions. "The shells must be made available for inspection within seven days. They will be moved to an area for the team to work on if needed. In addition, half of the shells must be turned over to the military within thirty days. The other half can be stored in a special preservation area while the party leaders decide if they stay there or also go to the military. That will be influenced by the outcome of the study. Lastly, no publication of any information regarding the story that has been discussed here—or the outcome of the research—is to be released without the express permission of the Chinese government. The person who will bear the responsibility for managing Cai Levee and your work will be Diao Lijun."

They were given a few minutes by Zhu to discuss the proposed agreement, after which George duly agreed and reached out to shake Zhu's hand, then Diao Lijun's hand. He reached toward Yi but no hand was offered. George could see that Yi was not pleased with how things were developing.

Zhu asked when they could see the shells. Cai advised that they, and whoever else wanted to see them, could all meet in his university office as soon as he was safely back in Beijing. He asked to be allowed to call his family and work to let them know he was safe, which Zhu agreed to, once again demanding that everyone in the room maintain secrecy; this project was not to be discussed with other colleagues and family members.

On a lighter note, Zhu announced that there would be a banquet that night before heading to Beijing the next day, adding that the professor and his team's projects in Wuhan were canceled—effective immediately. They should be ready to fly in a military plane by noon the next day to Beijing.

Diao asked if he could take the train, saying he was still anxious after the fighter jet flight to Wuhan, which explained how Diao had arrived there so quickly. Diao told everyone the last thing he needed right then was another plane trip. Zhu laughed, telling him there was an overnight train he could take if he really wanted to.

Cai was ordered never to attempt any concealment from the authorities in the future. George and his wife were told to be careful in these matters going forward. With that, Zhu stood and left, having asked that everyone be ready to head to the military's private club in Wuhan at 6 p.m. Diao stayed behind asking ever more questions about the team's findings thus far.

That evening they all headed out to an impressive provincial government guesthouse for the dinner. It was held in a very private area of the building so that they could be kept from public view and would all be able to talk freely. Zhu turned out to be quite the host, as the customary baijiu toasting got under way. Xiao Ping and Cai handled it pretty well, as did Zhao Feng, clearly relieved with the outcome of their situation, but George struggled to avoid having more than one glass. Diao Lijun however reddened in the face quickly, indicating that this infamous Chinese liquor at forty-seven proof did not sit well with him.

George could not help but notice how Ouyang spent most of the evening looking at him and the others as if each of them was being analyzed psychologically. Ouyang did, however, converse often with Xiao Ping, who he clearly found attractive. Yi tried to be affable, but

George had the feeling that all Yi wanted to do was drag him off to a room and beat even more out of him.

George had a stimulating conversation with Diao Lijun and Zhu, mostly about the history of China since the fall of the Qing dynasty. To his surprise, for the son of a coal miner, Zhu was smart and engaging. There was more to him than initially met the eye. Cai sat there generally silent, eating and drinking his way through the evening but joining in rarely. George sensed Cai's mind was clearly away from the party; he put it down to all his colleague had been through and was perhaps nervous that somehow the agreement could unravel and he would end up losing everything.

As far as George was concerned, at least they were not headed for prison. Whether the Chinese would censor everything his team was about to do was a gamble on his part. George's only regret was that there was no way to keep their find, in terms of the shells themselves, out of the military's hands. He'd prefer that they be housed somewhere like the Beijing Museum of History and that his team be allowed to share their find with the archaeological world.

During the evening, it did occur to George that Zhao Feng would need to be sent away as planned, although it was undoubtedly going to be awkward to arrange. For now, it was crucial that he be kept quiet.

The next day they gathered as requested, and at noon left their holding area. When they first arrived they had been blindfolded and transported in vans with no windows, ensuring none of them knew where the safe house was. This time, as soon as the officers felt their detainees were clear of being able to figure out the safe house location in Wuhan, they were allowed to remove their blindfolds with profuse apologies that the officers had been obliged to do this to them yet again.

The plane awaited them at the military base, where Zhu was standing by to greet everyone. He smiled and welcomed them to join him for the flight, laughing as he mentioned that Diao Lijun and Yi had taken the train after the banquet, Diao to avoid another flight, Yi to complete the arrangements for their arrival. Everyone was to go to the university immediately; there would be other guests waiting for them to arrive.

Charles told George later how Zhu's men had definitely wasted no time; they had gone right away to the hotel in Wuhan and packed everybody's things. They apologized to Charles and Arthur but told them that the professor and his wife were not there; they had left already for Beijing. Over Charles's expressions of concerns for his colleagues a full explanation was promised to them once they arrived in Beijing. They were advised to pack their things and head to Beijing taking both vehicles with them. Reservations had been made for them at a hotel near the university for a briefing; no one was to return to his apartment before that.

Charles told George that officers had accompanied them on the journey back, one in each of the vehicles. They were told not to worry, that nothing untoward would happen to them. George could imagine how concerned these remarks made Charles and Arthur, especially since the two were highly intelligent professionals; they would quickly understand that this was all connected with the infamous search for Ma's treasure, whatever that really was.

George could see that Zhu was a man of action; he was not going to wait to get to the shells. He advised George he would have a meeting later in the week with both a ministerial and military committee; he would "borrow" some of the shells for the meeting but return them right away. He said he needed to get the "theatrics" right for them and was also going to ask for approval to have Diao Lijun present.

When George expressed concern about too many people handling the items, Zhu just laughed. "Professor, if you'd seen what they tried to do to Cai's sample and how there was not a scratch on it afterwards you would have no concerns at all. You could run a tank over the piece and you would not see a mark of any kind on it."

They touched down a couple of hours later at the military base to be picked up in cars; this time with no blindfolds they headed through Beijing and off to Tsinghua University to meet the others waiting there. When they arrived at Cai's main building there was quite a reception committee including Diao and Yi. Zhu then decided who was to stay and who needed to leave; everyone sat together in Cai's office waiting for him to speak. Cai welcomed the esteemed group to his office and walked over to his credenza, took from one of the displays a set of three antique looking keys that at first glance looked like part of a work of modern art. He said he could not think of a better place to hide them, then asked everyone to follow him. Yi reddened slightly as Zhu gave him what was obviously a "How the hell did you miss that?" look.

Cai led them to the remote lab area and to a room that had signs warning of no unauthorized admission; he unlocked it and everyone filed in. There was nothing in the room but it had clearly been recently swept out. There were tables and chairs waiting to be set up and three old but comfortable-looking sofa chairs ready to be used. Cai mentioned this was the spare lab where he planned to research the writings on the shells before all the trouble of the last days had developed. He then strode over to the old strong-room door with all its warnings about bioresearch, the need for protective wear, etcetera, and proceeded to open the locks with the three keys.

Zhu and Diao stood close by as Cai pulled open the heavy door with Yi's assistance and flipped on the lights. There on a large table lay about eight hundred "shells," all slightly different but nonetheless similar in shape. Cai turned over one of the shells to show the markings on the underside and Diao let out a prolonged gasp. He commented that this was truly remarkable; he said he had no clue what the writing or hieroglyphics were. "This could be the greatest find of all time for China!" he exclaimed.

Zhu looked approvingly at the shells and told George they should get started as soon as possible. Diao was to be in charge of their efforts. They had thirty days starting the next day before handing over the shells. Until that time the team could do anything they wanted to research them, but no shells were to leave the room; there would also be a twenty-four-hour guard posted there. Passes would be issued only to those people that needed access. In three days, on the day of Zhu's update meeting, Diao was to bring about fifty shells to the meeting, along with photos of the entire cache. Diao could bring them back later that same day and two of Yi's men would escort him to ensure nothing was lost or stolen during the process.

Zhu turned to Yi, told him to coordinate this, and asked if he had any other suggestions. Yi replied that this all sounded very effective to him, but suggested video cameras be installed to watch everyone at all times. Xiao Ping raised considerable objection to this suggestion. Zhu interceded by declaring that video cameras would be installed at all entries and exits and at any windows accessing the rooms that were being worked in. This seemed extreme to George, who jokingly suggested they install metal detectors in the hallway too. Yi immediately turned to him and said that was a good idea. Zhu just looked at both of them with a smile and said it was fine and to get it done. George rolled his eyes in disbelief.

Diao decided they needed a meeting of the research group to discuss everything as soon as Charles and Arthur arrived from Wuhan. George asked Zhu and Diao to meet separately with him to discuss some scheduling problems that needed addressing. Zhu readily agreed and invited George into another room; Yi began to follow but was told to stay with the others. Yi did not look happy.

"What scheduling issues are you talking about, Professor? I'm sure they can be handled easily enough."

"General Zhu, we had prior arrangements planned for the team and in particular Zhao Feng. We have secured a new university position for Zhao Feng to take up in Fujian Province. It's important that he be released to that program before we get too far into this project."

"It seems to me, Professor, that he needs to stay with the project in view of everything he knows, don't you?"

"To be frank, I think we both know what kind of a team member Zhao Feng really is, and I'm sure I don't need to spell it out to you why. I have no problem living with the agreement we have, but I have to tell you if Zhao Feng remains here you will not have a cohesive team working to solve this mystery."

George could see the surprise on Diao's face at his determination to have Zhao Feng removed, but noticed the smile slowly appearing from Zhu.

"Professor, in regards to your request, I think I fully understand why you feel this way. I can assure you and Diao, however, that Zhao Feng will not be a problem and will keep all that he has seen and heard quiet. He is basically a weak man and we can control him easily. For now he stays with the project, but let Diao know what the plans are for him, and after the shells are turned over to us in thirty days we will organize his transfer." George was disappointed but not surprised that Zhu insisted Zhao Feng was to stay; clearly Zhu believed he was under their control. He would need to advise the others to be even more careful around their colleague.

With that they returned to the meeting room where Zhu reminded everyone they were under an oath of secrecy and called Yi into the same empty office next to Cai.

Yi followed Zhu, still aggravated about not being in the private meeting with Mathers. Zhu told him what had happened and to take special care of Zhao Feng.

"Yi, all will be fine here, do as I tell you without question. Do your work well. Zhao Feng is here for you to manipulate. You had good suggestions so go ahead and get everything done we talked about, or at least as much as you can. Please make sure the rooms are bugged before they come in tomorrow morning, and arrange twenty-four-hour surveillance of each of them until further notice."

"I have the security measures in motion and plan to attend Diao's meeting tomorrow. I'm going to use Zhao Feng carefully and watch him closely. I will also monitor Diao Lijun, just to be sure."

" Good. Your arrangements are thorough as always, but as regards monitoring Diao Lijun do so if you think we have to. But be very cautious; he's a Communist Party member of standing and highly regarded in government and party circles."

CHAPTER 18

CHARLES AND ARTHUR HAD DRIVEN straight from Wuhan to the university, driving most of the night. George was allowed to call each of them to give them a heads up as to what was going on, partially to alleviate their concerns, but also to save a lot of time when they arrived. While neither was overly surprised by the recent events, they were excited to hear about the full extent of the discoveries. George quickly outlined what had happened with Zhao Feng; both of them agreed that he had done the right thing in trying to get him out of the project before it began.

Both men agreed that it would be challenging to document eight hundred or so items in thirty days. They would need all the hands they could get. They discussed additional help but agreed that could be risky, and likely would mean someone from Yi's team simply there to spy on each of them whether Zhao Feng was there or not. George advised them to keep a close watch on Zhao Feng and to be careful what they said around him.

The kick-off meeting began at 10 a.m. with Diao already there, examining the shells with a large magnifying glass, mumbling in Chinese "fascinating, fascinating, oh my, fascinating, unbelievable" or words to that effect. While he was distracted George discretely passed a scribbled note to Charles and Arthur. He had talked to Xiao Ping that morning and also to Cai, but said nothing to Zhao Feng. The note said, "Take care what you say, for sure the room is bugged!"

At that point in walked Yi. He had certainly been busy overnight. The video cameras outside the rooms were in place, technicians were calibrating the metal detector that one had to pass through in the hallway to get to the lab rooms, and guards were in place. He smirked as he walked in asking everyone if they minded him sitting in. He said that he did not intend to spend a lot of time bothering them, but warned he would be keeping a close watch on all activities.

There was considerable activity too from Diao's side as boxes of equipment and computing gear were being stacked in the anteroom. Diao mopped his brow and told George he was not sure what they really needed; the equipment he was lending the effort was the most up-to-date items they were using. If the team needed more they could specify what they wanted.

Arthur glanced down the inventory listing, a copy of which Diao gave to Yi, and whistled. He told Diao he was impressed. Diao then initiated the first meeting by immediately focusing on the tasks ahead, telling them he did not want to dwell on the past. They had thirty days to get things catalogued so the work needed to commence right away. He wanted to know if there was anything more they needed. George said they should have at least two beds for guys to rest on during the long working nights. He also asked Cai if he could get them permission to use the showering facilities at the university.

George walked over to Yi and said they would need an explanation for the rest of the university administrators and faculty as to what was going on in this restricted section of the building, especially with all the military types running around. Yi looked over to Cai Levee and said it would not be a problem. He and Cai would set it up; they would let the dean of the university know a little more about their operation there; national security, classified information, and everything along those lines ought to take care of it.

They arranged the anteroom seating as a conference area with two desks for Arthur and Charles, along with a unit purposely set off to the side for Zhao Feng. The main examinations and classification of each of the shells was to be kept in the large strong-room. Arthur had to arrange to run a few more electrical cables for some of the equipment they would use. They determined that a digital record and 3D map of each and every shell would have to be created. Based on the testing on Cai's shell, however, it was obvious that handling and storage were not concerns. Nonetheless, George determined everyone would handle the shells with gloves and store each one in a simple zip-lock bag for the time being. The shells would be tracked using a serial number system that Arthur had already developed in line with the software requirements. The mapped shells would be stored in a locked cabinet when not under inspection.

One of the initial challenges would be to determine the sequencing of them. Perhaps that would come in the mapping of their shape, like fitting the pieces of a puzzle together, or when they broke the code to interpret the writings. They at least did not have to worry about defining what these things were made of; that was for the military to tackle with all their resources. None of them believed that the material was manmade. George was edging toward Professor Ding's theory more than any other. If it was accurate, if this was from some kind of prehistoric animal, it had offered that creature the best protection the world had ever seen. Whatever kind of animal the shells belonged to, it was definitely long gone from this world, like so many others in the evolutionary chain.

From that point on the team worked around the clock for the next thirty days, sometimes with everyone working, but always with at least two. It was a tiring and somewhat boring activity but they knew it had to be done. Zhu did not look like the kind of guy who would give any extension of time, and clearly Yi was pushed to make sure it was completed.

They did not discover anything new about the shells throughout this process. About the only strange thing they discovered was that the shells did not set off any alarms as the blank sample did. Xiao Ping discovered that difference by accident when she went off to the bathroom and carried one with her. The guard had stepped away and she was through the system before she realized it. George decided that for the time being only he, Cai, and Xiao Ping would be aware of this new information. They were not sure what they would do with this surprising turn, but it felt good to know something the authorities did not.

After the first week of activity the pace of mapping accelerated as a process and production line gradually evolved. Looking at the writings convinced everyone, Diao included, that they were just that: writings with a tremendous amount of information stored on them. The guards were still around and monitoring everything but Yi did not show up much after the first few days. Diao began leaving them to their own devices checking in with Cai and Xiao Ping often.

The guards were starting to lose their stiff edge with the team but as soon as Yi or some other official showed up they switched back to their full alert and sullen demeanor. Zhu was kept abreast of what was going on. He told them he was still intrigued by everything as their government scientists continued to try to determine how best to analyze the first sample; he said they kept begging him for more samples to test. He told George he was continuing to honor the arrangement in place but was growing concerned that information was leaking amongst the upper circles about the shells.

⟋ᴄ

Langley, USA

IN THE U.S., DICK JANSWIG, a key handler at the CIA headquarters in Langley, Virginia, was arriving in his office when he received a phone call from his superior. He was told to come to his office as soon as possible. Dick was used to this so thought nothing of it. He handled intelligence assets in developing countries, especially China; these early morning calls were nothing unusual when new reports came in. His boss, John Smythe, was a young up-and-comer in the agency, unlike Dick who had thirty years under his belt. But Smythe had field experience, whereas Dick, who had begged for the chance, had none. Despite the age difference, Dick respected Smythe, who reciprocated it and took care of Dick whenever he needed cover for his actions.

Smythe brought Dick up to speed on the newest intelligence from their highest-level asset, who neither of them was allowed to handle. That responsibility went all the way to the top to the current direc- tor of the CIA. The roots of this operative were established back in the days of the previous director, even before the current president came in to office. Someone had given this asset the code name of "Black Knight." Dick had always joked that perhaps they did not think "Black Tulip" translated from the Chinese version sounded manly enough, which always raised a chuckle between them.   On the desk in front of Smythe was a thick document covered in secret and classified stickers, "your eyes only," etcetera. "What do we have this time, John?" Dick asked. He was told this was a new report from "BK" in China; it needed their most urgent attention. John asked Dick to take an hour to read the file and come back for a meeting with the joint chiefs and the director at a confidential videoconference at 10 a.m. sharp.

At 10 a.m. the group in Langley turned on the video screen. An assistant punched in the phone numbers and access codes for the conference call to begin. It was a small gathering but the vice president had joined the call to listen to the discussion. The CIA director called the meeting to order and went around the room introducing the participants, one of which was a leading scientist in the U.S. military, one from the government's space program. The director turned the meeting over to John Smythe, who proceeded to summarize the purpose of the meeting. Everyone on the screen and in the Langley facility sat with the same blue files sitting in front of them.

Before John started to speak, the vice president remarked to the director, "Now, Fred, you don't really expect us to believe all this bullshit about coffins and treasures and so forth, do you?"

John Smythe interrupted and answered for the director. "Mr. Vice President, this is BK's material; how he got it I have no idea, and I can't ask since I don't have access to him. Whether or not all this ancient gobbledygook is right or not I don't know, but I do know this: our own asset has confirmed that the Chinese are testing some material they think is ours, maybe off a space rocket or missile. They can't analyze, destroy, nor mark it, and are rumored to be trying to figure out how to test it in a small nuclear explosion. There's been confirmed traffic to the DPRK asking if they have any tests coming up soon; they want to add a little experiment.

"If indeed they think it's ours, and our two scientific experts with us today say it isn't, then it must be Russian; they *have* been flexing their muscles of late. I will say this, sir. If the testing in these reports is correct, I for one do not want to be in the firing line with them if they find a use for it!"

The VP apologized, saying he wasn't trying to get the meeting off on the wrong foot. It all sounded pretty amazing so he would sit back and just listen. But first he asked one of the two scientists what he thought.

"Well, we can confirm first that no such material exists in our arsenal, and I must agree with John Smythe's comments that it would have to be Russian. If the Russians can manufacture this type of material in large quantities, apply it to all their military hardware and protective armor for military personnel, then outside of frying humans with nuclear weapons Russia would have a huge advantage over us. Likewise, if they apply this to all their evolving drone technology we won't be able to knock out their eyes and ears either here or in space. Unfortunately, until we get our hands on some of it we can really say no more."

The scientists knew their equipment was much more sophisticated than the Chinese at this time, so both felt they had a better shot at analyzing anything the Russians could make. One of the meeting participants asked what the panel thought about the section on Professor Ding, and if this could really be stuff from prehistoric times. The nuclear scientist just looked up at him with a smirk. "When my daughter's horse sprouts wings and flies!"

Moving the meeting along, the CIA director asked John Smythe what he wanted to do. His response was that they needed to get their hands on some pieces in any way possible. At that point Dick interjected, "Gentlemen, I manage the assets on the ground in Beijing. If the report is accurate they are already one week into the thirty-day period before the military takes over all the material. That gives us a very short window of time to do anything while these items are not under full military control."

The vice president asked the director for his recommendations.

"It's very difficult I know, Mr. Vice President, to accomplish something like this in three weeks, but I think we would be right to at least try. Unless you want to call up the Chinese, tell them it's not ours, and ask if we can give them a hand?"

The commander in chief of all the military preferred the Chinese be left guessing. The vice president agreed, thought for a moment then said, "Okay, let's do it. We can give it a whirl; nothing ventured, nothing gained. For Christ's sake though, everyone keep us out of it politically. And let's keep this mission top secret; that is, if anything can be kept quiet around Washington these days!"

With that, the call was over. They all chatted together as a team at Langley before John Smythe told those based at headquarters to be there at 0700 hours in the morning to develop a workable action plan. They were advised to come to the meeting with suggestions, not questions. All of them needed to carefully read the reports beforehand. All staff leave at their level was to be canceled for the next month.

Dick went back to his office and immediately started sifting through the classified materials from BK in China, still amazed that these documents had made their way out of the country intact. He wondered if in fact they were a plant by the Chinese; if so, it was a pretty bizarre approach.

Dick was an old hand at this game, and while computers were everywhere in Langley, he was something of the butt of numerous jokes at times like this. Dick always worked through problems like he now faced with his faithful short, somewhat blunt pencils, along with several foolscap pads of lined yellow paper. He was used to working on a large white board in his office as he did final analysis work or laid out strategies. That was, until John Smythe took over the department and insisted Dick at least have a digital writing tablet and an electronic white board with printer attached.

Dick fought both of these items for about a month before he finally compromised by taking the white board, but he insisted that his yellow pad could not be changed. John finally gave up the effort to bring Dick into the current century, and as a last gesture left Dick a gift on his desk, a box of one hundred lead pencils, new markers, and a new battery-operated sharpener with a card saying that Dick could at least keep his pencils sharp from then on.

Dick laid out on paper all the characters in the report, put down every detail in the story, and tried to connect every dot. He especially looked for openings with people, weaknesses that could be exploited in whatever plans they could come up with. He summarized the personalities as best he could, as well as who in all of the names would have sympathy with the U.S. and might be more pliable. He wondered aloud if one of these people was BK, a question Smythe said he had already put to the CIA director when the report arrived. He had been told no, none of the people in the report was BK but clearly there was a connection at a very high level.

Dick worked through the day. He had a basketball hoop over one of the doors to his large office into which he would toss balls of yellow lined paper all day long, as he made notes of this or that matter, then discarded them. The notes were classified but Dick enjoyed the comforting feeling of hitting the basket with his missiles 95 percent of the time. His assistant Betty had long ago been assigned the task of picking them all up, putting them in a basket, and either shredding them or taking them to the incinerator.

In a computer-dominated environment at Langley, populated by more and more young professionals, Dick's antics were quite an anomaly. John Smythe though got used to it, and used it as a weather vane as to how Dick's mind was working. A stack of yellow balls spread across the floor by the basketball hoop side of the office always indicated Dick was on a roll and on top of things. If there was little action at the hoop then things were going slowly. Usually though John would just ask Betty how things were at the hoop as he passed by; Dick would often hear her respond with "not good today, sir," or "looks like big points on the board today, sir."

From the pages of the pad, Dick would then move to the board where options and recommendations would flow, sometimes quite quickly; at other times it would take him hours. On this particular day Betty came by the office as she left for the day, cleared up a bunch of yellow balls as he moved to the white board with yellow sheets bunched together in his hand. She said good night and noted it looked like he would be working late. He responded that he definitely would be. He was working on a really tough one this time.

When Dick showed up at the meeting the next morning it was clear to John that Dick had not been home. He was unshaven (even though he kept a razor at the office) and was wearing the same clothes he'd worn for the videoconference. The meeting got under way with a brief review by John of the facts, as they knew them, and the time line ahead. He told everyone this was going to be particularly difficult to pull off with the instructions to keep this mission secret and avoid any international incident to disrupt the improving relationships between the two countries. China was a difficult environment to operate in at the best of times. The added security around this, and the importance the Chinese placed on their own efforts to unlock the secrets of this material, made it all the more challenging and dangerous.

With that John opened up the meeting to ideas and for someone to kick it off and get the juices flowing, so to speak, for the team.

He advised that this was going to be a long day. His idea was no one would leave the meeting until a firm plan was in place; there just wasn't any time to lose if they were going to try this.

Dick stayed quiet, always preferring to listen to others before commenting or committing himself to anything. The team went through five different power point presentations summarizing the objective of the mission, plan of attack, assets and resources along with a complete timeline for the proposed mission. They were all classic approaches; some though were extremely risky and ruled out right away. They often involved use of force; collateral damage would have been unavoidable. Two had merit; John wanted them put onto the "parking lot" working screen for further review by the team and perhaps refinement.

It was eleven thirty, just before Dick was next on deck, when John called a break for lunch. He told everyone to grab a quick bite in the dining room, clear their heads, and be back to hear Dick's thoughts. Dick was the only one that did not go with the others to lunch. He went back to his office and Betty brought in a lunch bag for him. She picked one up every day for him from a deli en route to the office. Dick was single and a confirmed bachelor; Betty had taken care of him this way for the last fifteen years.

When the meeting restarted Dick got up to speak, John quickly told his assistant to switch the projector off. "Dick's up. We all know we won't need that," he said amid smiles and friendly bouts of laughter. "My only hope is one day before he retires I get at least one power point presentation out of him, even if Betty does it for him!"

Dick took all of this humor in the way it was intended. He knew with some embarrassment that everyone in the room held him in the highest regard. Betty had as much told him so on occasions when he was struggling with life, not just from a work standpoint but also as a human being. Dick also knew there had been some rumors he might be gay, but they were completely unfounded. Early in his life he had a difficult romantic encounter with a girlfriend who was killed in a car accident while he was driving. He never forgave himself and had remained a bachelor, though he did date occasionally.

His story was well known in the office, but he had always been grateful to Betty, who was his great defender and had made sure newcomers knew about it.

Dick smiled as he walked to the electronic white board. Picking up a marker he noted that, in deference to his high-tech colleagues and John, he would break down on this occasion. Instead of using the flip chart in the room he would use the electronic white board. Everyone clapped until John screamed out to him, "Dick, don't use that pen, goddamn it!" It was a permanent marker for the flip chart, not an erasable one for the electronic board. "Hell, Dick, it took my secretary a whole day to get the board perfectly clean after the last time you did that!"

Further chuckles erupted and then Dick apologized and got down to it. He went through his analysis, options to be considered, and the pros and cons of each option. He closed with his personal recommendation advising that none of these options offered a guarantee of success and all had risk. He duly noted his preferred approach, which in his opinion carried the lowest potential for unanticipated results.

The room was quiet, the previous presenters all sitting in silence just looking at the board and the print-outs that came off the board as Dick went through his review. The look on everyone's faces said it all. Dick, with his lack of a PhD in anything—not even an MBA—together with a complete lack of computer skills had done it again. John had told him on many occasions he didn't know how Dick was able to come up with these programs, but that when Dick retired it would be a major loss to his department.

John asked for feedback from everyone. Which of the ideas presented had the most merit? To a man they recommended Dick's plan and gave Dick a round of applause, which embarrassed him some-what. John thanked all of them; there had been several good propos-als but he agreed their choice was the best. He asked the teams to stay together and thrash out the final details. He would schedule another video call in the morning; they would then present the plan to the VP; there was no time to lose. Turning to Dick, he smiled and asked that he make sure he shaved before next morning's call.

The next morning at 7 a.m., John Smythe presented the plan to the CIA director and the vice president. Dick was asked to walk every-one through it after John had summarized the options considered and explained why this plan should be approved. After a number of questions, John and Dick were given the go-ahead. The only thing lacking was a project budget, but both of them were told not to wor-ry about that, cost was not an issue. Again, however, avoidance of any harm to international relations or collateral damage was critical and anyone involved on the ground could find himself, or herself, an object of denial from the U.S. government if caught.

The director added, "We understand, Mr. Vice President, but we don't intend to leave anyone hanging out there on this one!" With that they had the green light; it was go for the operation. Dick fig-ured at that point he better bring a suitcase to the office; there were long nights ahead for many of them.

CHAPTER 20

IN THE BEIJING LAB THE team began working their way through the mapping process of the shells, first doing an accurate count of all the shells and then assigning a digital serial number to each one. They obtained bags for each one, nothing fancy, just plain old zip-locks bags from the local market, and assembled them into individual containers. There were exactly 825 specimens, plus the one the military already had. George thought Cai had mentioned 830 before, but Cai said that was a rough count. George didn't mention this to Yi or Diao; the last thing they needed was someone to think some were missing, especially given what they'd just been through. In any event, Cai had locked them all up; only he had access.

That morning a report on the cloth used to wrap the shells was received. A small sample had been sent to one of the specialized analysis departments for dating and a detailed report to be issued. They were all quite excited to open it up and Diao Lijun came over for a visit to see it firsthand. It turned out the report was somewhat inconclusive, but it did confirm that it was indeed ancient. The cover was a cloth made from flax fibers, twisted and cut; some kind of animal dye was present that could not be identified. The material was much older than the earliest example of textile found in a special place, the Dzudzuana cave in the former Soviet State of Georgia. Radio carbon dating had placed that cloth on the spectrum as around thirty to thirty-six thousand years old. Their cloth could not be confirmed, but tests indicated it was over one hundred thousand years old.

This was staggering; the analyzers suggested that perhaps the Americans had better equipment that could more accurately determine the age. George knew that could never happen but added it to the report. Diao was excited and with a glint in his eye said, "Let's see how Zhu and Yi react when they see this figure!"

George learned later that the pair had not commented too much about it, other than to say they were concerned that the latest classified explosive test performed on their shell had again not affected it at all. The test, however, had seriously damaged the concrete bunker it was contained in. The bunker had reinforced concrete walls one meter thick!

Dick Janswig was put in charge of the operation at Langley and a command center for the activities was set up. He called Lou Corr, one of his most experienced China operatives who traveled out of Langley, requesting him to drop everything and come to his office. He asked Lou if his visa and cover for China were current; Lou confirmed he was good for another three months before renewal. Lou was still operating undercover as the official "chief representative" for a heavy machinery company in Beijing. Dick very briefly outlined the mission and asked how quickly he could be ready to move. Lou told him as soon as they booked him a ticket. That was good news for Dick, but he was going to have to ask him to swing by Asheville on his way.

Lou looked puzzled. "My wife's sister and my brother-in-law, Scott Ramey, live there."

Dick smiled. "I know that; we need Scott's help, even though he's not one of our own. We need him to introduce you to the team working with this Professor Mathers without drawing any suspicion from the authorities handling them."

Lou worried that Scott would turn them down.

"This is precisely why we need you to talk to your brother-in-law personally to try to get you introduced out there as quickly as he can."

"I don't think we need Scott's help on this Dick. I'm sure I can introduce myself quickly enough. Beijing's not a big place for meeting ex-pats. We can keep Scott out of whatever this is; it sounds too risky to use him on something like this."

"That may be, Lou, but I have to insist on your at least trying. That way, you can use your family relationship so as not to arouse suspicion when you start nosing around. The connection's perfect. Maybe I should explain further why I want to do it this way."

Dick told Lou more of the history of how Scott Ramey had run into Professor Mathers and Xiao Ping through Diao Lijun, who was now leading their special program. He wanted Lou to persuade Scott to take him along, as his in-law, and introduce him to all of the team by arranging dinner or whatever while in Beijing. Scott's cover would be that he was there to see how the plans for his donation to the temple were being finalized with Diao Lijun. They should offer to meet with the professor and his wife again following their meeting in Zhangjiajie.

Dick told him there were many things he had to get working on. He needed Lou to be headed out as soon as possible. He already had a detailed playbook for Lou to review. They could talk it over the next day or two before Lou would be on a plane. Lou asked Dick what the "hook" was to persuade Scott to go along with this. Dick said he should use the "bit for your country" angle; tell him he and his wife would be invited to the White House for a private lunch with the president and his wife when he got back. When asked about what Lou should tell him about his own activities, Dick suggested

Lou tell Scott the same story applied to him and he was anxious to help his country.

Dick felt that as Scott was retired these days, he might welcome another free trip to China since he liked it so much. He also guessed that the lure of his wife getting to meet the first lady would be something he would jump at. Before Lou even asked the question, he told him they would definitely be having lunch at the White House whether they were successful or not, and the risks were minimal for Scott. They would make sure nothing untoward happened to him.

Lou was another matter, however; if Lou got into trouble he was going to be on his own. Dick spent as long as he could with Lou before calling Betty in to get him on his way, telling her to book Lou to Asheville as soon as possible, then within twenty-four hours to get Lou and Scott Ramey on a plane for Chicago and on to Beijing. He paused and then said with a smile, "Make it first class, Betty; I have a big budget this time!"

He told Lou to call him if he had any trouble with his brother-in-law and if he needed Dick to talk to him directly. Betty presented Lou with more background material; she told him the flights to Asheville were not direct but he could use the wait time to go through Dick's instructions. They were to be destroyed as usual after he had fully absorbed them. As Lou left, he asked Dick how he'd made the family connection with this whole thing. Dick laughed and looked to Betty. "She ran all the names in the file; our master personnel files came up with the link to you. She really should be out there as an analyst herself. She's better than all those college grads!" Betty left the room with an added spring in her step.

The two men shook hands as Dick wished Lou good luck. Dick then sent an encrypted message to a contact in China advising that they needed to get in touch; it was extremely urgent and the call needed to be that evening.

Activity in the lab had picked up as the documenting system began to run more smoothly; the way everyone interacted with the process became much better organized. It did not take long for each of the team to figure out they were being followed everywhere they went. Cai told George he suspected their apartments were also bugged, maybe even their cars too. Although the lab rooms were not under visual surveillance, the team acted as if they were. Anytime anyone needed to really talk about something they felt their "hosts" did not need to hear, they talked outside, in the university showers, or at some social event where they could disappear together.

The cataloging, though, was so important to get done in the allotted time that any effort in trying to understand the writing on the shells was rudimentary. The effort continued to reveal little of the shells' secrets. Diao had taken a photograph of a couple of the shells' writings to ask for help from China's leading experts in ancient writings, but to no avail. That the script was the earliest form of writing seen in China or from somewhere else was not an issue. Linking the scripts to any of the experts' previous work proved impossible; they knew there was a code lurking somewhere in the graphics, but how to break it was the challenge. Zhu agreed with Diao to have some of their military code experts try to solve the keys to the code too, but they were also stumped. George began to realize the effort was likely to take a long time before they could solve the mystery surrounding the writings on these shells.

Lou Corr took the next flight to Asheville after collecting some of his things. He called Vera Zhang, his assistant in Beijing, to advise he would be coming to China soon. She was to arrange to send her assistant, Mr. Han, to pick him them up at the airport as soon as he could confirm his arrival time. He told Vera his brother-in-law would be traveling with him, but to book him a room at the downtown Hilton. He would stay in his company apartment and asked Vera to be sure to have the ai yi (maid) "air out" the apartment and make up the bed for him.

Lou called his brother-in-law before arriving to advise he was coming to visit and needed his help. This obviously surprised Scott but Lou could tell it clearly intrigued him, especially the urgency. Lou said he'd be arriving there the next day and asked Scott if he was free to travel for a few days. Lou had read the game plan from Dick in transit and called back about three times asking for a bit more clarification on one particular item. He asked Dick again if he really had approval to authorize the special offer that was part of the plan.

Scott and his wife, Rebecca, insisted on picking Lou up and that he stay at their house. They had moved there ahead of Scott's retirement and this was the first time Lou had visited them in a very long time. The Rameys had a nice home in a good area, not far from the Grove Park Inn and Golf Resort. Lou knew that Rebecca had discovered Asheville in her travels and recommended the city to Scott; he saw it too and fell in love with the mountains, history, and diversity of the town.

After all the social discussions over their late dinner Lou asked Scott if they could talk in private, so the pair went down to Scott's office in the basement along with a couple of drinks. Lou did not tell Scott about what he had been asked to do, not in all its detail anyway, nor did he tell him his job in China was just a cover while he was actually a "company" man with the CIA. He basically told Scott the CIA needed their help to retrieve some valuable objects that were in China. For whatever reason they needed desperately to look at them or obtain samples as soon as possible. Lou was to contact one of the people involved with these objects to try to secure some of them. Apparently the people involved were friends of a Diao Lijun in Beijing; they wanted Scott to introduce him to Diao and hopefully the others.

Lou told Scott it was urgent; the guys at the CIA had come up with Scott's name in searching out contacts to these people. Scott advised he indeed knew Diao and told him how they met. He explained how he had just been over there a few weeks earlier so it might look strange his suddenly coming back. Lou assured him he had a good story for him. The real question was, would Scott help?

Scott confessed he wanted to help Lou all he could, but this sounded a little dangerous to him. He certainly did not want to get into any trouble with the Chinese authorities. He was keen to go back when the temple he was a benefactor to was ready to be inaugurated.

" Look, Scott, I have the same concerns as you, maybe more so because I still work in China. I have to say, though, the CIA convinced me they really need our help. Once we both get back, you and I, with our wives, will be invited to lunch with the president and first lady to show the country's appreciation. You know, that's one hell of an honor for us. Think how our wives would enjoy that!"

When Scott asked if there was any financial compensation involved Lou told him the thought had never crossed his mind, but if Scott wanted he could ask. Lou sat quietly as Scott thought for a few minutes about it before asking when they would leave. Lou laughed and said half-jokingly, "How about now? My bags are packed!"

Scott quickly asked Lou if he could think about it overnight and reply in the morning. Lou told him he could but he would have to be headed out the next day, with or without him. He would need to know quickly in order to cancel first-class tickets already booked for Scott and him. Nothing more was said about the conversation when Rebecca came downstairs. They had a good time talking more about what they had all been doing and how Lou's wife, Rebecca's sister Samantha, was these days. When they finally went to bed Lou sent a short text to Dick Janswig as promised; it simply said, "Bait set. Fish has not bitten yet."

When Lou first saw Scott the next morning in the kitchen, Scott shot him a thumbs-up; Lou knew right away that the fish was hooked. He asked Scott if he'd discussed the plan with Rebecca the night before. Apparently once they were in bed Rebecca pestered Scott about what was going on between the two of them, and he'd explained everything he knew from Lou. She was very concerned and initially told him there was no way he was getting mixed up in this. She was adamant that he was retired, and while she had no problem with him traveling to China on this temple thing (which had very nice rewards), she wanted him around Asheville.

"So did you change her mind?"

"Hell, she knows me well enough, Lou; she could see in my face I'd already made up my mind. I was going anyway but just looking for her approval. After she said no for the third time I told her that she could forget lunch at the White House."

"You took a while telling her that part!"

"Yeah, well I slipped that in for the final coup de gras! And it worked."

"What did she say?"

"Right away she says, why didn't I say that earlier? She then said, of course, we absolutely must go for the good of the country.

While Scott measured out coffee Lou slipped off to his room to text Dick with the good news.

CHAPTER 21

THE TWO MEN LEFT ASHEVILLE for China early the following day, leaving on a United Air Lines flight for Chicago, where they would change to a plane bound for Beijing. Scott told Lou he'd already contacted Diao Lijun to say he was coming through Beijing on the way to Hong Kong. Scott would be there for a few days and asked if he could meet with Diao to see how the temple restoration plans were coming. He would be with his brother-in-law, who worked in Beijing, and hoped they could all meet. He also mentioned his promise to look up Professor Mathers and his wife on a future visit; if they were in town perhaps they could have a reunion of sorts.

Apparently Diao responded that he was delighted Scott was coming back so soon, that he could definitely arrange something. He said he was working on a special project with the Mathers, so an evening would be best.

Lou was pleased to hear this and texted Dick, "Fresh bait laid. Hoping to haul in the big fish."

Diao apprised Yi of the impending visit by Scott Ramey and his brother–in-law, as Yi had instructed Diao that any visitors or meetings involving the team needed to be cleared. Yi was angry that Diao had gotten ahead of himself by agreeing to this visit without getting permission. He said it was not his decision to make and he would have to wait twenty-four hours for approval. He ran a check on both Scott Ramey and his brother-in-law. This Lou Corr was on file with the foreign ministry for residence and a work permit as chief representative for EXMACH, a leading U.S. manufacturer of mining equipment. Nothing showed up in any of their intelligence systems or reports that was suspicious.

Yi had his people check the airline tickets of both travelers, which confirmed Ramey was indeed ticketed to Hong Kong for a few days after Beijing before returning to the U.S. He ran it all by Zhu anyway, suggesting Diao should be told the visit was not allowed.

He was surprised when Zhu said he saw no real issue with it; he told Yi it might be good to get the team out of the lab. Confidentiality was to be strictly maintained and Zhu suggested that Yi have Diao organize a banquet for himself and all of the Mathers' team; Yi, however, was to specify where it would be held. Zhu wanted the party left alone in the restaurant but the dining room heavily bugged. He told Yi he was interested to hear what these people might say without the police or military around. Yi could tell Diao was relieved when he finally phoned back with full clearance, especially since Scott and his relative were already on their way.

The next time Diao spoke with George, he brought up the visit and suggested a banquet for the team. Diao told George he felt they all needed a bit of a break one night and it would be nice to have some outside company. George felt they were way too busy though to have everyone attend, but Charles and Arthur (who were not big on banqueting) agreed the rest of them should go; they had not met this Scott Ramey character anyway. They agreed to take the load while the others definitely needed an evening away from the lab. Their turn could come separately at a later date.

George and Xiao Ping were reminded they could not talk about what they were doing with Diao's guests; they should just say they were working together on a project associated with the museum. Diao then went off to make arrangements for the Thursday evening, the day after next, at an especially popular Chinese restaurant. He told them they had very good food there and a private room would be set up. Xiao Ping told George she was looking forward to some different company, as well as the chance to dress up and finally put on some makeup.

George wasn't so enthusiastic, but he could see she needed a break. Cai Levee would join them, with Diao of course, and for once their "babysitters" would keep their distance. George had no doubt they would still be watching them.

By the time Scott and Lou landed in Beijing, they had dined well and slept surprisingly long hours during the flight. Lou made a mental note that Dick owed him another first class flight like this; his usual inconspicuous "economy plus" seating just would not do it anymore!

The driver from Lou's office, Mr. Han, was as always waiting for him to arrive. He wrestled the large suitcase from Ramey's hand after introductions, led them to the car, and then headed for Scott's hotel first. Customs had been a breeze and no one had checked either of their suitcases, a good thing since the few gadgets in the false compartment of Lou's suitcase may have caused some concern. When Lou checked into the flight in Chicago one of the "company" staffers had been monitoring the process, following the bags to the TSA inspection area to make sure the bags got on the flight without being checked. Dick had made sure there were no hitches in the plan since time was so tight.

Dick was now literally living at the office. With the current time difference of thirteen hours between Langley and Beijing he told Lou he wanted to be available around the clock, at least until this phase of the mission was over. A lot could go wrong, and the plan called for certain things to go just right. His biggest concern was the part of the plan he had told no one about other than his special contact in Beijing. If all this blew up in his face he might be out of a job. He was convinced, though, in his gut that this would go okay; it had to.

The day after their arrival in Beijing, Lou was in his office catching up on some routine paperwork. Competition from local Chinese mining machinery manufacturers had increased over the last few years and the head office was losing interest in the market. He still had a front to keep up. Lou and his Langley handlers were already making plans for his future when the operation was finally closed; the CEO of the group had been very co-operative in the past, allowing Dick Janswig and his superiors to use their Beijing activities in this way. Of course, this was something few people in their company knew about and certainly nothing the shareholders would ever know. It was a good situation for Lou Corr because the mining activity allowed him to travel all over China with relative impunity; he had learned enough in the process to often joke that he might quit and take the business up legitimately.

Scott Ramey, although now retired, also had a history in China in earlier years, so he too knew China well. He told Lou that he had been amazed on his last visit to see how much development was going on. Things were constantly changing. He had worked as an IT consultant for a number of overseas entities, and had fallen in love with living in China, a life Lou knew Scott still missed, though he said he was thoroughly happy to have found Asheville to retire to.

On the flight over, Scott had told Lou that the opportunity to make another quick trip to Beijing had been an easy part of Lou's request for him to answer. But whether he would be able to assist in the real purpose of the visit was something he was nervous about. He said he appreciated the trip to Hong Kong too as he could pick up something nice there for Rebecca. Lou knew that part of the trip was essential in case someone in China checked on his brother-in-law's travel plans.

The activity in the lab was picking up and the pace of mapping the shells improved day by day. George and Xiao Ping figured they would make the deadline, but it might be touch and go. There had been quite a few nights that they hadn't used the two beds they had asked for, or used the university showering facilities. That Thursday, however, there would be no working in the lab till the wee hours. They had left early with Cai Levee to get changed and head with Diao to the restaurant to meet his guests. George was not pleased to learn that Zhao Feng was included.

A van was sent for them and despite the heavy traffic they made it to the restaurant by six thirty. Scott and his brother-in-law, Lou Corr, were already there and waiting in the restaurant lobby. The group knew the restaurant well; it was famous for fish heads cooked in a great-tasting sauce, on which they piled bite-size pieces of pancake to further absorb the delicious sauce. The heads of the fish were huge and meaty, coming from a special reservoir in southeast China. Xiao Ping was happy Diao had picked this place as it was one of her favorites.

Scott Ramey and Diao were obviously becoming real "lao pong you" (old friends). Lou Corr sat between Zhao Feng and Xiao Ping; having spent time in China too, Lou proved to be quite entertaining. He and Feng got along famously also. Scott told all of them that he was there for a few days only and wanted to see how the plans for the temple renovation were coming along, though his brother-in-law would be working in Beijing for a least a month, part of his regular work cycle in and out of China.

Lou explained he was trying to wind down his schedule; he needed to get his time in China during the year below 183 days to save on high China tax rates. He told them he would enjoy seeing more of them before he left.

After a few beers Zhao Feng decided it was time to make the evening special and break out a bottle of baijiu. George wanted them to stick to wine but went along with it anyway. By the time everyone left they were all well "lubricated," especially Zhao Feng and Lou Corr. They would pay for it in the morning, George thought, as they all said good night, declaring to be friends for life.

A text message was sent to Langley for Dick Janswig at 11 a.m. EST; it simply said, "Target confirmed. Wish me luck!"

Yi wondered to himself if George and the others had any idea what was going on at their banquet. The restaurant had always been one of his favorites, but not just for the food. It had separate rooms that were easy to bug. Since the restaurant was housed in a hotel, there were also rooms above the dining areas that could be booked. This was useful to Yi, not only to monitor what was going on with everyone, but to have people ready to move in on the party at a moment's notice.

Yi had been listening to the events at the banquet, and was a little envious of the obvious good time being had below. No unusual or suspicious comments were made regarding the work going on. The project had not been mentioned by anyone on the team, other than what they'd been advised they could talk about. His men had become hungry, so Yi had ordered fish heads to be brought up to their room. He would be reporting to Zhu later in the evening and there would be tapes on file of the conversations if anyone needed them.

One of Yi's men posed as a server too so they could secretly photograph the guests and know who sat where. Yi was disappointed that he had no reason to pull one of the team in for his own brand of special interrogation. He had to be careful how he used his own methods and when; Zhu was not one to appreciate anyone below him deviating from his directions.

Lou dropped Scott off at the Hilton hotel by taxi and then headed home. He had the taxi stop by the workers' stadium, Beijing's major sports' field, paid his 15 yuan fare, and continued on foot—nowhere near his own apartment. He walked to the ex-pat bar down the road called The Den. He waited there until after midnight when more of the homes would be dark, then walked along an unlit route to Chun Xiu Liu Street.

He headed to the Seasons Park complex where, from the banquet, he now knew Zhao Feng lived. He suspected he would have to be very careful; he had no doubt Zhao Feng was under surveillance. He made his way to the complex entry and walked straight through the gate past the security guard. He knew that a foreigner at that time of night who seemed to be walking to his apartment would not likely be stopped. In any event, he had a security pass in his pocket if he needed to show it.

He walked quickly down the car park entryway and through the complex underground; he knew this apartment development well, as friends lived there and he had visited the swimming area in the summer a couple of times. Taking this route, no one would see him. He had his scarf across his face acting as a supposed pollution safeguard; hat and glasses added to his disguise as he played around with his keys as if looking for a parked car. He used the security card to enter the building and took the elevator to the top floor. Zhao Feng was only one floor below, room 2202.

Lou stealthily made his way down the fire escape stairs, carrying his shoes to avoid making any sound, and checked Zhao Feng's floor. There was a guy in the hallway talking to the apartment security guy; they were chuckling to each other and were clearly both bored. He could not believe his luck after almost twenty minutes of waiting. One of them told the other he would join him in the basement for a smoke, but would have to be right back before his shift ended; he needed to use the bathroom anyway.

After they left Lou moved quickly out of the hallway to the apartment door, pressed a device he had brought with him from the U.S. to the door, and waited a few seconds. When the digital code breaker completed a cycle of clicking, a dull clunk indicated the door could be opened. He crept into the apartment and paused to both calm himself and get his bearings. He took a couple of other things out of his pockets to be ready to restrain Zhao Feng and headed to the bedroom area to see which of the three rooms he was in. At the dinner Zhao Feng had told him his family were visiting their father in his hometown; that was good news for Lou.

He located Zhao Feng quickly; he was snoring, thanks to an evening of drinking baijiu. Lou was heavyset and quite strong; he worked out every day and was highly skilled at restraining someone even larger than himself. He had carefully orchestrated his drinking as well. Zhao Feng was a slight man, an academic whose only exercise in life might be running for a taxi.

Lou took off his outer coat, tiptoed into the darkened room, and before Zhao Feng knew it Lou was practically sitting on him with a gag on his mouth, telling him not to make a sound. He taped the gag over Zhao Feng's mouth, pulled him into the bathroom, and taped him securely to a chair. He turned the taps on the bath and shower while he apologized profusely to Zhao Feng, who was clearly terrified. He told Feng he would take his gag off and untie him soon enough; he just had a proposal for him and needed his attention first without alarming his watchers.

Since they were likely being bugged Lou also needed to keep the shower running. Zhao Feng, knowing his attacker from the evening, eventually calmed down. Lou got down to the point of his visit very quickly. He told Zhao Feng his people knew what they were doing, that he was in a position to offer him two million dollars for four of the shells if he could get some out, and free passage for him and his family to the U.S. It was that simple.

He told him they knew Zhao Feng had tried to steal the treasure from the team but had failed. This was a way for him to get something out of it and he would be protected. If he failed then nothing would happen and no one would be the wiser. Lou asked Zhao Feng if he could take the gag off him with a promise that he would not raise any alarm. Feng nodded and Lou untied him and again said how sorry he was to have to do it this way. He told him he would give Zhao Feng twenty-four hours to let Lou know if he was in or not. He was to leave the lights on in his apartment the next night at 10 p.m., with the curtains open on one side, to indicate if he would help. Finally, he warned Zhao Feng what could happen to him if he mentioned any of this little discussion to the authorities.

Lou checked the hall before leaving the apartment to see if the "babysitter" was back before exiting as quietly and quickly as he came. He suspected that Feng would pass a sleepless night thinking about the lucrative proposal presented to him.

Lou walked far from the complex before taking a cab to his own apartment. The next day he would say nothing to his brother-in-law; Scott didn't need to know any more than he already did. He got to his apartment in forty minutes and sent a text message to Dick Janswig right away. "Real bait in place. Time and life in China limited. Confirmation tomorrow night."

Dick Janswig was sleeping soundly at Langley when he was awakened by the noise of the phone; he knew who it was and reached from the cot he was lying on to review the message. It was 4:30 a.m. He understood the message and knew that Lou was now at great risk. No matter how it all worked out he was sure this would be Lou's last trip into China. Depending on what the target did, it could be over very quickly. Dick was gambling on Zhao Feng's potential greed to keep what was happening quiet. It was a big risk they were taking with him but he felt they had no choice with the limited days remaining to access their quarry. On the bright side, step two was at least in place, but the time it would take to get their hands on the shells was slipping by way too fast for his liking.

CHAPTER 22

THE DAY AFTER DIAO'S BANQUET Yi received a call from Zhao Feng; he had not gone to the university that morning, he said, and wanted to meet with him and Zhu urgently. He stressed it was very important and he could not talk about it around the others. Yi advised him where they could meet and called Zhu. Zhu confirmed to Yi it was best they not meet at headquarters and advised Yi to dress casually. Zhu said he would change quickly into civilian clothes, which he kept in a side cabinet. They were to meet at one of the large Costa Coffee places in the Sanlitun shopping area.

Once everyone arrived Yi could see that Zhao Feng was nervous, his eyes darting around the coffee house; his hands were shaking. It was fairly quiet in the place, and they sat in a corner. Zhao Feng told them what had happened to him after the banquet, saying he didn't want any more trouble than he was already in.

Yi could see Zhu was intrigued, but Yi was concerned that his men had let this happen at Feng's apartment; things seemed to be slipping through his fingers. He was already planning how to reprimand the surveillance crew at the Seasons Park apartments; all other crews would be put on high alert too. Yi was ready to rush out and arrest both Lou Corr and his brother-in-law, but Zhu put a stop to it.

Zhu told Yi they were going back to HQ; he saw a real opportunity in this situation. He thanked Zhao Feng for coming to them. Zhu told him he was to keep this to himself and follow the

American's instructions; finally, he was to text the number given to him by the American and simply say he needed five days to obtain the shells. He was to keep Yi and Zhu fully informed of everything as it unfolded. Zhu told Zhao Feng they would be sending him bank account details to pass along to Corr.

As they all stood to leave, Zhu again told Zhao Feng he had done the right thing for his country and that his display of patriotic duty would go into his file. They would erase any past sins that were recounted in his security file. Yi wondered what Zhu was really up to.

As soon as they were back in HQ, Zhu called in two other intelligence specialists and brought them up to speed. Yi was instructed not to do anything out of the ordinary yet. "Just keep everything as it is, Yi," Zhu said. "Don't reprimand anyone either, as I expect you are planning. You'll have your opportunity later.

"The outside world needs to think everything is normal. We are going to play along with their game. We need to do more digging on Lou Corr's background so don't touch him yet. As for this Ramey character, I think he's clean. He was likely duped into providing access to the team. Nevertheless, keep a watch on him, even when he gets to Hong Kong."

"So what is your plan, General? Should I pull any of them in at all?"

"Certainly not! Hold back for now. First I want four copies of the shell in our possession to be made. These shells will be provided to our enemies through Zhao Feng. They need to be first class copies. They must survive a journey to the U.S., but I want them to eventually see they are fakes." Zhu joked to Yi that the party was going to appreciate the two million dollar donation from the U.S. He then explained the last part of his plan to them all. With everyone laughing he sent them off to complete their tasks. They had four days to get everything ready.

Scott Ramey met with Diao Lijun and the architectural team responsible for the temple renovation along with a group of preservationists; they all appreciated his interest and, of course, his support for this project. With that, Scott confirmed his flight arrangements to Hong Kong; he would be leaving in three days.

Lou Corr worked at his office getting things organized; he suspected this could be his last stint in China. When his cover would be blown was not certain, but he felt sure it eventually would. He thought it might well be time anyway for him to retire. He would make return travel bookings once he heard from Zhao Feng. That did not take long. When he walked by the Seasons Park the next night he saw Feng's confirmation signal: the lights were on and the curtains half drawn.

In the morning a text message came in from Feng saying it would take five days to acquire the shells. Lou didn't like it but thought he would have to accept it. It was pushing up against the thirty-day deadline though. He confirmed his flight out for a week later; he would need to get out quickly. Fortunately Scott would be on his way to the U.S. by then, having passed through Hong Kong. He would be happy at least knowing by then that part of the plan had gone off without a hitch.

Scott Ramey checked out of the Hilton on the day of his flight to Hong Kong and at the insistence of Vera was taken by Lou's driver Han to the airport. His brother-in-law could not see him off but had jokingly said he would see him at the White House once he got back.

Two days later Zhu gave Zhao Feng four shells. Although they were replicas, they looked perfect. No one would be able to tell the difference until they were tested. Zhao Feng looked them over carefully but made no comment, assuring Yi he would text Lou that he now had them and arrange pick-up.

Lou received the message that the goods were ready and would be available but Feng wanted half the money transferred before delivering all four. With time running out, Lou had to call Dick Janswig for approval before agreeing, finally advising Zhao Feng to watch the Swiss account in two hours. After an hour the account number was being checked and Zhao Feng received a call confirming the special account in Switzerland showed one million dollars deposited in it. Zhu and Yi had told him to demand this and haggle over it; there was no point in making it look too easy. If anything went wrong at least they had a million dollars for their trouble!

Zhao Feng sent Lou a text to meet him that evening at the Bookworm near Sanlitun; it was a popular café, restaurant, and book store. They were not to speak. Zhao Feng would have a stack of four books he would give to him. If he would open them, a shell would be in each hollowed-out book. Once Lou was satisfied, he could depart with the books, but Zhao Feng expected to see the balance in the account within two more hours or he threatened to go to the authorities.

The two met later and the transfer went smoothly. The shells intrigued Lou but his job was not to examine them, just to get them on their way. He thanked Zhao Feng, told him all would be well, and to enjoy his new savings and perhaps a future life in the U.S. Zhao Feng texted Zhu and Yi that the switch was done; the money should appear in the account within two hours.

Lou fired off a text message to Langley: "Goods received, transfer please, wish us luck."

A second text message was sent to Dick Janswig from China; it was not from Lou Corr. It simply said, "Your account is being checked." The sender knew Dick would understand what it meant, though no one else would. The sender suspected the next few days were going to be troublesome for the people involved.

Yi had confirmation that the account number Zhu provided to Zhao Feng showed a new balance of two million dollars; he reported the news to Zhu right away.

A few days later Lou closed up his apartment and gave it a final look, expecting that this would be the last time he would see the place. He held a banquet for Vera Zhang and the office staff, including her assistant Han. He could not say it was a farewell to them, but the staff suspected that he was going to be promoted or something and not have responsibility for China anymore.

Lou had packed the shells in his special case; a built-in floor contained the objects and would prevent a standard x-ray machine at the airport from detecting anything inside. Lou need not have bothered; Zhu had people waiting at the Beijing airport to make sure the bag made it on the plane. Lou and Mr. Han had an emotional farewell as he left; they had known each other for twelve years and Han was the oldest employee of EXMACH in Beijing. He had said his final farewell to Vera Zhang, his secretary and associate, at the banquet; he knew she was unaware that the dinner was likely the last time she would work for him. Lou was going to miss both Vera and Han, and he had already arranged through

Dick Janswig and the CEO of the company to provide the two employees additional bonuses. It was a way for him to thank them once the official news of his departure came out.

Lou passed through airport security for the United Airlines flight to Chicago with no problems. The check-in was straightforward; he was both a Platinum Card million miler and a first-class flyer anyway. He relaxed in the lounge, occasionally wondering if the special suitcase made it through. He knew that at the other end a special plane would be waiting to fly him and the goods straight to Langley.

Yi watched from his vantage point at the Beijing airport as the plane took off. Zhu's men had been there too with Yi to make sure that Corr got on the flight successfully and that his bag made it onto the plane. Yi could not help but secretly wish he'd had a few hours at the safe house with this real spy to see what it took to break him. As the plane left he sent a quick text to Zhu advising that "the goods" were safely on their way.

United 851 landed on time in Chicago. Lou had not slept much; his mind and body were still wired from the last few days' activities. He passed through customs quickly, accompanied by special security personnel, then was taken by executive bus to a hangar where a government jet waited for him. At Langley, he was whisked to a meeting with Dick Janswig and John Smythe. After that, he was free to head home to rest for a few days until they called him in.

Lou asked to be kept up to speed if anything happened there or at the Beijing end. Dick assured him he would be, congratulating him on getting his part of the plan completed. Lou smiled, then told them to let him know when their families would lunch with the president; he expected Rebecca Ramey to be asking him as soon as she heard he was back.

Dick laughed and said not to worry about that. Their wives would be receiving a courier pack the next day with a very impressive invitation to lunch at the White House for the following month, all expenses paid by the department. "Economy tickets," Smythe had chipped in, "none of that first-class crap!" He smirked at Dick.

Lou left, and as he passed Betty's desk he told her Dick had approved a round-trip ticket to Asheville to see his brother-in-law to calm him down after their escapade.

Yi was invited along with Zhu to meet with their superiors and bring them up to date on his actions. They all noted that the funding was very welcome, and congratulated Zhu and Yi for getting the better of their counterparts in the U.S. Zhu confirmed that through this incident they now knew the material was not American; they were after it too. Clearly it was Russian. That concerned them even more as none of them had imagined the Russians capable of developing anything like this.

Dick Janswig and John Smythe inspected the four samples of shell material and the strange markings on their other sides before sending them off for analysis. Dick told Smythe neither the team in Beijing with Daio Lijun nor the Chinese military had been able to translate any of the strange writing on the shells. Smythe told Dick that before their scheduled meeting with the V.P. and others he wanted to at least let their people have a look at them. He asked Dick to attend the meeting since he had orchestrated this successful mission and should take his share of the glory.

The group would be smaller than the time before. The people in the know would be strictly controlled to avoid any leakage back to the Chinese. Dick made the arrangements for the conference and who would be involved. Two of their top scientific minds would be invited, one who was looking at the material itself and the code breaker, who was to take a crack at the script on the back of the shells. Dick then sent a text to Lou Corr to make sure he too could be back for the meeting. Lou would not be invited into the meeting but should be available to answer any of the group's questions Dick could not handle.

In Beijing the thirty-day period came to an end. Zhu and Yi came along to the university with their staff and carefully logged out all the shells, packing them into military steel containers, locking them securely, and taking them off to be further examined. George and the team were left with everything else in place, the shells mapped and logged and given identifiers. They suspected, however, if they saw the shells again the identifiers and package IDs would all be gone. Of course, they would be able to re-map them; however, that would mean repetition of everything that had been done so urgently over the prior four weeks.

In the next few weeks security gradually eased, the metal detector was removed, and only one guard remained on permanent watch. Within a few more weeks the video cameras were removed. George was reminded of their original deal from time to time and that they were still under the authorities' supervision.

Now that the military had the shells to play with and received regular reports of the university team's inability to crack the language of the writings, they seemed content to leave George and the others alone. It was George that reminded Diao of the agreement to get rid of Zhao Feng once the thirty days were over. Diao told

George he would talk directly to Zhu and he should wait for his feedback. It was made clear to George that if they did not go directly through Zhu, then Yi would insist Zhao Feng remain in the program.

After a few days word came back that Zhao Feng was to move to the position that Cai Levee had originally arranged for him. It was Yi who visited the lab to deliver the final message but George could see Yi was not happy about it. The reason given was lack of funding. Zhao Feng became very angry about being the only one leaving the program; everyone could see the atmosphere was turning nasty. Yi at that point excused himself and practically dragged Zhao Feng off into another room. Diao told George and the others to calm down so as not to inflame the situation further. About fifteen minute later the two reappeared; neither looked happy but Zhao Feng finally muttered a few words of disappointment at having to leave the team; he thanked Cai Levee sarcastically for finding him a good position. With that Yi left with Zhao Feng and Diao stayed behind; he reminded George that General Zhu was a man of his word, not like some of the others involved in this affair.

Lou returned from to Langley from Asheville the morning of the meeting. He said everything had gone fine; Rebecca was overjoyed with her invitation to Washington, proudly displaying it around the neighborhood. Aside from that, Scott was fine too but wanted to know more about what Lou had really been up to in China. Dick told him to say nothing about what went on, to make up whatever story he felt appropriate. He was advised to stand by in case he was needed; meanwhile Dick gathered all the things he needed for his meeting and Lou wished him good luck as he left.

The vice president, CIA director, and commander of all the military forces, as well as a top level scientist with full security clearance, had flown in for the face-to-face meeting with the teams. Aside from congratulating the people involved, they too were fascinated by what had been going on and wanted a look at the shells.

Dick headed down to the secure bunker room for this conference, mentally rehearsing his presentation; he had no power point slides despite John Smythe's pleas for him to prepare them. He strolled calmly along the halls and took the appropriate elevator down to the lowest level in the complex.

Dick entered the meeting room to find everyone already waiting for him. The atmosphere was warm and friendly. Everyone shook hands with Dick and welcomed him in. They sat down and gave Dick the floor. Dick then proceeded to recount the entire story and series of events, as well as the most recent activities. He then ceremonially pulled out the four shells that Lou had successfully brought back with him. They were passed around while everyone touched them, turning them over to see the strange writings. Dick waited for the shells to tour the room before inviting in the CIA's top scientists, advising the group that they would first review their findings so far.

Steve Braden, the material specialist, stood by Dick smiling slightly but looking very nervous. "Are you sure you want to do this?" Braden whispered to Dick.

"Absolutely, Steve, don't worry about it, it's my show."

"Glad it's not mine! You're crazy, Dick. You know that, don't you?"

Dick told everyone that based on the latest intelligence the Chinese still had not figured out what the shells were made of. He calmly told the audience, however, that Steve Braden here had been able to do it in fifteen minutes.

Everyone including Smythe immediately sat bolt upright with expressions of surprise and pride; that is, until Dick took a shell in his hand, raised it above his head, and brought the edge of it down full-force on the conference table. The shell exploded into pieces showering the two men sitting nearest to him. With that, Steve walked out as planned and in walked Phil Stephens, language specialist and obsessive code breaker.

Picking up another shell and turning it over while the room was still in shock Stephens said, "Gentleman, the script on these shells is a fine example of the earliest known form of Chinese writing and similar to that found on a 4,800-year-old piece of pottery unearthed in the Shendong Province of eastern China in Juxien County.

"The hieroglyphics were dubbed the Davenkoy Pottery Inscriptions by archaeologists; they pre-dated inscriptions on ox bones and shells that were found from the Shang Dynasty dated 1,600 years BC. Dick has asked me to give you a brief summary of what the words say. One of our contacts at Harvard University, a Chinese linguistics expert, confirms what they basically say, and that is 'The Chinese Military sincerely appreciates the two million dollars that you transferred to our account in Europe.'"

As Dick gave him the nod, Phil left the room.

Everyone in the room was glaring at Dick. John Smythe was red in the face and the vice president looked like he was going to come unglued. Dick advised everyone to stay calm while he further explained.

"Gentlemen, I need to tell you about the other plan."

Smythe immediately broke in. "Jesus, Dick, there was no other plan as far as you told me! What the hell are you playing at? Now all we have is some junk on our floor and the government coffers and taxpayers down two million dollars. Have you lost it?"

Dick tried to speak as the group railed at him, but to no avail. Finally, the VP cut in and forcefully said they should hear Dick out. At that point Dick opened a package of four more shells and circulated them to the group. "Gentlemen, these are the genuine ones we extracted according to the real plan."

John Smythe fairly snarled at Dick. "For Christ sakes, what the hell plan are you talking about, Janswig?"

Dick wondered if maybe this time he'd gone too far with his antics. "The truth of the matter is I was concerned there were too many leaks around here, and getting the shells out was going to be difficult without the help of assets on the ground. Part of the plan had to be kept secret, I guess, though I have to apologize to everyone here—especially John—for not telling anyone about it or getting approval.

"I needed the Chinese to think that no shells were unaccounted for to avoid risk to the various parties involved in the shell effort. I also took to heart the desire for no collateral or international embarrassment from our efforts to obtain them."

Dick nodded politely to the vice president in that regard before continuing.

"When our operative Lou Corr returned to his apartment he was met by a young Chinese woman who gave him a box containing the shells that you see before you; real ones, that is. Lou gave his brother-in-law a special suitcase to travel with on this trip, a gift from his company, he claimed, but told him nothing about the case. We didn't want Scott to look nervous at any stage of the plan, especially leaving China.

"Lou had taken the package of real shells with him, gained entry to Scott's room while he was meeting with the temple architects, and placed the package in the false compartment of the case. He replaced the clothing and left Scott to unknowingly carry the real shells back to the U.S.

"Lou flew to see him just yesterday and retrieved them without Scott knowing it. So now we have the shells to work on; the Chinese think we don't, and they think they've pulled a fast one on us. They will not be trying to find out who really smuggled them out and that will protect our high-level asset who helped us pull this off."

Despite the complaints about the money that was transferred to the Chinese military the vice president sat back, loosened his tie, and smiled. "Dick, John, good job. I like the way you handled it." He nodded toward the joint chief. "At least two million bucks would've probably been spent by the general here and his friends on a midnight attack in Beijing that would have started a war!"

After a moment of total silence, a burst of chuckling all round followed. Even the general shook his head and laughed.

The meeting adjourned, Smythe walked with Dick back to his office. He said that while he was pleased with the outcome, he was concerned with how easily things could have gone wrong. He also questioned Dick as to who his asset was. When Dick got him over to his office, he closed the door and again expressed to John his concern they had a leak somewhere and apologized for leaving him out of the loop. His asset had confirmed the leaks as such with the coded text message Dick had received that said, "Your account is being checked."

John then complained again about Dick having outside assets that he was running off the books; he demanded to know who it was. Dick told him he could not tell him, put his fingers to his lips to request silence, and calmly turned the box that the shells had been in over on his desk. Smythe could clearly see the writing; after a minute he looked straight at Dick then turned and left. Dick could hear Smythe muttering "Holy cow, you old fox, Janswig! Son of a bitch, Janswig, frigging brilliant!"

The writing on the box simply said, "To Dick Janswig from the Black Tulip."

When Janswig saw Lou, the pair of them had a good laugh over the theatrics Dick had used with the big-wigs. Smythe had also told Lou that the looks on everyone's faces when the shell exploded were priceless. Of course, at the time he still thought they had been hoodwinked by the Chinese.

Dick called Smythe to say that Lou Corr was in his office, and Smythe came back over to thank him for risking his neck—and his in-law's. He was sorry Lou would likely never get another visa for China but told him the chairman of EXMACH had agreed to place Lou in any of their other offices if Langley requested it. The chairman also passed along to Lou that if he wanted to work for them as his own man he was more than welcome. Lou had laughed at that and said once Dick retired he would retire too—or accept the chairman's offer. "Hell, Dick! They have better benefits than we do, and they get to fly business class all the time!"

Dick's last action was to make sure that news of the agency getting duped would reach Beijing.

Zhu and Yi received high recognition from the Chinese military and government for three things: recovering the shells and playing the trick on the Americans, which of course led to the gift of two million dollars. Zhu received a reward of fifty thousand dollars; Yi received twenty thousand. He secretly wished he had given the Americans his own account information instead of the intelligence group's number.

After the meeting Dick was pestered continually by John Smythe; John wanted to know who had *really* removed the shells. At first he thought it must have been Cai Levee; then he wondered if the Black Knight and Black Tulip were the same people. Dick would simply smile at him and decline answering. John even wondered if Zhu might be the Black Knight. No answer from Dick. Was it someone inside the military doing the testing? Was it a scientist working on them? Who was the woman who delivered the package to Lou Corr that night, Xiao Ping?

CHAPTER 23

THE SEASONS WERE CHANGING IN Beijing, weeks were rolling by, yet the passage of time seemed even slower to George. They were making no progress at all on deciphering the scripts. They'd had them computerized and tried multiple ways to decipher them. They were allowed to let out snippets of the text to experts in the field without revealing their origin; however, that effort was to no avail. George could sense that Diao's interest was waning, and neither Zhu or Yi was seen around the university. The last guard disappeared one day from the hallway.

Occasionally Professor Ding visited; he would always leave waggling his finger, still convinced he was right. "It's animal, I tell you, ancient animal. Nobody listens to Ding, but one day you'll find out I'm right!"

The fact that no one had been able to pull any DNA from the specimens was a mystery in itself. George knew full well that if it were animal, that would have come to light at the onset.

The team was frustrated and began to question why they were still bothering. It was Arthur who finally suggested trying something different.

"What do you mean, Arthur? We've been down every path we can think of."

"I mean let's focus on the shells, not the writing. We know they're all similar, and we've been trying to figure out if they will fit together somehow. If they did, we could maybe view the translation as a whole rather than piecemeal."

"How would we ever do that if we can't figure out what the shells say?"

"Look at this material here, George, I've shown it to Charles too; he thinks it's worth a try. I've researched the availability of software to help with this and I've come across some programs. They were developed for re-assembling pieces from such things as explosion damage or archaeological pieces that are then re-assembled to their original shapes, that kind of thing. It's the very latest in this type of software; it was developed in the States over a number of years. I think it could work."

"Sounds expensive. Do you know if it's restricted for sale to foreign countries? Can it even be purchased in China?"

Arthur sighed and looked at Xiao Ping for support.

"George, I think it's a great idea," Xiao Ping said. "Diao likes the idea of getting the software for the museum and other entities in China to use for archaeological purposes."

George looked from his wife back to Arthur. "You still haven't answered my question about cost."

"Diao was taken aback by the cost when we told him about it," Arthur said. "He was almost laughed at when he talked to the university administrators about obtaining it."

"I'm not surprised," George said.

"But, George. Let me finish. Diao ran it by Zhu, and his group's willing to help purchase the program—if the university will meet them at least halfway. Zhu's people think it could have some military use for them in the future."

There was only one thing George could say to all this with Xiao Ping sitting there smiling. "Well, of course we should pitch this to the head of purchasing for the university right away. Would you set that up, Arthur?"

It took only one week for the research team to get funding approval from the university, and for the U.S. State Department to approve the sale—to everyone's surprise, given the usual red tape. Unfortunately, it took several more weeks before the software finally arrived in Beijing, accompanied by two engineers to assist the team with the setup.

Once it was installed, the engineers demonstrated what George thought were some pretty impressive examples of what it could do. They also showed the team examples of projects successfully accomplished in the past. Arthur went ahead and showed them what he wanted to do with the software, but the engineers told Arthur he would have to reconfigure the way the data currently was stored and coded. It would take a few weeks to get the program up and running.

The U.S. engineers had to leave in a week, however, so they began walking Arthur through the steps he would have to follow. Arthur enlisted Charles to back up the effort, which Charles appreciated; he finally felt he was doing something positive.

About two weeks later, Charles and Arthur were still working hard on the project, all their efforts beginning to show progress. It was mesmerizing to those watching the program at work, especially George and Xiao Ping. They put the images on the large screen in the anteroom, but all anyone saw for days was this mass of shapes in three dimensions floating around the screen, trying to come together, looking like a shape was forming, then blasting apart and starting all over again. It was actually quite hypnotic and George frequently had to look away; otherwise he found himself almost in a trance.

After another week, Arthur finally called one of the software engineers by phone to tell him what was going on. "Peter, hello again, it's Arthur. How are you?"

"We're all fine, really enjoyed our stay with you guys. John's over his stomach bug but he's already anxious to go back. How's the project going?"

"Well, that's the reason for my call, Peter; it's going nowhere. The program looks like it's about to complete the assembly of our objects then blasts apart every damn time. Do you have any suggestions on what we can try next?"

The rest of the team listened quietly as the two of them talked on a speakerphone discussing everything that had occurred to that point. After giving it some further thought Peter finally said, "Look, Arthur, there's only one other potential issue I can think of right now. In a way it's obvious and I can't understand why we haven't factored it in. You know, if these shapes are incomplete, and you're trying to assemble one hundred percent of the pieces to the shape, then the program will simply be continuing to try to assemble the ones in the system to each other.

"You need to work through the probabilities of that progressively, use lower percentages; see where that leads you. We don't need to be there; I can easily talk you through it."

"That makes sense. It's so logical I can't understand us not considering that either. I feel pretty foolish."

"No worries, Arthur, we all get lost in the trees sometimes. Anyway, it's worth a try."

He sent a lengthy set of program instructions to Arthur highlighting the areas that were important. He told Arthur to start adjusting the probability percentages to see if that would help bring the assembly together. The theory was this would eventually confirm where any pieces were missing and would show gaps in whatever structure this was. Arthur played with different guesses the following week. The team could tell he was on the right track because the pieces stuck together longer than before until blasting apart for the program to recycle itself yet again. He had picked a figure of 80 percent and started working towards 100 percent in steps of 1 percent. He had no idea where it would end up, or even if a rounded percentage number would work. He wondered aloud how long that would take if it were, say, something like 91.336 percent.

Actually it took only a short time; the software itself had an algorithmic function that would recommend the next percentage to try. Within two hours at 96.6 percent something happened. Arthur ran around the offices pulling everyone back into the lab. Crowding around the screen they watched the software lock the pieces together. Arthur ran it several times to prove it was no accident.

"Well, what do you thing about that, Professor!"

"That's incredible," George exclaimed. "Look! The configuration shows at least eight shells are missing. The clarity of the image is amazing; I can hardly believe what I'm seeing. Xiao Ping, call Diao right away and ask him to get over here; tell him we have something interesting for him to see. We should also have Ding look at this."

Xiao Ping quickly rang through to Diao Lijun, then to Professor Ding. Both would come as soon as possible.

George could see Arthur was really pumped; this was the first real break. Diao was a good hour away, so Arthur saved the entire program result to a separate hard drive as well as on the current program. He then maneuvered to the reverse side of the shells where the scripts were now all lined together, except of course for the eight shells missing in random places. He then threw a cover over the screen so the team could have a show and tell to both Ding and Diao as soon they were both in the room.

Diao arrived clearly anxious to see whatever it was that was so exciting to everyone. Ding rushed in moments later. Arthur gave his little professorial tutorial on the software, how he had used it, the processes that had gone on over the last few weeks, and what he was about to let them watch. Charles took a couple of chopsticks and gave a lengthy drum roll on one of the cabinets while Arthur uncovered the screen.

Diao and Ding watched, as everyone had done earlier, in amazement and utter fascination at what began to happen. Over a ten-minute period the shells, or whatever they were, moved over the screen, joined, parted, aligned with others, added more shape and formed gradually into a 3D image. Diao let out a long whistle. Ding smiled from ear to ear and remarked in his Chinese English, "George, some of a bitches, I told you it was prehistoric; it is! These are no shells; they are scales of animal and what you are looking at is part of a huge tail."

"Professor Ding, you may have been right all along. This must have come from some huge crocodile, bigger than anything we've ever known about before."

"No, George, not correct; no not correct at all. This is part of a tail—yes, I will give you that—but no crocodile. I give you one other comment." With that he looked at the screen for a few more minutes, peered at the shape with his nose almost on the screen, stepped back and looked around at everyone in the room. He then took off his glasses and wiped them with his handkerchief. "Gentlemen, it is Professor Ding's opinion that what you are looking at is tail of huge flying predator, oldest we have seen—never a trace of anything like this in China, intact or fossilized. Not just China, not anywhere before!" Ding then shuffled out of the office, a little taller than when he came in, clearly proud that his earlier prediction that the shells were animal and not manmade was correct.

Diao headed over to Cai Levee's office and proceeded to call Zhu with the news. The only comment Zhu had, Diao reported when he came back to tell everyone, was that he wished he had never seen the damn things. The experts on his end were still trying to test them and learning nothing. Diao laughed as he repeated the exact comments for them, changing his speech to a deeper Zhu-like tone. "Ai yo, Diao, we might as well line the insides of the president's limousine with them . . . protect him from a cruise missile strike."

Diao grinned. The military, it seemed, were giving up the whole project and gathering the shells from the different research centers. The political leaders had apparently decided the pieces were to be locked away in storage, but not returned to the team or to Diao. Zhu had wished Diao well with the translation efforts and told Diao to call him if anything more was found out, though he highly doubted that would happen.

The project's funding became more tightly controlled, even though Zhao Feng had been moved out after the shells were shipped to the military. Charles at that time also decided to move on and was convinced they would never interpret the writing. Xiao Ping, Arthur, and Cai Levee were left to continue the project with George, although Cai was now focusing more of his time on other university projects. Diao still came by, but he was under increasing pressure to give up the effort. Identifying the articles as a prehistoric (maybe) animal's tail had saved the project for a while, but it looked like interest was waning with him too.

Fortunately for the team another lucky break again came at one of their daily brain-storming sessions, thanks to Arthur. George looked a little more upbeat than he had before as he asked them to gather around. "Listen up, everyone. Arthur reckons he might break our logjam here; go ahead, tell them what you told me earlier."

"Thanks, George. Well, I've been following an interesting paper that's just come out from a Professor Hansen. He's working at the Massachusetts Institute of Technology (MIT). I'm sure you know it's a private research university located in Cambridge. They've continued to develop computer program logic to be used in deciphering ancient languages. In 2010 they were successful in translating a written language from 3000 years ago, the Ugaritic language used originally in western Syria. The language was first discovered by archaeologists in 1920 but couldn't be deciphered until 1932.

"When this Professor Hansen and his team applied their computers to the task they fed in every known language in that area as part of their analysis effort. The program scanned these multiple languages at the same time along with the Ugaritic script and successfully translated the text in three hours!"

Xiao Ping spoke quickly in Chinese to Cai as both of them leaned forward, now far more interested in what Arthur was saying. "Go ahead, Arthur," Xiao Ping urged. "You've got our attention now!"

" Okay, good. Again, Hansen has continued to improve the software. According to this paper, they're doing extensive work on ancient Asian scripts. I already asked Diao for permission to release the text of one shell to Professor Hansen, see if we could interest him in coming to China and running their programs alongside our digital mapping. Maybe they can somehow shed some light on our shells . . . or scales. Whatever.

"I showed the paper to Diao and he's gotten approval—from the Chinese government *and* the university—to proceed! The one stipulation is that this Professor Hansen must be willing to do this work in China."

Xiao Ping looked elated, but—for once, George thought—she was speechless. George said, "Okay! I think we all agree it's a good idea to follow up with this Hansen fellow. Arthur, why don't you continue with that?"

"Actually, I have already, George. I've even sent him a sample."

Xiao Ping narrowed her eyes and scowled at Arthur. "Why don't we just announce this whole project on the front page of the *New York Times*?" she said.

"I'm sorry," Arthur said. "I should have told you, I know; I just got carried away, I guess. But I didn't want to get everyone's hopes up and then have him refuse us."

"Humph," Ziao Ping grunted.

"Anyway," Arthur went on, "Hansen says he would need a lot more samples to have any chance of success."

George sat up and cleared his throat. "Arthur, what did we just say about running off on our own without keeping the team fully abreast? If we all run off on our own we'll never get this thing cracked."

"Sorry again, George, but he's really keen to work on this! He's fascinated by the digital image of the script I sent and the chance to make a major breakthrough in their field globally, let alone have the chance to visit China."

George sighed. "All right, Arthur. I'll support you in this. But in the future, please remember that we are a team. I repeat, a team. This isn't a one-man show, you know."

Arthur hung his head and rubbed his forehead.

George looked around the room. "I just hope getting this software into China won't be a problem."

CHAPTER 24

~

"Dick, John here. Can you come to my office right away? There's a new report in from BK over there in China."

"Give me fifteen."

Dick headed to John Smythe's office; he told Betty to hold any calls for him but he expected the meeting would be short.

"So what do we have, John?"

"Grab a chair, Dick. It's not much but the report says their military has given up. The only part of the project remaining is this crazy effort to translate the damn writings or whatever they are on the backs of these things. The report claims this guy Zhu is giving up but other folks claim to have determined the shells are the scales from an enormous prehistoric animal. They think the scales are part of the animal's tail. You think that's all bullshit like me, right? What're you smiling at?"

"John, maybe good old American technology has won the day. Our scientists determined the shells were animal and perhaps prehistoric a week ago. Apparently one portion on the edge of one of the shells, about the size of a pencil tip, succumbed to the efforts of a diamond-tipped tool and broke loose. They haven't determined the exact age, but they've settled finally that it's not manmade."

"You've got to be kidding me. This is getting weirder!"

"I know, they tried to use this one flaw in the particular shell— I guess we should call it a 'scale' now—to penetrate the rest of the piece but failed to even make a mark, just like the Chinese. One of the scientists believes this animal material was fired to its hardness with some ridiculously high temperature. Perhaps certain gases could have aided the hardening and abrasion resistance of the pieces."

"What the hell do they think could do that?"

"When I asked what kind of natural phenomenon could cause that he wasn't sure. He thought maybe a direct lightning strike, but doubtful, or maybe the mouth of an erupting volcano. That might generate the kinds of temperatures needed. In the end who will ever know?"

"Seems like this is turning into a complete waste of the agency's time, Dick. We've got enough problems without screwing around with this any longer. Maybe we can convince the uppers to pull the plug, huh?"

"I doubt it. Those military guys are anxious to stay on it. I do have an interesting situation we might want to follow, though."

"Is there something new I don't know about?"

"Maybe. Anyway, we've been asked for our views about some special translating software being released to China. Apparently the folks over there have been in touch with some whiz kids at MIT."

"Code-breaking stuff?"

"Not exactly; that was the first thing I checked on. I mean it could help but our guys don't think it would assist the Chinese too much more than where they are now. They've talked directly to a Professor Hansen up there and don't see a problem. It's been given to India already for some of their archaeological finds."

"Well, why should we let the Chinese have it? The sons of bitches are already stealing everything we have these days?"

"Actually, we may have an opportunity here. The software is already out there, as I've said. I'm shocked they haven't figured that out for themselves yet."

"What particular opportunity are you seeing?"

"Simple, John. It would take a couple of weeks or more, but it might be worthwhile to us. First we use the software here ourselves to see what we can make of it, but then we have our techies work with the MIT folks before it's released. We build in a Trojan horse, maybe some malware, something like that. Not only can we understand what they're doing but also our techies suspect the software could find its way into even more interesting areas. I bet their military will look at it. Right now they think the only place they can get the software is from MIT, but as I said it's already in a few sensitive places if they look harder."

"So much for protecting our intellectual property." Smythe got up mumbling to himself as he paced around the office a couple of times. "Okay, Dick, go ahead with State and clear it, but absolutely get our boys in the back working on something to get us more out of this than just helping them translate some dumb text from their past.

"Try not to let it get in the way of your other stuff. Remember your retirement's on the horizon, Dickey boy. No need to create more headaches for yourself."

Dick smiled. "Headaches I don't need, but I still think something's going to come out of this. I'm not sure what yet, but thanks for giving this old guy a little more rope to play with."

"Okay, do what you need to, but watch the damn bucks. I wouldn't know how to explain why we're playing around with animal shells . . . or scales . . . whatever the hell they are."

With Smythe's help, Dick was able to convince everyone in the loop to approve the release of the software to the Chinese. The Langley team, who'd had no success in translating the four scales either, requested their people be allowed to work with the software people under Hansen. They were asked to see what kind of intellectual protection, Trojan horse, or self-destruct programs could be built in before it left the U.S.   There were also a competitive few on his team who wanted to decipher the language ahead of the Chinese. Dick could never understand China's techies' obsession with that aspect, as more people were interested in what could be done with the material itself. Then again, the guys involved certainly fit the image everyone had of a bunch of geeks hidden away in a back room.

Hansen and two of his leading programmers received all the clearances, invitations, and visas needed for them to leave for Beijing in February. In China Diao organized everything; he arranged to set up the America team with an independent lab to work out of. Arthur told George he was a little surprised that the approval came so quickly, but George felt his personal contacts had made the difference; in any event it would give them one more opportunity to break the code.

They all met with Hansen and his team the day after their arrival. A welcoming lunch was held in the famous Quanjude Duck restaurant on the south side of Tiananmen Square. Diao planned the location such that after lunch he could give them a private tour of the Forbidden City and take them through the museum, the domain he was responsible for. The team had a bit of jet lag but certainly enjoyed the Beijing duck lunch and the guided tour that Diao laid on. They planned to begin work the next day, inspecting the lab set up for them and discussing what exactly they would need to do to press forward. Andrew Hansen, "Andy," was a likeable individual, obviously highly intelligent, brilliant with computers (Arthur of course raved about him), yet surprisingly unassuming. He was quite in awe, as most people were, on this first visit to Beijing and China. He was clearly going to make the most of it, if everyone else could keep up with him.

The one challenge in the lab was satisfying Hansen's addiction to soda. He would gulp twenty-ounce beakers of the stuff all day long. How drinking that amount of sugary soda did not have any effect on him was beyond George. Diao, as always, was able to fix him up with what he needed. Between the team's coffee addiction and Andy's soda addiction George imagined they were all going to get along fine.

Setting up the software and computer configurations with the lab servers took the whole first day for Arthur and the software engineers; meanwhile, George and Diao filled Hansen in on what they knew about the scripts. Despite the amount of research the team had done, their success in that regard was very limited. It didn't concern Andy Hansen, who seemed to relish the challenge.

As they were getting set up and preparing the materials Andy's team had requested, George suspected the specialists from Zhu's cyber team were monitoring and tracking everything they were doing in the lab. There were too many warnings out there in the overseas press about hacking efforts going on in both China and the USA, but by then most of the team were getting numb to it. For Cai and Xiao Ping there was no question about it; they repeatedly warned George that as far as they were concerned the authorities were wired into everything they did. Cai was convinced that was one of the main reasons behind the approvals to import sophisticated software. They said nothing to Andy Hansen, however, and if the computers were being monitored, his engineers never noticed.

The first day's efforts generated few results. Andy asked through their Chinese associates at the university to obtain every ancient written language they had, as well as the neighboring Asian ones; the library of both written and hieroglyphic texts was becoming the largest Andy and team had ever assembled.

As the days went by patterns of script started to emerge but the magic solution to this mysterious language still seemed out of reach. Eventually as they brain-stormed further actions some began to wonder if the way they were trying to translate them was wrong; perhaps the scales had been assembled in random order. Arthur was concerned that if this were true, then trying to figure what the right sequence was would take forever; these eight hundred plus scales would end up forming millions of potential combinations.

Andy's team met separately for two days reviewing all their data to date and came back to George. "I believe we need to change our approach. This is truly a unique challenge that we feel may need a different plan of attack based on the last few days. We think we can use the rhythms in the text as well as the common characters to approach the scales by selecting a pattern first, and then try the translation effort. I'm recommending we pick the ten most promising rhythms, as we call them, and focus on those first. The big problem is we can only stay with you for one more week. We can get you through the process, of course, and leave you with the skills to proceed. If we can find a potential breakthrough rhythm we will be more than pleased to help you by coming back later, or being involved remotely from the MIT campus. Unfortunately, we have other commitments scheduled and really can't stay too much longer."

"It's your call, Andy; we appreciate that you have other projects to work on. Believe me, it's happened to us before. As you say, we can work with you remotely if we need help."

George looked over at Arthur. "How comfortable would you be if you have to work with them that way, Arthur?"

"I hate to see them leave, frankly. It's obviously easier for me with them here, but if I have to, well, I guess then I have to! As long as I can easily contact Robert here in particular, I think I can do as well as anyone."

Andy spoke up. "Robert thinks very highly of Arthur . . . I do too, George. I see no problem with Arthur plowing ahead with the new strategy; in fact, if he ever wants to leave China we'll take him on in a heartbeat!"

George looked around and saw there was a clear consensus in the room. "Okay, so that's the plan; let's do it. I'm sure Arthur appreciates your confidence in him, Andy, but we hope to keep him around here a little longer!"

A week later the teams had generated seven promising rhythms before Hansen and company readied themselves to leave. Arthur had run some of the translation software and was encouraged; he resigned himself to following the game plan, continuing the scanning and random computing programs until he had the ten programs to really focus on. Everyone suspected they were stepping up to a roulette wheel or worse against a staggering number of potential combinations, especially with a few scales missing.

Diao came back from a meeting with the authorities and looked nervous as he briefed George and his team on his discussions. Diao seemed to always have his emotions on his face for anyone to see; it was obvious to George that he was not a happy man this morning.

"I guess there's no easy way to tell everyone this, but I'm afraid our leaders gave me bad news today; the funding for our work is being withdrawn. The situation is certainly not good and I can tell you that I was very much against this. I negotiated hard with my peers and they agreed to give us three more months before we either shut down or self-fund our efforts. I know this is terrible news but we must look at the results from our superiors' viewpoint. If only you can progress on breaking the language code in this time then maybe we can save our program."

George wasn't surprised it had come to this; he just was not expecting it at this time. Xiao Ping looked particularly worried, and Cai Levee was about to speak when Andy Hansen jumped in. "Look, everyone, before we take our leave, I think I can speak for my department in offering the services of MIT under a grant. I believe I can get it if that helps, assuming we can bring everything to the U.S. for study."

Diao shook his head. "I'm afraid that would be difficult; in fact, impossible. The Chinese government and my peers would be very protective of what we have; on the other hand, I might be able to use a formal offer from you—and MIT—as leverage to continue if I need to. But I do thank you for your kind offer."

"I appreciate that, Diao, but understand this is not just kindness on our part. First, it's professional fascination with what you have here; secondly, it's a personal challenge. I've never failed to unlock a translation to date. Lastly, and most important, if we're successful and your peers acknowledge to the world our accomplishments here, future grants for our programs will go through the roof in the U.S.!"

George tried to calm the concerns of everyone, especially his wife, assuring them he was confident that within three months they would have the translation codes broken anyway. What else could he really say to everyone? That they had no chance of doing it?

A nice farewell banquet for the team from MIT was arranged before they left. A number of other professors joined in and new friendships were established for the future. Whatever relations were like at the government level of the two countries, at this level, as usually is the case, relations were quite positive.

With the MIT team gone, things at the lab returned to the seemingly endless routine of programming. They were always waiting for the computing to complete its lengthy cycles before the progress and outcomes could be reviewed.

After three more weeks of frustration and reviewing the results from the ten scans Arthur had finally put together, Cai Levee spent a whole day poring over the data. He told George he wanted to look at them without Western thinkers around him so he could view the results with a purely Eastern eye.

Later Cai reported to the group that four of the programs showed promise. The word accumulation, as yet still random, was somewhat improved but program eight seemed to stand out above the others. Cai, like all Chinese, considered eight a very auspicious number; he recommended they gamble on that program. Time was running out, he reminded them, and this was as good as he had seen.

The team met and reviewed Cai's suggestion; none of them had a better call. Xiao Ping certainly did not like the number four run, as the Chinese translation was similar to "death" in Chinese—definitely a bad choice. In many hotels in China there is no fourth floor and in certain deluxe Western hotels neither a fourth or thirteenth floor!

Arthur also ran multiple combinations at the same time for those scales that did not seem to advance in translation, leaving the ones that made some sense. From what little had emerged George and Xiao Ping realized that this was not going to be a language as developed as theirs; to make anything readable in today's world they would have to use some freedom of expression. They had agreed that "Up go door," for example, would have to be worked into "he got up and went to the door." For sure they would need to augment whatever finally came out of their efforts to unlock the code.

~~&~~

CHAPTER 25

DICK JANSWIG HAD CALLED ANDY Hansen in from MIT for meetings at Langley as soon as he got back from Beijing, Andy did not have much choice as to whether he came or not; after all, the CIA was to a degree one of the sponsors. They met with the people who worked on the software side and in the code-breaking area. Hansen seemed tired after his long trip; other than that he showed no discomfort about being surrounded by a bunch of specialists. Dick suspected Hansen could run rings around them in his field anyway. After introductions and pleasantries Hansen gave a review of his time in China.

"Tell us more about the people involved, would you please, Mr. Hansen?"

"I'll do my best, but please call me Andy. Frankly I can't understand why the CIA is even interested in what's going on there with the relics. And I'm still a little uneasy about the work done on our software for your own purposes. Obviously you are using us as a Trojan horse for whatever it is you're trying to do. My big concern is if it is uncovered the good relations with our Chinese counterparts will be ruined for the future."

"Don't worry in that regard," voiced one of the specialists. "Anytime they start looking we have built in mechanisms that will render any unauthorized party's access meaningless."

"Don't kid yourself, young man; these people are smarter than you think and getting better by the day."

Andy bristled and was about to say more when Dick stepped in before any argument developed. "Okay, gentlemen, can we move on please? Mr. Hansen—sorry, Andy—your thoughts please."

"Look, I really don't have much to say about the people involved. Professor Mathers is a pleasant enough American, but I will say that thanks to his charming Chinese wife, Xiao Ping, he sits in two camps. He is still one of us, so to speak, but I think push come to shove he would stick with the Chinese side. He is undoubtedly very smart, as is his wife, but she and their Chinese associate Cai Levee are certainly more aggressive. This Diao Lijun is a real gentleman and I was impressed with his professionalism and knowledge of Chinese history and antiquities. Arthur, their main computer guru on Mathers' side, is very good."

"Actually we do know a lot about them. Did you meet anyone else while you were there that stood out?" Dick asked.

"Not really, well except for one rather unsavory character, I think his name was Yi. He stopped by asking a lot of questions of us, but we only saw him once. I took George's advice to heart when he whispered to me the guy was security and to say nothing in front of him. He was definitely security or military, in my mind, walked like he had a steel rod in his spine. His English was poor but precise and pointed, just like an interrogator. Not the kind of guy you would want to meet on a dark night. He and Diao seemed close but I had the impression, even though I don't speak any Chinese, that Diao was having to put up with the guy. I put it down to the Chinese watching over everyone, even their own."

"How about the software materials and installation? Did everything go off smoothly enough?" asked one of the specialists.

"No problem on that side; we did make limited progress, as you know, on the translation side and we've left them some advice on that, but we have of course successfully copied all the scale details they've been working on. I've brought them back to you on the special hard disks your people gave us before we left. As we all know, anyone checking those disks will find nothing of any importance; the copied details of the scales are well-hidden in the drives. The only thing we don't have on these disks are the last few random programs Arthur will have run. Clearly eight hundred to the power of eight hundred in terms of permutations is literally too huge to comprehend; they have limited computer power at their university."

The meeting didn't last long before the CIA specialists asked Hansen to stick around for a while to assist them while they reviewed the disks and MIT's software. They were keen to duplicate Beijing's efforts making full use of Langley's unique and extensive computing power, which outstripped either Hansen's or the Chinese capabilities. After some time they managed to produce some strange language that looked pretty fantastic but was still incomplete. Andy Hansen thought this start by Langley could be very useful, especially since they were able to plug in four of the missing scales that Beijing did not have.

After several days of running programs Dick decided they needed to give up playing around with these disks. What they saw had no intelligence interest, although Dick hoped that the software had indeed been being taken over by the Chinese military and introduced some surprises to their systems. In fact, those that saw and read some of the print-outs thought they were a joke, though no one could figure how the language came into being, or more importantly where these scales gained the properties they held. Like their Chinese counterparts the U.S. military people kept asking for more samples if the CIA could get their hands on them.

The impetus to discover the origin and properties of the scales was waning in the U.S. just as it was in China. Dick was moving on to other more urgent matters; Lou Corr was now in place in Moscow with EXMACH as their new general manager (still with the CIA and reporting to Dick), actively developing contacts among the influential industrial leaders for future use.

Dick decided to get a message on something he thought would be of interest to Mathers and crew. He knew he would have to arrange it through a third party; after all, the Chinese understood nothing of any outside CIA involvement to the level it was, or so Dick hoped. Likewise he understood his superiors wouldn't be too happy if they knew he'd decided to give the Chinese a little help.

In Beijing George received a strange note to be in a bar, The Den on Dongxhiman Avenue in Sanlitun, on Saturday evening at 11 p.m. to receive a package of interest for him. The message was delivered to him on Friday evening. It was special delivery; he recounted later to Xiao Ping how it had been delivered by one of the many delivery services in Beijing. The man was dressed in his company uniform with a scarf and helmet on so there was no way to identify him. When George called them back later to ask who delivered it they apologized and told him they had no record of any such delivery. This whole episode intrigued George so much he determined he and Xiao Ping should visit The Den as requested.

Xiao Ping and George arrived at the popular expat hangout around 7 p.m.; they had decided they might as well eat there and perhaps run into some people they knew. The couple ended up at the table of an old friend, Eric Mowatt; they'd known him for years and he was almost a fixture at The Den. Eric was a Scotsman who practiced the ritual of heading to the "pub" every night when in Beijing, as so many Brits seemed to do. Lisa, one of the main waitresses of the bar, always served him; she made sure his beer glass was full and generally took good care of him when he was there.

George was surprised in conversations with Eric to learn they had a new mutual friend—Lou Corr, who had visited them with Scott Ramey. Apparently, Eric and Lou worked for the same mining business and knew each other well.

The bar was full of people, come to see some Australian rugby match on the big-screen TV. Xiao Ping wasn't enjoying herself with all the noise and told George she had a terrible headache, so about 10 p.m. he suggested she head off and he would wait. She appreciated the consideration, gave Eric a big hug, and left.

The bar was crammed with every seat filled; talking became more like a shouting contest around the room. George was anxious to get "the package" and go home. Eric left and George stayed until the appointed hour but no one showed up. He decided to give it fifteen more minutes before leaving, then asked the waitress, Lisa, to watch his drink while he slipped off to the men's room.

On returning, he noticed a package sitting on the table beside his drink and waved Lisa over. She immediately smiled, came over, and before George could say a word, she pointed vigorously toward someone pushing through the crowd. George saw the back of a Chinese girl, very similar in build to his wife. She was heading toward the exit door. He knew going after her would be useless. By the time he got through the crowd she would be long gone.

The package was clearly labeled in large print: "Attention of Professor G. Mathers. Private and Confidential." George thanked Lisa, who'd kept an eye not only on his drink but the mysterious package as well. As she went to serve the table behind him, George quickly finished his drink, grabbed up the package, and left.

Finding a taxi had taken a while, but George finally made it back to the apartment after midnight. Xiao Ping was still awake but sitting in bed reading. George sat down in the chair beside the bed and opened the small package; there were some computer disks inside and a note. It was not signed and there was nothing to indicate where the disks had come from.

"Well, read it to me," Xiao Ping, sounding a bit impatient.

He cleared his throat, then: "Dear Mr. Mathers, we hope you are making progress on your special translation project. We hope these disks will be of some value to you in your efforts. We do want to draw your attention to three of the symbols that in our opinion are "dra" "gon" and "fire." Draw your own conclusions; good luck. Do not try to find out where this is from or advise the authorities that you received it."

George looked at Xiao Ping in shock. "Dragons? Are we really dealing with the scales of dragons that no one believes ever existed?"

For George, the thought that this text truly was a story about the dragons of mythical Chinese legends was suddenly very exciting. It could certainly revitalize the team's interest in the project, which George admitted to Xiao Ping had been waning fast for him too.

George slept poorly that night, as he knew Xiao Ping did. Both were anxious to get the disks into Arthur's hands as soon as they could to see what was on them.

CHAPTER 26

THE TEAM IN BEIJING WAS on a new and exciting path from then on, thanks to the information contained on the disks. Week by week Arthur was able to unravel more of the story contained on the "drag-on scales," as they now referred to them. Cai was drawn frequently away from his other university projects to study the scripts, while Diao again became a regular visitor to see the progress. After several months the full extent of the dragon scripts began to make sense. It was clear, however, that the full story was incomplete; they were all convinced that the *final* answers lay within the other coffin material that had been lost to them. George decided everyone should review the draft independently, then meet together to discuss their views.

"Is Diao coming along to the meeting this morning?" Cai asked.

"No, I decided we'd all get together first before reviewing it fur-ther. You know how the authorities view all this anyway, right?

"Of course, but look at what we have, George! It's a fantastic story that we Chinese would love to be true. What do you think, Xiao Ping?"

"George, I'm with Cai. I think we need Daio in on this too. It's an incredible story; if this is truly the story of the earliest dragons it's surely one of the most remarkable stories ever told."

"I think that's supposed to be the bible, isn't it?" Arthur added with a smile.

"Well, maybe for you, Arthur, but not for us Chinese. We've already been through that with the Taiping Rebellion and our infamous brother of Jesus there."

Xiao Ping turned to George. "Whatever this is, the rest of the story is in that damned coffin we couldn't find. Look again at that section starting on page two-twenty. I'm sure that's what has Cai so excited."

"No question about that!" Cai said. "You may be doubting everything here too, but your lovely wife and I agree that this reference to the treasure of the dragons and the so-called dragon keepers means there's more out there."

"Cai's right, George," Arthur said. "Look at the text; we've seen so many of these legends in recent years, but this one smells the sweetest of them all. It clearly tells us that what we have is part of the story and that a fantastic treasure awaits us to find. It ties in with what Ma Jun told Xiao Ping too."

"I'm sorry, everyone," George said, "but I can't believe that; something would have turned up—well before us—over the centuries. And we didn't find the second coffin anyway, did we? I'll give you it's a terrific story and our finding it makes another one in and of itself. What more can there be?"

George could see Cai growing more frustrated with him; it wasn't that George did not want to believe in what they had, it was just the way he always approached these things with a certain skepticism.

"I know what Xiao Ping really thinks about this," Cai said. "Arthur isn't saying much but I think even he sees more in this than another legend of old China. As far as I'm concerned the other coffin is out there and I for one intend to find it. We have an old Chinese proverb 'qi er bu she,' don't give up and make steady efforts. Don't give up on us, George. We need to go over all this again, just like in your American crime movies."

George tried to end the meeting on a positive note; the story the dragon scales revealed was fantastic. It told of the very first dragons and how they eventually assisted the earliest warriors of China before disappearing. It detailed how a group of guardians called the Dragon Keepers was formed and how a vast treasure was accumulated over the years with the dragons. It was easier to explain now why the emperors of more modern times had woven the image of the dragon into their elegant robes and architecture.

Cai left the meeting in a bit of a huff because he couldn't get George to believe they could ever find the second coffin. Arthur was noncommittal and ready to go either way; he was just pleased to have cracked the code, so to speak. Xiao Ping wasn't happy with her husband at all; George knew as they left he was in for a tongue-lashing later from her on Cai's behalf. As far as he was concerned, if Xiao Ping and Cai thought there was more to this then they could certainly have at it. Meantime, his feeling was they had another Chinese story in hand to tell—a legend, plain and simple—with terrific elements of truth in what Ma Jun and all his ancestors did to preserve it.

Later that day Cai Levee came back to the offices with a huge grin on his face. He had never stopped believing there were indeed two coffins as Ma indicated to Xiao Ping. He waved an envelope in his hand as he approached Xiao Ping and George, his excitement almost infectious. Certainly Xiao Ping became especially animated.

"Look everyone, tickets to Zhangjiajie again for the coming weekend. I've made us all reservations with Sam and Ivy at the lodge; hopefully the old jeep will fire up again."

"You've done what? Made reservations there again, what the heck for?"

"Treasure hunting of course, George, treasure hunting!"

"The scripts are the treasure, Cai, I've said that so many times!"

"Oh no, George, not so. There may be more scripts but there is treasure for sure. You must read the scripts again!"

He refused to tell them where he thought the other coffin might be, but simply looked at Xiao Ping. "Ma Jun told us where it is."

"He did? When was that? I don't remember him telling us."

"Remember he said to you, 'I am my father's son; I am my father's son'? Now both of you go pack and be ready to go."

With that Cai laughed and left them looking at each other completely puzzled. George could still hear Cai laughing as he walked down the hallway.

George looked at Xiao Ping and knew right away he couldn't say no; it was clear in her face that she would be going with Cai, with or without George. He stepped over to her and took her hand. "Well, one thing is sure, we'll document everything we can again on this visit; I think the dragon scripts are the real treasure but I know Cai's absolutely sure there's even more awaiting us. And you, my dear, you look as excited as I've ever seen you!"

"The coffin, darling, I just know we'll find it . . . somehow I really do. You must believe!"

George wished, for his wife's sake if nothing more, that they would find something. He just hoped that Cai knew what he was doing.

The next day the tickets to Zhangjiajie were sitting on George's desk. Cai was busy getting everything together for their departure. For the time being nothing had been said to Diao Lijun about Cai's ideas or the plans to travel there again. Cai still would not tell either of them what he had in mind; all George could drag out of him was the same words from Ma Jun over and over. George was sure Cai delighted in driving him crazy with them, but Xiao Ping just smiled at her husband and shrugged.

"Later, George, later. When we get there he'll tell us where the key is; it's there, of that I'm sure."

As George walked by Cai's office the lab board had two sentences written on it in both Chinese and English. Cai insisted that, until they got back from their trip, those words would stay right there.

我是我父亲的儿子　　　　我是我父亲的儿子
I am my father's son.　　　I am my father's son.

www.ingramcontent.com/pod-product-compliance
Lightning Source LLC
Chambersburg PA
CBHW071459170626
46811CB00007B/2631